SHORES OF *Resilience*

SHORES OF *Resilience*

Restored

Part 8

Mary E. Hanks

www.maryehanks.com

Scriptures taken from the Holy Bible, New International Version®, NIV®. Copyright © 1973, 1978, 1984, 2011 by Biblica, Inc.™ Used by permission of Zondervan. All rights reserved worldwide. www.zondervan.com. The "NIV" and "New International Version" are trademarks registered in the United States Patent and Trademark Office by Biblica, Inc.™

Suzanne D. Williams Cover Design:
www.feelgoodromance.com

Cover photos:
MJTH @ shutterstock.com
EpicStockMedia @ shutterstock.com

Visit Mary's website:
www.maryehanks.com

You can write Mary at
maryhanks@maryehanks.com.

For the readers who have read this whole series

Thank you!

For Jason

Thank you for cheering me on!

"The Lord bless you and keep you; the Lord make his face shine upon you and be gracious to you; the Lord turn his face toward you and give you peace." Numbers 6:24-26

One

"Let us go, now!" Paige Harper tried articulating around the gag wedging her mouth open. She jerked as hard as she could against the ties binding her wrists to a chair in the coffee area of her gallery. "Please. I beg of you—"

"Silence!"

"We won't tell anyone what you've done."

What could she report about the tall, darkly dressed guy wearing a ski mask, pacing across the gallery, anyway? Nothing about him was familiar. Except maybe his voice. When the guy shoved her onto the chair and told her to be quiet, his voice sounded familiar. Who was he? Did she know him?

Her phone vibrated inside her coat pocket. Was Forest calling her? Too bad she couldn't answer. If she could, she'd shout, "Call 911! We've been kidnapped!" Or else, she'd silently connect the phone, leave it in her pocket, and keep it on so he'd hear what was going on. Then he'd know something was wrong!

The stranger dug his hand into her coat pocket and yanked out her phone. "It's Judah. Are you two close now?"

How did this masked person know her brother-in-law? He must be someone local. Why was Judah calling her?

The guy hurled the phone across the room. The device slammed against the wall, breaking into several pieces. There went her only means of communication with Forest!

"Why'd you do that?" Her words came out garbled.

How had things spiraled downward so drastically? A masked man subdued her assistant, Sarah Blackstone? Then waited for Paige's arrival and tied her up? Those things happened in espionage films. Not in Basalt Bay. Although, her sister, Paisley, had been kidnapped a few months ago. Now, it was happening to Paige and Sarah?

The fabric gag rubbed against Paige's face, making her lips dry and sore. No wonder Paisley's cheek still bore scars from her abduction. How many hours would this standoff, or whatever was taking place, last until Forest found her? Would she have scars on her cheeks and lips too? How many days had Paisley been locked up in Edward's closet before someone rescued her?

Paige shuddered. She didn't want to be like this for even one hour!

Sarah, tied up in a chair next to her, made muffled pleas. Above the cloth covering her mouth, fear emanated from her dark brown eyes. Poor Sarah. Paige hired her only four days ago. What must she think of being an employee in the gallery and coffee shop now?

"It's going to be okay," Paige attempted to reassure her. Although, her voice sounded more like someone who'd just had a root canal.

"You'd better hope your hubby meets our demands, or you won't be 'okay!'" the kidnapper said, his voice as gruff as his manner.

How dare he tie her up and threaten her! Of course, Forest wouldn't meet his demands. But he would figure out a way to find her. Judah, too. Maybe even Craig. Those men would barge in here and fight to get her and Sarah away from this creep. But how long would that take? Would they have to spend the night here? Horrible thought!

Maybe it was best to keep a captor talking. "What do you want? Why are you doing this?" She tried speaking clearly but failed.

"How many times do I have to tell you to shut up?" The man strode toward the door, taking long strides. Then he stomped back into the coffee prep area. "How long does it take for the detective to get here from the inn?"

Not long. But she didn't answer him. She wouldn't cooperate unless it was absolutely necessary.

The guy stared at his phone, tapping the screen.

Paige sent Sarah a couple of visual instructions—widening her eyes, she nodded toward their attacker and jerked her shoulder. If they both rocked their chairs inward at the same time, they might be able to collide against him. Knock him over. Or knock him out! What then? Their hands would still be tied up. How could they break free?

As soon as the hostage-taker strode to the door again, both Paige and Sarah tugged furiously at the ropes binding their wrists. If one of them loosened their bonds, she could untie the other one. As far as Paige knew, the masked man didn't have a gun. He'd subdued her by sheer force. She should have fought harder, but he was a tall muscular man. She hadn't stood a chance of getting away from him. She pulled against the ties at her wrists again.

"Stop that!" The guy charged toward her. "Stop pulling on those ropes." He squatted down in front of her. "You don't realize how serious this is, do you?"

"Why don't you tell me?"

"You want your little girl to remain safe, correct?"

Every muscle in her body tensed. "You leave her alone! Stay away from her!" If a strong man like this went after Piper, would Dad be able to fight him off and protect his two-year-old granddaughter?

The guy pointed toward Paige's nook of paintings and photographs. "You want to live in safety? Walk away from this business, away from this town, and today's chaos disappears."

"This kidnapping is about getting my building?"

How ridiculous! Yet hadn't Mia Till warned her that she'd own the gallery one day? Was this guy working for her?

"Please, just leave my daughter alone." Even she heard how weak her protest sounded through the gag.

"Say goodbye to your life in Basalt Bay, then." He leaned his face close to hers, his dark eyes peering intensely at her.

Where had she seen him before?

Shivers raced up her spine. Should she go along with what he said? Act complacent to keep her, Sarah, and Piper safe? Or should she fight, resisting anything this oaf said or did, in hopes that Forest would come to their aid before it was too late?

Two

Seven Days Earlier

Judah closed his eyes in the lounge chair on the seaside veranda behind his and Paisley's cottage. In a few minutes, he'd get up and continue job hunting online. For now, the New Year's Day air that was warmer than usual for January enticed him to relax for a little while longer. The sunshine caressing his face and the gentle sea breeze lulled him to sleep.

A tender touch. *Ah, Pais.* He scooted back, making room for his wife on the chair. In his state of half-sleep, half-oblivion, he curled his arm around her waist, letting her nestle against him. Her lips touched his neck. Her delicate hands spread over his chest.

Delicate? The perfumed air didn't smell like Paisley's. Who was—

Mia Till?

Judah leaped from the lounge chair, scrubbing his hands over his arms, trying to rid himself of her scent. "What are you doing here?" he demanded of the woman stretching upon the chair like she just woke up too.

"Hey, Judah." Mia grinned.

How long had she been here?

"Judah?" Paisley called in a worried tone from the open doorway. "What's she doing here?"

"I have no idea. I woke up and she was beside me." He jogged over to his wife, clasped her hand, and silently begged her to understand he had nothing to do with Mia's presence here.

"Judah, I must speak with you. Alone." Mia pushed up from the lounge chair and shot a glare toward Paisley.

"Not happening. Where have you been?" He marched back toward her. Thankfully, Paisley clasped his hand and walked beside him. "Forest and Deputy Brian have been searching everywhere for you. They assumed you were missing! Possibly kidnapped. Or had a serious accident. Everyone's been worried about you since the day after Christmas!"

"Here I am." She swayed out her hands, laughing. "The other stuff is just a misunderstanding."

He doubted that. What was really going on? Why was she here?

"Why were you sitting with my husband?" Paisley asked in a tense tone.

"Sitting? Is that what you call being curled up with a handsome man? How about some coffee?" Mia jerked her head toward the house as if ordering Paisley to get her some.

"Why are you here?" Paisley scowled at Mia.

"I have my reasons."

"Were you vacationing and not showing up to work so people would be worried about you?" Judah asked.

"You are so naïve. Cute. But naïve" Mia squinted at him. "You don't see what's at stake in Basalt Bay, do you?"

"I see you've been making people search for you when they had better things to do with their time."

"You should go," Paisley said firmly. "We won't let you mess with us again."

"No?" Mia grinned as if her statement was a personal challenge. "Take my advice, honey, and stay out of this. I'm here to see Judah. Not you."

"Speak respectfully to my wife or get off my property!"

"And don't call me honey!"

"Fine. You don't have to get all huffy." Mia wrapped her arms around herself like she was cold. "About the coffee?"

Paisley didn't move. "Say what you came to say, then go."

"Can I have a moment of your husband's time in private, pretty please?" Mia asked with fake sincerity. She lowered her head and batted her eyes toward Judah.

"Not on your life." Paisley slid her arm possessively around his waist.

"Whatever you have to say can be said with my wife here." He tugged Paisley closer to his side. "I want her to be my witness."

"Afraid I'll throw myself in your arms again?" Mia's eyebrows danced and she thrust her hands through her blond hair.

"You have one minute to explain," Paisley said sternly. "Then I'm calling Deputy Brian!"

"Okay," she dragged out the word. "Judah, Edward wants to talk with you before the trial."

His shoulders stiffened. His whole body felt tightly wound. "You're doing all this, pretending to be missing, lying beside me, to get me to visit my father? Unbelievable."

"I'm finished at C-MER." Mia strode forward until she stood six inches in front of him. "Lying in your arms was just a nice side benefit."

"Mia, so help me—"

Judah tugged Paisley back, stopping her from retaliating against Mia.

"It's time for all the parts to move into place before Edward's trial, including yours." Mia skimmed the pads of her fingers over his wrist. "Promise me you'll visit him?"

"No." He pulled his arm away from her touch. "I'm not promising anything."

"Leave now!" Paisley said.

"I had something else to tell you, but now I won't." Mia winked at Judah then sashayed down the beach. "See you later, handsome! That's a promise you can take to the bank."

Clearly agitated, Paisley marched away from him. "Oh! She makes me so mad! Now, do you believe me when I say she's up to trouble?"

"I believe you."

"You woke up and she was just here?" Paisley sounded doubtful.

"I thought she was you."

"How could you think *she* was me?"

"I was sleepy. Wasn't aware until the smell of her perfume nearly gagged me. Nothing happened."

"She got close enough to be in your arms, didn't she?" She met his gaze and sighed. "Look, Judah. I trust you. But I trust her as much as I trust a scorpion. She's up to something dirty."

"I'm sorry she came here like this."

"You and me both. She was right about one thing. You should see your dad."

"I'd rather not." After all his father had done to harm Paisley in his attempt to take her away from him, he didn't want anything to do with Edward before his trial. Thankfully, Judge Greene had already ruled that he didn't have to testify against his father in this case.

"I mean it. In a week I must face him in court. If he has some last-ditch attempt to be released, or for something bad to happen, I want to be aware of it. For us to be aware of it." She glanced in the direction of where Mia traipsed down the seashore. "And keep your distance from her."

"That goes without saying."

Three

"Look at this article from a year ago." Eyes bleary from days and nights of reading through newspapers without taking many breaks, Craig thrust the water-stained paper toward Al. Even though she went by Alison Riley in the newspaper articles she wrote, or Ali to her friends, he still thought of her as Al. "See what your uncle wrote here? He mentions a private group that was gathering to decide the fate of the waterfront in Basalt Bay. Not the city council, either. Doesn't that ring a warning bell?"

"Sure does," Al said as she squinted at the article, her eyelids barely open. "This could be what we're looking for. The evidence we need." She sounded groggy. Not the usual dive-into-the-problem woman he knew her to be. "I'm sorry. I can hardly read a word of this."

He snagged the newspaper from her hands.

"Hey!"

"It'll keep. Time to get some rest."

"Craig—"

He grabbed a pair of scissors off her desk and clipped the article. Then using a magnet, he secured the piece to a giant whiteboard where a dozen other articles were posted. Each time they found something of significant interest, they put it on the board.

"Let's go. We both need sleep, preferably before daylight." He held his hand out toward her.

"Fine." She clasped his hand and stood. "I'm sure you've had better dates for New Year's. Not that this was a date," she amended.

"No, it wasn't." He let go of her hand. "But you being here with me, looking aloof and gorgeous? I could get used to that."

"Aloof, yes. Gorgeous?" She scoffed. "I look like I haven't brushed my hair in days."

"Your hair is—" He stopped himself from touching the strands he'd been captivated by since the one time he had kissed her. Her lips looked soft, opened slightly as if welcoming him to draw closer. As if she were inviting him to do what he wanted to do right then.

But he was tired. They both were. Even though this was a holiday where people stole kisses at the brink of New Year's, he'd told himself he wouldn't. And he hadn't. But the temptation was still there.

"I should go." He nodded toward the door. "So should you. Let's catch a few hours of sleep before it's time to start this fact-gathering marathon all over again."

"You're hot and cold. You once accused me of being fire and ice."

Was she going to flirt with him now?

"So I did."

"One minute you're staring at my mouth as if you want to—"

His heart pounded a heavy beat. Wanted to kiss her? So she knew. Of course, she did.

"Sorry. As you said, it's late. We already agreed not to go there." She glanced over at the whiteboard. "I'll read the article you showed me in the morning. Which stack did you find it in?"

"There." He pointed at a waist-high pile of musty papers.

Stepping in front of him, she touched the button on his shirt. Maybe he shouldn't have stayed this long. But if she was going to keep working until the wee hours of the morning, he'd do the same. He refused to leave her alone until they figured out who was behind the threats against her uncle, Milton Hedge. Did the group mentioned in the article have anything to do with those threats?

"Craig?" Al's eyes looked extremely tired.

He lifted his chin, steeling himself against any tender emotions toward her.

"You're a lot nicer than I first thought when I came to Basalt Bay and saw you wearing that neon-green vest." A teasing smile crossed her mouth.

The air he hadn't realized he was holding expelled from his mouth. "Thanks, I think."

"Don't look so worried. I'm not going to kiss you." She stepped back. "You should have seen your face!"

"And yours." He grinned, glad for their snarky playfulness. That was better than lunging into something emotional they might both regret. "You looked ready to fall into my arms and kiss me until morning."

Her jaw dropped. Good. He surprised her.

"In your dreams, Craig Masters. In your dreams."

Yeah. She was right about that.

* * * *

The next morning, Ali slammed the phone into its docking station. Some people in this town annoyed her beyond her tolerance level. The innkeeper was one of them!

"Who was that?" Craig stood next to the counter piled with stacks of papers, a cup of coffee in his hand.

"Maggie Thomas. She wants me to pay an outstanding bill to her inn."

"You stayed at Maggie's inn?" Craig's face scrunched up as if he found that, or his coffee, distasteful.

"Not me. Uncle Milton!"

"What date is this bill from?" Craig's dark scruffy cheeks advertised he needed a shave.

"A week ago."

"So your uncle was staying at the Beachside Inn then?"

"So she says." Ali rolled her eyes.

"Maggie is a gossip, but I doubt she'd conjure up a fake bill." Craig thrust his fingers through his dark hair and sighed. "When you came here to run the paper, perhaps Milton wasn't as far away as you thought."

"Why would he hide right here in town?" Her exasperation had to be evident in her tone. Why was Uncle Milton putting her through all of this? He was the one who should be here getting his paper put out.

"Beats me." Craig shrugged and sipped his drink. "Why did Maggie keep his secret?"

"If only I knew." Ali rubbed her hands over her face. She hadn't applied makeup in days. "I guess the newspaper will have to cover the bill."

"And the meeting your uncle wrote about?" Craig rocked his thumb toward the article he'd put on the whiteboard.

"More for us to unravel. I'll have to make some phone calls."

"Let's get started, then."

What would Ali have done without Craig Masters sticking with her through all the late hours of scouring newspapers? Through all the microwave food and the bazillion cups of coffee they devoured?

He was becoming someone upon whom she was depending. Someone she might like a tad too much. Did she want to be dependent on a man like him? Did she want him to be more than her security detail?

One glance at his scruffy face, his soft as pudding lips that she longed to kiss, and she knew the answer.

Four

Paisley clutched Judah's hand as they waited in Pastor Sagle's office. Sitting in the chairs in front of the pastor's desk brought back memories of their post-vow-renewal counseling sessions. Like then, she didn't want to come here today, but Judah said he thought they should. She saw the wisdom in talking with someone they respected and valued about what they were going through. But that didn't mean she wanted to expose her deepest emotions and thoughts to Pastor Sagle.

He would probably ask her if she forgave Edward. What would she say? That she'd tried? One minute, she thought she'd put the harrowing kidnapping experience behind her. The next, thoughts of lying on the closet floor in the dark made her throat tighten and her heart throb nearly out of her chest. She still had to pray some more about forgiving the man who'd caused her such trauma.

With the trial coming soon, would Pastor Sagle understand her need for more time and more prayer? Did God?

Imagining herself facing her attacker at the trial in seven days made her feel close to having a panic attack right here. She felt the precursors—hot and cold alternating through her hands and feet, prickles of tightness pulling at her temples, eyes, and forehead, and the nauseous churning in her middle. Since discovering she was pregnant, she'd held at bay a full-on panic attack about testifying against Edward. She was truly trying to trust in God to carry her through the ordeal. To carry her through everything concerning her pregnancy, too. With Him guiding her and comforting her, she could do anything and face anything, right?

Then why was she shivering? Why was she still so fearful about looking Edward in the eye? Would she ever get past the way she felt?

Judah put his other hand over both of their linked hands. "Are you okay?" His gaze met hers tenderly.

"I'm having a tough time being here." She wouldn't say she was fine about the situation when she wasn't.

He leaned his forehead against the side of her head, closed his eyes, and prayed quietly for her.

The door opened and Pastor Sagle strode in, heading for his chair on the other side of the desk. "Sorry for the delay."

"Thanks for seeing us on short notice." Judah sat back in his chair but kept their hands clasped.

"Certainly. Let's dive right in, shall we?" Pastor Sagle stared intently at Paisley. "Since your announcement on Christmas Eve, how have you been feeling?"

"Excited. And tired."

"Congratulations to you both."

"Thank you."

"Does your pregnancy make participating in the legal proceedings more difficult?" The pastor tipped his head, his eyes shining as if he sympathized with her.

"Not really. I'm excited to be having a baby. I just want the part about me facing Edward to be over. I'd rather skip it altogether."

"I understand." He nodded. "Judah, you mentioned in our phone conversation that you were planning to go by and chat with Edward. Are you still going to do that?"

"Yes. We felt it might be wise for me to talk with him before the trial. I haven't seen him in a while." Judah stared at the opposite wall as if hunting for the right words to say. "He's my father, but with all that's transpired, there's a wall between us."

"Sure, sure." Pastor Sagle gave him the same sympathetic expression he bestowed on Paisley a few minutes ago. "What would you like to have happen when you talk to him?"

Paisley and Judah had discussed what they should and shouldn't mention to Pastor Sagle. While they trusted him, he was visiting Edward in jail. They didn't want him accidentally saying anything to him about their conversation here.

"I have questions. Private things to ask him."

"I see." The pastor squinted at a piece of paper on his desk. "Paisley, you mentioned having to face Edward. What concerns you the most about that?"

She drew in a breath and let it out slowly. "How I'll feel sitting across from the man who hurt me. The man who seemed to hate me with his whole being."

"Are you afraid of him?" He gazed at her again.

"Yes. However, I want to be brave. I don't like feeling controlled by fear." She took another breath. "I'm going to be a mom. I want to be strong for our child. I want Judah to be proud of me, too."

"Oh, sweetheart." Letting go of her hand, he hugged her. "I am proud of you. God's going to help us through every step." He pulled back from the hug but kept his arm resting comfortably over her shoulder. She leaned into him, thankful for his inner strength and his strong arm around her.

"Practicing might help." Pastor Sagle rubbed his hand over his whiskered chin. "Have you thought of doing that?"

"Practicing how?" Paisley imagined herself practicing for speech class back in high school.

"You and Judah might try acting out a courtroom scenario. He could ask you some questions like the lawyers will do." Pastor Sagle nodded toward Judah. "You can do that, right?"

"Sure. Practicing sounds like a good idea. What do you think, Pais?"

"I guess." Although, she didn't see how it would help.

"That way you're working on conquering the fears together." Pastor Sagle spread out his hands toward them. "You two are close, praying together, and you're trusting God. All good things. I'm proud of you both."

"Thanks, Pastor." Judah drew his arm away from Paisley and leaned forward. "There's still the matter of our feelings about the wrongs Edward has done. The cruelty he displayed toward Paisley, and toward my mom. How do we get over that? How could anyone?"

Now it was time for the forgiveness talk—the part Paisley dreaded. The part she probably needed to hear the most.

"Remember the assignment I gave you a while back?"

"About praying for Edward?" Judah shrugged. "Sure. Over the last month, we've prayed for him daily. We've asked for God's help in forgiving him too."

"Good, good. And have you?"

Thankfully, the pastor's question was aimed at Judah. Not her.

"About the time I think so, anger wells up in me again. I wish speaking with my father wasn't as difficult as it is. If he were a more reasonable person, we could talk things through."

"We previously discussed the atrocities Jesus went through." Pastor Sagle tapped the Bible on his desk. "How he forgave everyone, even those who did the worst to him and still had grace for everyone."

"We did. That's how I want to live my life. However, I confess to failing sometimes." A grim line crossed Judah's mouth. "The trial is going to be a struggle. It might bring all the awful stuff we went through, particularly what Paisley went through, to the surface again. That's why we're here."

Judah met her gaze and smiled softly. Such tender feelings rushed through her for her husband. She loved him more now than ever. She appreciated how he was strong yet humble. Loving yet struggled to forgive. She was thankful he was able to be honest about his weaknesses and not try to pretend he wasn't upset with Edward.

She was so blessed to be Judah's wife. So thankful he was her baby's father.

How had he turned out so right when his father turned out so bad?

Five

Inside the Beachside Inn office, Forest waited to talk with Maggie. He'd spoken with Alison and Craig this morning. They told him about the newspaper article they found concerning a private group meeting to discuss the coastline. Were they investors? Concerned citizens? If only he could find Milton, he had questions for him pertaining to the piece and finding out what else he might know about Edward. Since Alison mentioned the bill Maggie called her about, he came straight to the inn.

"Yes, what is it?" Maggie strode into the office from a back room, a grumpy expression on her face. "Be quick about it. I have important things to do."

"I won't take much of your time. How long did Milton Hedge stay here?"

"I can't give out information about my clientele." Maggie fiddled with the edge of her purple sweater. "Last I knew staying at my inn wasn't a crime."

"Alison told me you called her about a bill for Milton's stay, is that correct?"

"If you heard about that, you must know how long he stayed." Lifting her chin, she peered at him with owlishly wide eyes.

"Why didn't you tell me Milton was here?"

"My overnight guests have a right to their privacy! Do you want folks broadcasting your whereabouts?"

"No, but this isn't about me." Forest took a steadying breath, controlling his tone of voice in the next question. "Did Milton ask you to keep his presence in the motel a secret?"

"He may have asked me to keep it under my hat." She chuckled. "We used to compare notes after heated community meetings since both of us had grudges against the ex-mayor."

"Why was Milton staying secretly at the inn?"

"Did I say secretly?"

"Sort of."

"Well, I didn't!" She marched to the window and peered out as if looking for someone. "It's the only overnight accommodation in Basalt Bay. If that's all—"

"Did Milton act suspicious while he was here?"

Maggie was the one acting suspicious right now. Forest took a glance out the window in case someone was out there watching them.

"He kept to himself." She returned to her spot behind the counter. "No law against that."

"Did anyone come looking for him?"

"I think you should leave!"

"Who asked about him?" He was determined to get his questions answered. "Did you recognize this person, or people?"

"Did I say anyone came looking for him?" Maggie pointed toward the door. "Goodbye, Detective."

"Did you feel threatened by anyone while Milton was here? Get weird phone calls? Any strangers asking for his whereabouts?"

Huffing, Maggie picked up a clipboard and tweaked the clasp like it might be broken. "I don't want to get involved. Now, please, leave."

"Involved in what, exactly?"

"Them," she said in a hushed voice.

"Them, who?" Forest took another gander out the window. A beige pickup was parked in the lot. "Do you have guests staying here now? There's a vehicle with Oregon plates."

"Privileged information. Can I get back to cleaning my supply closet?"

"All right. One last question. Did Mia Till stay here?"

"That viper? She's not welcome in my inn, ever!" Maggie turned and stomped out of the room.

Interesting reaction. Why did she have such a strong response to Mia's name? And why was she protecting Milton?

Six

Impatient to get this chat with his father over with, Judah waited in the sterile-looking visitation room, clenching his hands together. What was taking so long for the prisoner to be brought in here? If Paisley hadn't asked him to make this visit, or if he was required to testify against Edward, Judah wouldn't be here now. He'd see his father in court next week. That was soon enough.

The door finally squeaked open and closed with a clang. A mid-fifties officer dressed in a navy uniform escorted Edward into the room. The prisoner's handcuffs and chains rattled with each step. Edward looked haggard. His scowl seemed engraved on his face.

Judah took a deep breath. *God, help me to be kind to this man. He's my father, but—*

"Judah." Edward nodded once as the officer clasped his handcuffs to the table.

"Good morning." The two words felt as dry as cotton in his mouth.

"How's your mother?"

Judah clenched his jaw. After the cruel way Edward had treated Mom, any inquiries about her were off-limits.

"Why did you ask me to come here today?" He rotated his shoulders to relieve some stress.

"Give us some privacy!" Edward frowned at the police officer who'd moved to stand in front of the door.

"No."

"He's my son! Not a conspirator."

"Sorry. Rules are rules." The gray-haired man crossed his arms over his chest.

Edward grumbled and rattled his chains against the table.

"What's this about? There must be a reason you arranged" —Judah avoided saying Mia's name—"this meeting."

"Can't a father ask to see his son?"

If only fatherly emotions were the reason for this summons. Judah bit his lip, not replying. Hadn't he avoided the awkwardness between them since Edward was transferred to Florence?

"I've been incarcerated in this dump for seven weeks and you haven't been by to talk with me. Not even for Christmas."

Was he going to use this time to scold Judah? His hackles rose. Should he remind Edward that he lost those familial privileges when he kidnapped and hurt his wife? Sitting across from his father brought back too many injustices. Too many grudges.

Lord, help me.

"The trial's next week." Judah rubbed his forehead with his fingertips. "It'll be difficult for all of us."

"So what?" Edward bunched up his lips like he was getting ready to spit.

"That's why I came here today."

"I thought you dropped in because of the sweet-tart who asked you to visit me." A raunchy gleam sparkled in the man's eyes. "Mia has a certain sway, if you know what I mean."

Judah gritted his teeth. "She said you needed to see me. What's going on?"

Edward squinted at the lawman like he was worried about him listening. "Your mom sitting in my mayoral seat is killing me."

"Is that what this is about? Someone else being mayor besides you?"

Edward seemed determined that the focus of this conversation was on him, on his demands and wishes. Not on apologizing or admitting his wrongs.

"It's only temporary." Edward buzzed his lips together, making a rude sound. "Half a year and I'll be back governing the town. Wait and see."

"Half a year?" Judah coughed. More like a decade. "How do you figure?"

"I have a golden plan. A perfect opportunity that won't fail."

Judah didn't want to hear about any of his grandiose plans. "Are you going to tell me why you called me here? I have things to do."

"Look. I put something in the crawl space under the house." Edward's nose flared with each word. "Remember where you used to hide and pout when you were a kid?"

Judah tensed at the criticism. "What does this have to do with anything?"

"For once in your life, do what I want you to do!" Edward huffed out a loud breath, then spoke quieter. "I've made arrangements for getting out of my predicament. But in case the worst happens, there's information I want you to see."

Why should Judah listen to anything he said? "What is it? Why not have your special emissary do your bidding, since you two have such a meaningful bond?" He stared hard at his father, silently questioning his ethics, his morals.

"You don't know the half of it, Son." Edward snickered. "It's a private matter. I should have told you before, but never got around to it."

Was he having a pang of conscience? If so, maybe Judah could use that to his advantage.

"Will you do something for me in exchange?" He was putting Edward on the spot this time.

"What's that?"

"Confess to your guilt. Tell the truth! Let my wife live in peace without having to go through the courtroom fiasco." Judah felt emboldened to speak his mind. "Why drag our family through the mud of a public hearing when you know what you did to her? How about stepping up and being honest about your mistakes?"

"Edward Grant doesn't make mistakes." He hawked and spit on the floor. "You think I care a bug's wing about your wife?"

Bile crept up Judah's throat. "You should." He shoved away from the table and stood. "She's carrying your grand-child!"

"Well, well. It's about time you did something right. Let's hope your wife has the stamina for being questioned by my lawyer." Edward's grimace showed his yellowed teeth. "She might not do so well when *her* character is challenged. When *her* fairytale story about me hurting her is ripped to smithereens."

Judah clenched his fists. For a second, he was tempted to ask Judge Greene to reverse his ruling. Maybe he should testify against Edward! "Do the right thing, please. For Mom. For Paisley."

Edward's guttural laugh sounded like machine-gun fire. "I'm not doing squat for the Cedars girl or for your mother."

"I'm done here." Judah met the guard's gaze. "Let me out."

"Don't forget to look in the crawl space."

Judah didn't agree. Nor did he glance back at his father.

Seven

Ever since Paige's gallery opening, the business had been going well, even without the grand celebration she'd hoped for. Sometimes, more customers were in the shop at a time than she could handle, some looking at art, others ordering coffee. Occasionally, she felt pulled between the two positions, gallery owner and barista, not knowing who to serve first. That's why she was thinking of hiring some part-time help.

Sarah, who'd been staying at the project house for the past two weeks, seemed like the perfect candidate for her to ask first.

After making herself a cup of coffee, Paige carried her hot beverage over to the window overlooking the bay. She loved this view. The thick window between her and the rolling waves provided the perfect amount of distance and safety she preferred, too.

The front door opened. "Hello?"

"Hi, Sarah." Paige smiled at the dark-haired woman. "Welcome to my art gallery."

"It's lovely in here." She gazed around the space as if admiring everything in one long glance.

"Do you like art?"

"I do. I used to sketch. Just for fun." Sarah stepped closer to the window. "What a view! You're lucky to have such a glimpse of the sea every day."

"I know. I love having my coffee right here."

"Kathleen is teaching me about creating shadows and the illusion of movement with mosaics, especially with the waves. I'm fascinated with the art form."

"Me too. Check out her display." Paige walked toward the table covered in black fabric with six mosaic pieces resting on top.

Sarah followed her. "These are amazing. Kathleen is working on another one like this dory on a sandy beach." She touched the corner of a mosaic framed by distressed wood.

"That's good to hear since the customers love her stuff."

"I can see why. They're lovely."

"Are you working on a mosaic of your own?" Paige asked.

"I just started one. It's more therapeutic for me than artistic." Sarah whisked her shoulder-length hair back and gazed around the room again. "Where's your work? Callie says you're quite the artist."

"Over here." Paige led the way to her nook by the coffee shop. She swayed her hand toward a tall easel displaying an acrylic painting of Lookout Point Lighthouse that Piper spilled juice on before Christmas. Fortunately, Paige had been able to rescue it from permanent damage.

"Wow. You do great work!"

"Thank you." She met Sarah's gaze. "You're probably wondering why I asked you to come by today."

"I am curious."

"Would you like some coffee or tea?"

"No thanks. I'm fine." Sarah clutched her hands together.

"Let's sit down then. Some customers might pop in while we're chatting." Paige strolled over to a table and sat down. "I'll assist them. Then we can resume our discussion, if that's okay."

"Sounds good." Sarah scooted into a chair opposite her.

"How long will you be staying in Basalt Bay? I don't mean to sound like I want you to leave," Paige hurried to explain. "But if you're going to be here for a while, I was wondering if you'd like a job."

"Really? Are you hiring?"

"Yes, I am. Sometimes, there are enough customers here to keep two workers busy, especially during peak hours."

"You're not inventing a job for me, are you?" A wary expression crossed Sarah's face.

"No. I am creating a part-time job for someone." Paige chuckled. "Although, I can understand why my doing it just for you might seem like a possibility. Are the ladies at the project house offering suggestions for what you should be doing with your life?"

"Yes!" Sarah pulled her clutched hands to her chest. "While they are the best trio in the world, hearing Callie say, 'Bad things happen. Move onto the next phase,' makes my skin crawl!"

Paige smiled at her rendition of Aunt Callie.

"Kathleen is the sweetest, always looking out for me." Sarah took a trembling breath and lowered her hands to her lap. "Bess has been so understanding about me losing my husband."

"I'm sorry for your loss." Paige reached out and patted Sarah's arm.

"Thank you."

"They are great ladies, each one with their own strengths." Paige took a sip of her drink. "What would you think of working here with me? I'd train you. Give you a chance to settle in."

Sarah stared longingly toward Kathleen's display of mosaics. "I'd like that. It's what I hoped you were inviting me here to ask. Thank you for even considering me."

"You're welcome. When can you start?"

"Is tomorrow too soon?"

"That would be perfect."

The door opened, bringing their conversation to a temporary end.

Relieved their discussion went so well, Paige stood and smiled at the young woman who entered. "Welcome to the art gallery and coffee shop. How can I help you?"

Eight

After his difficult meeting with Edward, Judah hated being here at the house on the cliff, doing his father's bidding. This was where Edward dragged Paisley, bound and gagged. This was where he harmed Mom. Intense emotions struck Judah as he stood in the front yard of the house he grew up in.

"Are you okay?" Forest asked as he exited the truck.

Fortunately, Judah brought his brother-in-law along. Otherwise, he'd surely turn around and head back down the hill without searching for the mystery item in the crawl space. If there even was such a thing. These days, he doubted anything Edward told him.

"I knew it wouldn't be easy. But this—" He shuddered. "Might as well get it over with." He marched around the side of the house and stopped in front of a short door. "This is where I used to hide. Edward said I did that when I was pouting. But it was more than that. Even as a kid, I had to prove myself to him. Did I ever fall short!"

"Sorry." Forest gave him a sympathetic expression. "You want me to go in there with you?"

"Yeah. Who knows what he's talking about? He might be leading me on a wild goose chase, manipulator that he is."

"If so, why would Mia have gone to all the trouble to get you to see him?"

"Who knows why she does anything?" Judah thought of her curling up on the lounge chair with him two days ago. She probably did that just to cause trouble between him and Paisley. He shook his head to wipe away the image.

He pulled a small flashlight out of his pocket and squatted down in front of the door. With his free hand, he unfastened the metal hook, then cautiously ducked into the crawl space. He shined the flashlight between the dirt and the floored ceiling above him, but nothing caught his eye.

"See anything?" Forest asked.

"Not yet."

"Where did you hide when you were a kid?"

"Back there beneath the kitchen." Judah shined the light toward the far corner. "I could hear my mom puttering around upstairs. Singing sometimes." He crawled deeper into the earth-scented space. Then flicked the light around the area that had been his favorite place to get away from his father as a kid. "About here."

"Why didn't you just climb a tree?" Forest asked. "This is like crawling into a bear cave. Spooky."

"Gives me the creeps, even now." Judah leaned his elbow against a beam. "I'm not seeing anything unusual either. It's a waste of time. Too bad I fell for Edward's manipulation again."

"Are you sure?"

"Yeah. Let's go."

Forest gripped his arm. "What's that? An object is catching the light right there." He cast a beam of light from his cell phone across a metal box.

"I see it." Judah scrambled forward on his knees. Between the cement pier and the wood, a slim box the size of a small toolbox had been crammed into a crevice. He tugged on the metal, but it didn't give easily.

"Might need a screwdriver to pry it out." Forest pulled a set of keys out of his pocket. He unclasped a Leatherman multi-tool with a tiny knife extended. "Try this." He handed it to Judah.

"Thanks." Holding the flashlight aimed at the metal, Judah pried the knife between the metal and the cement.

"It's like the box was made for this space," Forest said.

"No doubt." Judah kept working with the knife, prying the slim container forward until it fell into his hands. "Now, let's get out of here."

Outside, he felt a sudden release of tension. What a relief to be free from under Edward's house. Free from under his manipulation too.

At his pickup, Judah worked with the lock on the box using Forest's multi-tool. He was impatient to discover what was inside and be done with this task.

"What do you suppose Mia has to do with any of this?" Forest leaned his forearms against the hood of the truck

"No idea. Other than her being Edward's pawn. What do you think?"

"I think she's participated in his crimes. Although masked beneath—"

"Her being a receptionist? The biggest flirt known to mankind?" Judah snorted.

"All that, and your father's confidante?"

"Maybe. I learned to keep my distance from her a long time ago. Paisley has warned me about her multiple times."

"Warned you how?"

"About her flirting. Of her having a scheme to cause problems between us." Judah twisted the tool in the keyhole. The lock gave way, and he opened the box. One small scrap of paper rested on the bottom with the words "Too late!" written in block letters.

"Is this a joke?"

"Too late for what?" Forest asked.

"Just another trick." Judah scooped up the box, tempted to hurl it into the woods, and climbed into his truck. The empty box and the brief message screamed of Edward's doing. Or Mia's. "Sorry to have wasted your time. And mine."

Nine

Ali's phone buzzed. "Unknown" displayed across the screen. Uncle Milton?

She sat up on the bed in the attic where she'd been sleeping at the project house for the last week. Staying with the older ladies was like tiptoeing around three grandmothers who wanted to offer lots of advice. She was eager to get back to Uncle Milton's house, and some peace and quiet.

"Hello," she answered. Hopefully, this wasn't one of those early-morning scammer calls.

"Alison?"

"Uncle Milton! It is you." Hearing his voice brought tears to her eyes. She batted them away, but tenderness rushed through her. "Where are you?"

"Please don't ask."

"Can I drive to where you are and meet up with you?"

"No," he said tensely. "I don't want you to do that."

"You aren't far away, are you?" She thought of that Beachside Inn bill Maggie wanted her to pay.

"Look. Stay out of it."

"Out of it, how?"

Surely, he didn't know she and Craig had been hunting through his old newspapers, reading everything he published over the past few years. Or that they were digging up information about Edward and his group of cronies. Or that Forest—the man who Milton's source said was in league with Edward—was helping them.

"You've been working long hours at the *Gazette*." Uncle Milton's voice sounded accusing. "I told you not to get involved. To leave town! Why didn't you listen to me?"

"How do you know anything about what I've been doing?" She thrust her hand through her tangled hair. She needed coffee. And a shower.

"I've been informed of your doings."

"Informed?" Her muscles tightened. She didn't like anyone telling her what to do or looking over her shoulder. "Do you mean you have someone spying on me?"

"I told you we were being watched. Back off before it's too late!" His voice lowered. "They're probably listening to this conversation. You don't know who you're dealing with here. How big this thing is."

"No, I don't. Why don't you tell me?"

"Dangerous people have serious plans. Get out of Basalt Bay while you can!"

"Sorry, Uncle. I can't do that. We've found some things in the papers. Things you wrote." She debated saying what was on her mind, especially if Uncle Milton's phone was compromised. "Perhaps you purposefully left some crumbs for us to follow?"

"No, that's not what I did!"

"You wrote about Edward's buyout schemes over a year ago. About a group of people—"

"Alison—"

"—who were making plans for the coastline. Something you disagreed with." She stood and shuffled to the window. A thick fog hung over the trees between her and the bay. "Suddenly, you were agreeing with Edward. Supporting his views. Like you converted to his way of thinking. Why would you do that?"

Uncle Milton swore. "You had no right to analyze my writing."

"I had every right. It's public record." Ohhh. Public record! "That's why you kept all the papers from the last decade! You left a record of everything you've written. Of everything that was going on in Basalt Bay. You did that on purpose, didn't you?"

"No, I did not!" He lowered his voice. "Talking like this will only cause us more trouble."

At least he said "us."

She leaned her forehead against the cool glass. "I want to help you, Uncle Milton. Where are you? Please, tell me what's going on."

"I can't. Just leave it alone. Leave me alone!"

She wouldn't agree to that.

"Can you hear the sea from your motel?"

"Yes," he said, emitting a long sigh.

"If I stopped in Florence for coffee, would you meet me there?" After a silence, she asked coaxingly, "How about lunch in Coos Bay? I'd drive down there to speak with you."

"I called to tell you to back off. That's all!" His tone went down to a whisper. "I've been getting email threats."

"What do they say?" She matched her volume to his. Was her uncle in any real danger?

"The same thing. 'Talk and you'll be sorry. We're watching her.'"

Her. Ali gulped. Now she felt more thankful to Callie, Bess, and Kathleen for letting her stay here, even with their bossy grandma personas.

"Be careful, Alison. Watch your step, because they are watching you!"

His warning sent goosebumps scampering up her shoulder and neck. "I will. I love you."

"Love you too."

She had one more question. "Are you going to testify at the—"

Click.

She groaned. Uncle Milton was her only close relative. Someone she looked up to since she was a girl. Someone she wanted to pattern her life after as a writer.

What had he discovered about Edward, or his circle of greedy men, which caused him to go into hiding? Was someone watching her? Someone who might be dangerous?

She was no closer to finding out where her uncle was, other than his admission of hearing the sea. Yet that didn't comfort her. Not with three-hundred-sixty-three miles of Oregon coastline possibly separating them. How was she ever going to find him?

Ten

Forest had two interviews scheduled for today—one with Evie Masters, and the other with Clyde at C-MER. Right now, he was waiting for the deputy to bring Evie into the interrogation room at the Basalt Bay Jail. Would she cooperate with his questioning this time?

Her chains rattling outside the room alerted him to her arrival. Deputy Brian led her across the tiny space and attached her handcuffs to the hook without speaking.

Evie's faded jailhouse orange clothes bore the words "Basalt Bay Jail #105." By her sullen features, she seemed down emotionally, until she lifted her chin and grinned. "Hey, there, cutie."

"Good morning, Evie."

"The deputy's scowl is getting dull. You're more my style." She winked at him.

Brian made a muffled moan and clicked the door shut on his way out.

Ignoring Evie's flirtation, Forest tapped the icon on his cell phone to start a recording and set the device on the table. "Have you had any contact with Edward in the last week?"

"Contact? The deputy said I couldn't talk with anyone until after Eddie's trial. Says he can make that order, which I doubt. I have rights!"

"Have you had any contact with Edward?" he repeated.

"No! Jealous?" Another wink.

"What did your letter mean when you said it would happen at the gala?" He was veering away from his scripted questions, but he needed an answer about that. Paige still wanted a grand opening, even though he'd convinced her to hold off for a while.

Evie rolled her eyes. "Who says I wrote that?"

"Are you saying you didn't?"

She shuffled her shoulders. "Got a cig?"

"No."

"Gum? Candy? You expect answers without bringing me anything in exchange?"

"Did you write a letter to Edward stating something would happen on the night of the art gala?"

"What's it to you?" She tipped her head and peered at him as if she were the investigator and he the criminal.

"My wife owns the art gallery. I'm an investor. It matters to me."

"Keeping it all in the family?" she asked in a sarcastic tone.

"The family?"

"The brat child married the Cedars wretch, who happens to be sister to your wife. Did I get the legacy correct?"

Forest kept a calm façade despite his rising irritation. "Is it Judah you dislike? Or the Cedars women?"

"You have sexy eyes." Evie leaned forward as far as her locked chains allowed. "Mia was right. You are handsome. Love your eye color!"

Subduing his exasperation, he continued in a monotone voice. "Before Edward kidnapped Paisley, did the two of you discuss her capture?"

"I'm not stupid. I know you're trying to trap me." She slouched against her chair. "Not happening."

"So, you didn't discuss if Edward got rid of Paisley, and Judah stepped up to become mayor, you two could be married?"

"We talked about lots of things, sugar. He and I are madly in love. Lovers talk about everything." In contrast to her upbeat declaration, a sour expression crossed her face.

Maybe things weren't all rosy in Edward's and her relationship.

"Did you discuss Edward passing the title of mayor onto his son?"

"He wouldn't take my advice, anyway."

"What advice did you give him?"

"I told him to let Craigie be the mayor. He's smart like me." She thumped the table with her knuckles. "But nothing was good enough for Eddie in comparison to his brat child!"

"Did you feel bad that he didn't own up to being Craig's father?"

"Who says he didn't own up to him?" She jerked against her chains.

"You've referred to Edward and Bess's son as a brat child. You recommended Craig be the mayor instead of Edward's choice of Judah." He still attempted a passive voice. "Edward wouldn't listen to your suggestion. Didn't approve of your advice. How did that make you feel?"

Evie leaned forward, glowering. "You're trying to make me upset so I'll say something I'll regret, aren't you?"

"Settle down. You love your son, right?" He tried a different tactic.

"Of course. I always did right by him."

"When you performed tasks for Edward, you were probably just trying to provide for Craig."

"It's about time someone saw that!"

"Edward should have noticed you were making sure your son grew up healthy and strong." Forest hoped he sounded empathetic. "He should have appreciated your efforts, right?"

"I'll say! But he had the brat child to take care of. Craigie came in second or third," she said scoffingly.

"Third?"

"Oh, uh, never mind. I didn't mean—" She coughed. "Don't repeat it, or Eddie will be mad."

"Are you saying he has another child?"

"I said don't mention it! The deputy is listening. He'll blab to Mia!"

"All right." Forest palmed the air. Despite his curiosity, what she said in this interview was confidential, except for what he'd include in his reports to the sheriff. "Let's stay focused. Talk about when things were better between you and Edward, okay?"

A flirty smile replaced her scowl. "He's such a great guy. He used to bring me presents."

"What kind of presents?"

"Perfume. Candy. Cutesy clothing for our dates."

"And Craig? Did he bring Craig gifts?"

"He did until *she* told him to stop seeing us! I hate her. She ruined everything!"

"Bess?"

"That piece of work he married when he loved someone else!"

"You?"

"No. Someone else before me." She slumped in the chair like she lost all her energy. "He met me on the rebound. He was sad and lonely after another woman broke his heart. Poor man."

"Sounds complicated."

"I would have been the best wife." She pushed up her sleeves a little. "He told me that before he sent me away. I knew he'd send for me again when the time was right."

"So, after Bess left him, he called for you to come back?"

"He needed my help. Needed me."

"He must have realized how valuable you were to him."

"I'd do anything for Edie." Her face took on a rosy glow. "We were so in love, even after those years apart."

What was that saying about love being blind? Forest kept the thought to himself.

"When Edward called you back, what important thing did he need you to do that only you could help him with?" Was he finally on the precipice of getting a truthful answer?

"I'm not falling for any of your tricks!" She squinted at him.

"It's a beautiful love story you have with Edward, spanning so many years. He needed you to do something important. What was it?"

"He would have been a great father to Craigie, if it weren't for his preferred son. And *her*."

Her hate toward Judah and Bess was almost a tangible stench in the room.

Still walking a tightrope between her feelings for Edward and her hate for his other family, Forest pushed a bit more. "What did the man who you considered to be the love of your life, your child's father, need you to do?"

She gnawed on her dry lip. "We were going to be partners."

"Partners in—?" Crime, no doubt.

"Love." She spread her elbows as if she were trying to spread her hands but couldn't. "Power. Living in his mansion. Him, me, and Craigie, a family as we always should have been." She stared at the wall as if lost in a daydream.

Why had she placed her life's hopes on such a vile man?

"What did Edward want you to do about Paisley?"

"He hated her," she muttered.

The words twisted in his gut. "Why?"

"He told me not to talk about it, so never mind!"

Forest contemplated how to proceed. "You know I'm helping Craig, right? He and I are becoming friends."

"How is my boy?" A softer expression crossed her face. "He hasn't been by to see me."

"He's working hard to pay off his debt to society. I'm helping him stay out of jail." He wouldn't mention how Craig was helping Alison search for her uncle. He didn't want that information leaking to Edward.

"Can you get me out of here too?" Evie shifted back and forth in her seat. "Like you helped Craigie?"

"I'm sorry." He wouldn't give her false hope. "I wish I could."

"If I tell you what you want to hear, can you get me out?"

An enticing offer. Some investigators might lie to get the answers they needed. He wouldn't.

"Before Edward tied Paisley up in the art gallery, did you two discuss it?"

"Maybe." She sighed.

"Did you come up with ideas about how to get Paisley out of the picture?"

"Of course!" Evie leaned over and wiped her forehead against the back of her thumb. "My idea was better than his."

"What was his idea?" Forest held his breath.

"To bump her off," she stage whispered. "She's alive because of me. She should thank her lucky stars I spoke up for her."

Forest expelled the breath he'd been holding. "Your idea worked better, huh?"

"You bet." She winked like they were sharing a secret. "Just like Eddie sent me and Craigie away, he could send her away. Make his snotty son pine for her the way I pined for Edward all those years." She spit on the table. "Make that usurper wife hurt too."

With her own words, she declared herself embroiled in Edward's crime toward Paisley from the beginning. Forest almost felt sorry for her. For Craig too. Both of his biological parents would be going away to prison for a long while.

"Did you argue with Edward about what to do with Paisley?"

"Sure." She cast a skittish glance toward the door. "Will you protect me if he hits me?"

"Did Edward hit you before?" The weightiness of his question hung in the air.

"He was always sorry. Said he loved me. Always loved me."

What a wretched mess Edward Grant had brought to the people in his life.

"I'm tired. I want to go back to my room now." She said "room" like she was staying in a motel room, not a jail cell.

Forest had one more question. "On the day Edward took Paisley captive"—he avoided using the word "kidnapped"—"were you at the art gallery?"

"There you go acting like I'm stupid." She clunked the chains together. "Deputy! Get me out of here! The detective is asking snoopy questions. I'm not going to tell him anything."

But she already had.

Deputy Brian sauntered in and unlocked Evie's cuffs. As he led her out, she glanced back. "I would have made a perfect wife for Eddie. The best mayor's wife. I had to show him I was worth it."

More proof of her involvement.

What had she been willing to do to prove her worth to Edward?

Eleven

Forest was running late when he arrived at the C-MER parking lot. He'd stopped by the house for a few minutes and before leaving took a call from his sister, Teal. She wanted to update him on how her counseling session with Danson went. Not good by the sound of it. She railed at her estranged husband's flaws for ten minutes straight. Forest had to intrude on her monologue, promising to talk with her later and ending the call.

Now, to his dismay, Craig and Alison were waiting for him in front of the C-MER building.

"What's going on?" he asked as he approached them.

"Sorry to show up uninvited, but we hoped to observe your meeting with C.L. Is that okay?" Alison shrugged. "I can pursue my own interview with him. However, I'd like to hear what he has to say to you."

"I don't think this is a good idea."

"Why not? What's wrong with us being here?" Craig's

neck tightened visibly. "We've done the research. Under-handed stuff is going on. Let's find out what."

"Three against one will put Clyde on the defensive." Forest strode toward the front door.

"He's already on the defensive." Alison followed close behind him. "Maybe my feminine smile and easy-going ways will put him at ease."

Craig chuckled. "Yeah. That'll do it."

"Come on, Forest," Alison said in a pleading tone.

"Okay. You can come in with me." He didn't want to argue with them, and he was already late. Plus, they had put in a lot of hours trying to discover more information about Edward and Milton through the newspapers. "When I say we're leaving, it's time to go. No questions asked."

"Fine," Craig said.

"You got it, boss." Alison gave him a fake salute.

He opened the heavy door and a mid-forties woman with black hair met them. "Hello. I'm Betsy. How may I help you?"

"We spoke on the telephone. I'm Detective Forest Harper. I have an appointment with Clyde. These are my friends, Craig and Alison."

"Oh, dear." Twisting her hands together, she peered back toward some doors on the far side of the room. "C.L. is on an important call. Doesn't want to be disturbed."

"We can wait." Forest nodded toward a lounge area with a couch and a couple of chairs.

"Any chance your meeting might be rescheduled?"

"I need to see him today. It's important."

"All right." Betsy glanced over her shoulder. "It may be a bit of a wait."

"No worries. Clyde is in the building, right?" The receptionist's nervous demeanor concerned him.

"Yes. But he yelled at me." She made a gulping sound. "I'll tell him you're here. But if he bites my head off again, I'm leaving. They don't pay me enough to put up with his overbearing attitude."

"Thank you for your help." Settling onto the couch, Forest remembered a few tough bosses he'd had in his career. Although Clyde didn't seem like the type to be rude to his employees, especially considering he'd run for interim mayor. However, appearances could be deceiving.

Alison dropped onto a chair and picked up a magazine off a small table. In jerky movements, Craig traipsed from one side of the window to the other, then back again. Did being in his old place of employment unnerve him?

The sound of Betsy knocking on Clyde's office door reached Forest. "Some people are here to see you," she said with a timid voice. "A detective and two others." As if Clyde had yelled at her, she scurried back to her corner of the room, her head tucked down and shoulders slumped. Would she leave as she threatened?

Forest gazed out the windows at the dunes, listening for sounds of the manager's approach.

Fifteen minutes passed.

"I've had enough waiting." Craig strode across the room.

"Craig! Wait up." Forest marched after him.

Alison followed too. "What are you doing?"

"C.L., open up!" Craig pounded open-palmed against an office door. "The guy's a flake," he muttered over his shoulder. "Open up!"

"This isn't the right way of handling this," Forest said.

The door opened slowly.

"What do you want?" Clyde scowled.

"Look, we're here—"

"Hello. I'm Detective Harper." Forest nudged Craig out of the way.

"I know who you are. Why are these two here?" Clyde stepped out of the doorway, straightening his tie. "For that matter, what do any of you want?"

"I'm here as a representative of the Coastal Task Force." Forest pulled out his badge and extended it toward the C-MER manager. "Official business as I explained on the phone."

"Yeah. Fine. What about you?" He jabbed his finger at Craig.

"I'm here to observe." Craig's tense features screamed that he was angry at Clyde, or here for retribution. He had been fired from this place.

"You should leave now. And stay away from my office!" Clyde said forcefully.

"Why should I?"

Chins lifted, muscled shoulders back, the two men faced off.

"Hey, hey, hey." Forest stepped between them. He eyed Craig. "Leave this to me, will you? We don't want any trouble."

After several seconds of glaring at Clyde, Craig stepped back. "Yeah. Sorry."

Alison smiled widely. "Mind if I listen in on your conversation with Forest?"

"And you are?" Clyde stood taller.

"Alison Riley, a reporter for the *Gazette*."

"Then, no. Get out of here!" Clyde thrust his finger toward the front door. "No reporters are allowed in here. Company policy. Betsy!"

"Don't want anyone discovering your falsifications of data?" Alison asked pointedly. "Are you in Edward Grant's pocket, too?"

Clyde's jaw dropped. "How dare you!"

Forest held out his palms toward Alison. "This isn't helping, either."

"Betsy!"

The nervous receptionist came running. "Yes, sir?"

"Call security. I want these two removed from the building immediately!" He pointed at Alison and Craig.

"Will do." Betsy rushed back the way she came.

"Is that necessary?" Forest asked in what he hoped was a calming voice. "Let's go into your office and talk. My friends will wait in the lobby."

"No. I want them out of my building, now!"

"You both should leave." Forest rocked his thumb toward the exit. With Craig still serving community service hours, he couldn't afford to have law enforcement called in. "I mean it. Please, wait outside."

"Okay. Fine." Craig put his palm on Alison's back and led her toward the door. "Come on."

"He can't make us leave." She grimaced over her shoulder. "He's not the president. Not the owner of the company, either!"

"That's the truth."

A guy dressed in dark clothes and wearing a security badge jogged past Forest, huffing.

"It's about time, Jeff!" Clyde shouted at him, his face red and his fists clenched at his sides.

"Shall we?" Forest swayed his hand toward the office, trying to take control of the situation. Was a peaceable dialogue even possible between him and Clyde now?

In his office, Clyde parked himself on the opposite side of the desk, arms crossed, not inviting Forest to take a seat. "I'm expecting an important phone call. What's this about?"

"Have you spoken with Mia since her return?"

"Briefly." Clyde squinted at him.

"Did she have a reason for her disappearance?"

"Why not ask her?"

"I've tried."

"It was, uh, a mistake. My assumption she went missing, that is." Clyde shrugged like it didn't matter. "She planned to quit all along."

"Yet she didn't give two weeks' notice?"

"Thus the horrible, useless temp receptionist. Is that it?"

"Can you tell me why Mike Linfield was fired?" Forest retrieved his notepad and pen from his jacket pocket to take down information.

Sighing, Clyde dropped into the black chair behind his desk. "I can't comment on private employee records."

"Is it true he was let go suddenly?"

"As is often the case in this company." Clyde tapped his fingers against the surface of his desk. "No doubt, that's what will happen to me if I don't get my work accomplished."

"Was there anything suspicious about his firing or leaving town?" Forest was digging for information but was falling short of getting any satisfactory responses. Why was Clyde being so evasive?

"Suspicious, how?"

"You tell me."

"Nothing to tell." Clyde ran his finger beneath his shirt collar, loosening the top button like he was uncomfortable.

"Why were you chosen to replace him?"

"Am I under suspicion now, too?"

"Maybe."

Clyde scoffed. "You're wasting your time. And mine. You should go."

"If I subpoenaed your computer—"

"You can't do that!" Clyde's face reddened.

"If I did, what might be in there about Mike Linfield's firing?"

"I didn't have anything to do with his getting busted! That business was between him and—" He abruptly closed his mouth.

"Between him and who?"

"That's all I'm saying without a company lawyer present." Clyde stared at his computer screen.

Forest shoved his notepad and pen back into his pocket. It seemed this interview was a waste of his time. He gazed around the cleanest office he'd ever seen. Almost bare.

"Are you aware of any connection between Mike Linfield and Milton Hedge?"

"Milton Hedge ..." Clyde said as if pondering the name. "No, can't say as I do." His cell phone buzzed. "I must take this. See yourself out." He turned away from Forest and answered, "Hello."

"If you remember anything about Mike and Milton, give me a call," Forest said on his way out the door. But he doubted Clyde would contact him.

His uncooperative behavior and his unwillingness to speak without a lawyer present was suspicious. Was that company policy? Or was he hiding something?

Twelve

"What's the harm in me talking to my mom for five minutes?" Craig forced his jaw not to clench as he stood by the deputy's desk. "I need to ask her a couple of questions. That's all."

"Detective Harper was already here earlier," Deputy Brian said.

"Was he?" Craig's temper rose. He was still frustrated by not getting to hear Forest's discussion with C.L. But he didn't need to get riled and have the deputy kick him out too.

"He said you should stay off the premises while Evie's here."

"Is he your boss now?"

Deputy Brian laughed. "No. But he's your taskmaster."

"Don't I know it?" Craig rolled his eyes. "I should have the right to speak with my own mother without his approval."

"All right. Five minutes. I'll let you talk to her with bars between you."

"Fine." However, observing his mom locked up would be heartbreaking. He knew firsthand how horrible that claustrophobic feeling of being behind bars was.

"Craigie!" Mom squealed as soon as he entered the small room with two cells in it.

"Hey, Mom."

She reached her hands through the bars. "My boy! I've missed you."

Craig extended his hands toward hers, but Deputy Brian cleared his throat loudly. "No contact."

Craig pulled his hands back and stuffed them in his jacket.

"Aww, Deputy. This is my son," Evie whined. "I want to pinch his cheeks."

"No contact means no contact," Deputy Brian said sternly.

"How are you, Mom?" Seeing her pale features and dark bags beneath her eyes made him feel bad for her. Did she hate being in this jail cell as much as he had?

"As good as can be expected. I'm still waiting for Edward to spring me out."

"Mom—"

"What? You don't think he'll come for me? Just wait." A cheesy grin crossed her face. "He always takes care of me."

"Was he taking care of you when we lived in our car those times?" Craig gritted his teeth. "Was he taking care of us when we didn't have money for food or gas? Or you couldn't get the insulin you needed?"

"Now, Craigie. What's this about? I can see you're worried."

He glanced around her cell. Messed up blankets on the cot. A few books on an end table. A journal and pen. Bare survival in a box. Is this what her life would look like from now on? What his life would have looked like if Forest hadn't stood up for him?

Some of his angst toward the detective lessened. Forest made him leave C-MER earlier because he was trying to do his job. That's all.

Craig cleared his throat. "I need your help with something."

"Anything, Craigie." Evie gripped the bars between both hands. "Mommy's here for you."

Inwardly, Craig groaned. Deputy Brian snickered. But even he must have a mother who made a fuss over him!

"Do you know anything about Edward meeting up with a group of guys to discuss the coastline?"

"Why would I know anything about that?"

"How about C.L.? Have you heard of him?"

Ever since his wasted trip to C-MER, Craig felt suspicious of the manager. Why had he been so adamant that Craig and Al couldn't be present?

"C.L.? Oh, sure thing, sweetie. We double-dated at the big house."

"Double-dated?"

"Edward and me. C.L. and Mia." She grinned as if proud of the fact. "I made baked chicken and scalloped potatoes to die for. Having all those ingredients at my fingertips was a dream come true."

Craig tried mentally wading past the vision of her and Edward as a couple, or of Mia with C.L. "Why did Edward meet with C.L.?"

"Why do you want to know?" Her eyes glinted at him. "Did that reporter put you up to these questions?"

"Who told you about her?"

"Mia, who else?"

"Mia's been here?"

"Not lately. But she told me about the troublemaking journalist. How she'd like to stuff a rag in her printing presses!" She chortled like she'd told a funny joke.

Craig tensed at even the possibility of Mia being violent toward Al. Any chance the threats toward Milton came from her?

"Were Edward and C.L. making plans about the town at this dinner?"

"Stop pestering me, Craigie." She crossed her arms and lifted her chin defiantly. "Your mama's no snitch."

For a minute, he felt like the parent; she, the child.

"I need you to be honest with me." He made his voice sound more desperate than he felt. "Please, Mom? What did they talk about?"

"I'd do anything to help you, but I can't rat out Edward. He and I are going to be married."

"No, you're not!"

"Yes, we are. He loves me!"

"Edward loves himself. He's looking out for Number One." Craig raked his hand through his hair.

"I am his Number One now."

"Craig—" Deputy Brian barked. "Time's up!"

"Mom," Craig appealed to her again. "What was so important that C.L. and Edward met like that?"

"Wrong question. You shouldn't be asking why they were meeting. You should ask why those handsome men were meeting with Mia and me!" She cackled like she solved the whole dilemma.

"Time's up!" Deputy Brian grabbed Craig's forearm and tugged him toward the door.

Craig took one last look at his mom, his heart aching for all the trouble she was in—and she didn't even seem to realize it.

Thirteen

Ali tried concentrating on the editorial she was writing about Forest. It was hard for her to admit she was wrong about anything. Apologizing publicly? That was exponentially difficult. But she'd promised Forest, and herself, that if she discovered she relied on erroneous facts about him, she would write a retraction. Since she believed that was the case, she wanted to clear his name, even if she had to eat crow in the process. In the future, she'd vet every piece of information that came into the newspaper office. She wouldn't rely on anyone else's viewpoint—not even Uncle Milton's.

With Craig stalking around the maze of papers like a prowling lion, focusing on her writing was even more difficult. Forest had called and asked for a meeting between the three of them, and Craig was wearing out a path on the floor. What was bugging him today?

A few minutes later, Forest strolled in, his expression downcast. "I had a call from Sheriff Morris. He's thinking of pulling the plug on my involvement in Edward's case, again."

"What?" Craig said strongly.

"Why now? When we're so close to solving this thing?" Ali asked.

"Are we?" Forest wiped his hand over his forehead. "We've followed leads. Looked under stones. But with four days until the trial, we don't have the necessary proof I thought I'd find. No hard evidence."

"I wish we knew where my uncle was."

"I went and saw my mom yesterday." Craig peered at his thumbnail.

Forest groaned. "I told the deputy—"

"I asked her about C.L. She says the four of them had dinner together—her, Edward, Mia, and C.L."

"Is that right? Did she say why they met?" Forest's forehead puckered into furrowed lines. "Or what they talked about?"

"No. She doesn't want to rat out Edward." Craig shrugged. "She said I shouldn't be asking what they were talking about. But I should ask why they were discussing it with her and Mia. Like they were the important parts of the equation."

"Like she and Mia are in it deep?" Ali saved her document then faced Craig. "C.L. too?"

"Maybe. However, I don't know if anything she says is dependable. Even though she is my mom, there have been too many lies. I don't trust her where Edward is concerned."

"Thanks for trying to get her to cooperate." Forest unfolded a sheet of paper and held it out. "Here's my other news. Milton's phone records tell an interesting story. See the repetitive number I highlighted?"

Ali peered at the phone numbers.

Craig came around the end of the desk and looked over her shoulder. "I recognize that one." He pointed at the paper. "It's Mia's."

"Correct," Forest said.

"My uncle was corresponding with Mia Till?" This couldn't be right. Uncle Milton wasn't involved—

"Repeatedly. I tried her number this morning, but she didn't take my call, again. As far as I can tell, she hasn't been to her apartment." Forest glanced at Craig. "Has she contacted you?"

"Nope."

"Your phone number shows up on her phone records also. Care to explain?"

"I'd like to hear that one too." Ali met his gaze, searching for possible guilt.

"I texted her. So what? I asked if she was okay."

"Did she answer you?" Forest asked.

"No. Thus my answer about her not contacting me."

"If she reaches out to you, notify me immediately." Forest folded the phone log.

"Will do."

"When you find her, throw her in jail, will you?" Ali said. "Maybe then she'll answer our questions."

"If I had solid evidence against her, I would have already done that." Forest turned toward Craig. "Did Evie say anything else that might help us find Milton?"

"Not really. She believes Edward's going to get her out." Craig rolled his eyes. "That they're going to marry. Live happily ever after. Yada. Yada."

Taking advantage of the pause in their dialogue, Ali said, "I had an epiphany concerning the meeting we read about in the paper. We should question Callie Cedars about it!"

"My wife's aunt?" Forest was obviously confused by her suggestion. "Why waste our time?"

"Before Christmas, she offered to tell me something about Edward if I followed through on what she wanted me to do, which was to clear your name." Ali tapped her fingernail against her keyboard. "I didn't fulfill my part of the deal, but she knew something. If anyone has information, it's her."

"That seems like a stretch." Forest stroked his chin as if he was deep in thought. Then he strode to the door. Pausing with his hand on the handle, he asked, "Are you coming? I'm nearly off the clock for the Task Force. If we're going to do this, it must be now."

"Count me in!" Ali glanced at Craig who stood with his arms crossed, leaning against the counter. Then she ran out of the office. She couldn't miss this opportunity to confront Callie!

Fourteen

Paisley woke up experiencing some cramping and spotting, and immediately feared the worst. Another miscarriage? *Oh, Lord, please, no.* She knelt on the floor in the bathroom, crying and praying, begging Him to save her child. Asking for this chance to be a mom.

Heartbroken at even the possibility of losing another baby, she silently wept all the way to the ER in Florence.

As he drove, Judah sent empathetic glances her way. He had to be aching inside over the possible loss too, but he obviously didn't know what to say. What could he say? Nothing would comfort her right now, anyway.

"Are you okay?" he finally asked.

"I don't know." She sniffed and wiped her nose with a tissue. "I want this baby."

"I do too. Pais?" He clasped her hand, keeping the other hand on the steering wheel. "We're going to get through this together and trust God, no matter what, okay?"

She nodded despite the tears flooding her eyes.

Judah prayed quietly for her and their baby. A couple of times he let go of her hand to steer around a curve, but otherwise, he clutched her hand as firmly as she held onto his.

She kept replaying her previous problems with trying to carry a child to term. What if she miscarried again? What if she couldn't give Judah a son or daughter?

More tears. More weeping.

In the ER patient room, the process of waiting for answers felt like it took forever. Didn't the medical professionals see her distraught features? Couldn't they tell she needed to know what was happening? Was something wrong with her baby? Would she and Judah have to go through this same loss again and again?

Each nurse or technician who entered the small room asking questions, taking her blood pressure, getting a blood draw, requesting a urine sample, or performing an ultrasound was kind to her, but she wanted more than sympathy and polite responses. She needed to hear the truth. Not knowing what was happening was too devastating.

Judah stayed beside her, holding her hand, his face looking anguished but hopeful. "It's going to be okay."

"How can you be sure? We both know it doesn't always turn out okay."

"I have a sense the baby's going to be all right." A slight smile crossed his mouth.

Was he just saying that to try and comfort her? Or had God given him wisdom or knowledge about this child? Surely, a sense about the baby being okay wasn't enough. She wanted to have children with him. She wanted this child. Stroking her flat stomach, she prayed. *Please keep my baby safe. We want this baby so badly.*

Judah kissed her forehead. Then he whispered a verse she recognized, "'So do not fear, for I am with you; do not be dismayed, for I am your God. I will strengthen you and help you. I will uphold you—'"

The door opened. A short brunette woman in a white lab coat entered carrying a chart. "Hello, I'm Doctor Mallory."

"Hello," Judah said.

Paisley pressed her lips together, willing them to stop trembling. Silently, she begged the ER doctor to tell her good news, this time. Judah's hand still clasped hers.

"Take a deep breath," Doctor Mallory said, "and let it out slowly."

Paisley followed her directions, but her breathing felt stilted. Empty of oxygen.

"Do it again." The doctor raised her chin as if guiding Paisley through the steps of breathing. "I've reviewed your history. Considering your previous experience with pregnancy loss, what you're going through today must be extremely scary for both of you."

"Yes." Her one word came out on another breath.

"The baby's heart is still beating strong."

"It is?" The air whooshed out of Paisley's lungs. She unclenched her fist that had been gripping the sheet. "The baby is okay?" She met Judah's gaze. He grinned and nodded.

"Yes," Doctor Mallory said. "Let's hope for the best, shall we? You need to take it easy for the next week or two. Bed rest for a couple of days. No heavy lifting. Drink plenty of liquids. And try not to stress out."

Paisley cried again, but this time with tears of relief, joy, and gratitude. Judah wrapped his arms around her, holding her gently.

"It's going to be okay," he whispered.

She nodded.

"Any questions?" Doctor Mallory patted Paisley's leg.

"Just take it easy and we'll be all right?"

"There are no guarantees, but that's what we're hoping for. Think positively. The nurse mentioned you've been under a lot of stress?" The doctor's dark eyebrows drew together.

"She's the key witness in a trial against my father in a few days," Judah explained.

"Do you have to testify in public?"

"Yes," Paisley said.

"Until the day you absolutely must go in, I want you resting and being in a positive frame of mind. A safe and comfortable environment, too. Okay?"

"Yes. Thank you, Doctor."

"You're welcome." Doctor Mallory smiled at Paisley, then Judah. "You two have a lot to look forward to."

Judah gave Paisley's hand a squeeze, meeting her gaze tenderly. "We know that. And we're so thankful."

After the doctor left the room, Judah helped Paisley stand, then he held her to him and murmured a prayer of thankfulness to God for protecting their baby.

"Amen," she whispered.

All the way to the project house, the doctor's words about them having a lot to look forward to played through her thoughts.

Thank You for keeping my baby safe. Thank You. Thank You.

Fifteen

As Forest approached the project house with Alison, his phone vibrated. It was probably Teal. He hadn't gotten back to his sister in two days. They still needed to have a conversation, but not right now. He let it go to voicemail. Hopefully, she wasn't having an emergency. If she was, she'd surely contact Mom.

Scowling, Callie opened the door. "What are you two doing here? What's this about?"

"We're sorry to barge in on you like this," Forest apologized. "May we come in and ask you a few questions?"

"Me? What do I know?"

"Plenty, by what you implied to me in a conversation before Christmas." Alison pegged Paige's aunt with a dark look. "I'm writing an article clearing Forest of any wrong-doing, so it's your turn to talk!"

"Now, hold on!"

"We just need to ask a couple of questions, then we'll be on our way," Forest said, hoping to tone down any annoyance.

With the nonverbal darts flying between Callie and Alison, would that even be possible? "Please, Callie? May we come in?"

"I rarely forbid someone to enter my house, especially a guest who's staying in our attic." She glared at Alison. "Keep your voices down. We have a patient here who needs quiet and rest."

"A patient? Who's that?" Forest asked.

"Paisley. She had a nasty scare about the baby this morning."

"Oh, no."

Alison's expression softened. "Sorry to hear that."

"Let's talk in here." Callie led them into the kitchen. "She's resting in the living room."

"Is Judah here?" Forest stopped by the center island that he and Judah had placed here during the renovations.

"No. He drove back to their house to get supplies. They'll be staying here for the time being." Callie tapped her index finger against the butcher-block surface. "He's concerned for Paisley's safety. I wonder where he got the idea someone might try kidnapping her again, hmm?"

"Just precautions." Heat rose up Forest's neck, alongside the blame Callie was sending his way.

"Let me get right to the point," Alison said.

"I wish you would." Callie lifted her chin and squinted at Alison. "Then I can get back to helping my niece!"

"Before, when you wanted me to write a retraction, what did you plan to confide in me about Edward? It's of dire importance that you tell us now!"

"Excuse me?" Callie's chest puffed up. "Don't you dare come in here telling me what to do! Since you're a guest here, you might feel you have the right to say what you want, but this is my house."

"Callie," Forest said gently. "We don't want to cause trouble. Do you know anything about Milton Hedge that might help us find him? Anything about a secret group he and Edward may have been involved in?"

"Secret group?"

"That's right." Forest wanted to set up his recording app, but if he did, it would surely put Callie more on the defensive. "Was there any shady business dealings between Edward and Milton that you caught wind of in your social circle?" He purposefully avoided saying, "gossip circle."

Callie crossed her arms. "I'd wager Edward was the master of shady business dealings. What's this about Milton?"

"With only four days until the trial, I need to find him and discover who has been threatening him, possibly trying to keep him from testifying." Forest rubbed the back of his neck. "I've come up cold, so I'm here asking for your assistance. If you know anything about a secret group of dissenters who were plotting—"

"Plotting?" Callie set her palm over her heart.

"Yes. If you know something, please tell me."

"Well, that is, I may have heard some gossip." She shifted her weight from foot to foot. "Nothing believable, mind you."

"Such as?" Alison pressed.

"Does she have to be here?"

"Yes. It's her uncle we're trying to protect. And her. Paisley, too." Forest patted Callie's shoulder. "Please?"

"I'd do anything to protect Paisley."

"I know you would. I'm sure she knows that too."

"I heard about something suspicious a year or so ago." She met Forest's gaze, her eyes moist. "Nothing came of it. The ones who spoke of it are good men who didn't know that I overheard them talking."

"Who did you overhear discussing what these men were up to?"

"They won't like me telling you." She pressed her fist against her lips as if to subdue a confession.

"I'm sorry about that, but who was it? We really need to hear this from you."

"Come on, Callie," Alison coaxed.

Callie's lips quivered and she shook her head like she was having an internal battle about whether to say anything. Finally, she heaved a sigh. "It was Pauly and James."

Sixteen

During the drive to Paul Cedars's house, Ali contemplated how she'd sat at the same table with Paul and James for Christmas Eve dinner and enjoyed their company. How could either of those friendly guys have been aware of pertinent details concerning Edward's greedy plans and not come forward? Especially when Paisley had been kidnapped?

"I'll take the lead," Forest warned her before he knocked. "When I called, Paul wasn't happy about this interview."

"No doubt. But I'm not going to remain quiet if that's what you're implying." She was a reporter. She'd ask the questions that needed to be asked, regardless of his familial ties or possible hurt feelings.

"Try to be less intimidating then, will you?" Forest knocked firmly on the front door.

She pressed her lips together, not agreeing to anything.

Paul opened the door and glanced nervously back and forth between them.

"Hey, Paul. Mind if we come in?" Forest asked.

"If I do mind?"

"You might as well let them in and be done with it," James said from somewhere inside.

"He's right." Ali attempted a less-intimidating tone but probably failed. "You'd be doing your community, and Paisley, a service by talking with us. And possibly saving my uncle!"

"I'm sorry about this intrusion," Forest said. "You want your daughters and your granddaughter to be safe. So do I. Please, can we talk?"

Paul's expression went from defensive to sickly-looking. "Sure. Come in." He backed up, tugging on the bottom of his well-worn tan cardigan.

Once they were all seated on the mismatched furniture in Paul's living room, Forest spoke first. "As I said on the phone, we have reason to believe you and James may have been privy to the plans of a local group of disgruntled men a year ago."

"Privy?" Paul pushed his glasses up his nose. "Sounds like you mean guilty!"

"Now, Paul," James said. "He didn't say that."

"No, I did not." Forest leaned his elbows on his knees. "Paul, you're my father-in-law. I want the best outcome for our family. I love your daughter and granddaughter. Yes, I'm here to do my job. But I care about them foremost, and about you."

Paul's face turned so red that he seemed about to explode, yet he remained silent.

"Don't you have anything to say?" Ali wasn't the type to wait patiently. She had things to do. Tomorrow's paper to get out. Her piece about Forest to finish writing. "Did you or didn't you overhear the conversation Callie says you did?"

Forest glanced at her sharply.

"Callie?" Paul huffed.

"She's the one who said we heard something?" James scratched his forehead.

"I told you it was my sister's big mouth!"

"Don't blame her. We put her on the spot," Forest said soothingly.

"Once a blabbermouth, always one." Paul crossed his arms.

"Can you tell us anything about the discussion you overheard? Who was there?" Forest asked.

James and Paul exchanged worried glances.

"My uncle's life could be in danger! My life could be in danger. The information you share might keep your daughters from having to testify."

"Alison—" Forest shook his head. "We can't promise anything. All we can do is seek evidence. And find Milton. Now, Paul, did you overhear a conversation between Edward and Milton?"

"Yes." He sighed. "James and I were having breakfast at Bert's."

"What did you hear that concerned you?" When Paul didn't answer, Forest turned to James. "Anything you can share?"

"Paul's been my friend since grade school. We've had arguments, but the one that day was a doozy."

Paul shot James a glare as if telling him he'd said too much.

"What was your argument about?"

"About whether we should tell the authorities what we heard. A couple of braggarts talking about their wealth and plans. Big deal!" James drew in a shallow breath. "What was to tell?"

"Besides, a year is a long time for a man to remember a conversation." Paul adjusted his shirt collar.

"Yet Callie remembered hearing you and James discussing it," Ali said.

"She had no business meddling in my affairs!" Paul punctuated the air with his finger. "Sisters!"

"I have one too." Forest cracked a smile.

"Guys! We're going in circles here." Scooting to the edge of the seat, Ali put her hands together in a begging pose. "Put me out of my misery. What did Edward and Milton say?"

"And the other fellow," James added. "Don't forget the C-MER hotshot."

"Hothead, you mean," Paul said.

"Mike Linfield?" Ali clutched the vintage chair's arms. "Was he there too?"

"That's the one." James stroked his whiskery chin. "Braggadocious. Red-faced. Got angry at the server."

"He fired Judah too." Paul tsk-tsked.

"And stopped the dike's progress." James nodded resolutely.

They were getting off the subject again.

"About the conversation between the three men?" Ali asked impatiently.

"You going to tell them? Or should I?" James stared at Paul.

"What if we do the thing they do on TV shows?" A crooked smile crossed Paul's face. "Plead the Fifth?"

Both men turned toward Forest.

"Why would you want to do that? You weren't involved in this meeting, right?"

The older men shook their heads like a choreographed dance move.

"Yet you're reluctant to explain about it a year later." Forest shrugged. "Why?"

"Because of the threats." Paul glanced over his shoulder like someone might be listening in on the conversation.

"You were threatened because you heard their discussion?" Forest's brows furrowed.

"Yes." Paul jammed his hands into his cardigan pockets. "They threatened me about Paisley. Judah, too."

"Me too," James chimed in.

"Like if you told anyone, something bad would happen?" Forest asked.

James and Paul nodded.

"It sounds like the same thing that's happening with my uncle." Ali met Paul's gaze, then James's. "He's being threatened to stop him from testifying. Yet his eyewitness account might guarantee Edward gets what's coming to him. So you two should speak up. Haven't you kept this to yourselves long enough?"

"Edward was—"

"James!"

"Sorry, Paul." James ran his hand shakily over his hair. "Edward demanded the other guys' help in swaying the town in his favor. Milton with the paper. Mike with the C-MER bigwigs."

"He didn't want to just be the mayor of Basalt Bay." Paul pursed his lips and shuffled lower in his chair. "He wanted to rule it! He planned to convert this stretch of the Oregon Coast into an empire of resorts, spas, and fancy golf courses. Upscale stuff."

"Did Milton and Mike pledge their allegiance to his plan?" Forest asked.

"You bet they did! He had rot on both." Paul made a sucking sound against the back of his teeth. "He threatened to expose them, and deal harshly with them and their loved ones, if they didn't cooperate."

"The debt they owed him would be quadrupled." James shook his head. "He's a bad man."

"What did he want them to do?" Ali prodded.

"Milton had to persuade residents of Edward's integrity." James spit out the last word. "Like he had any!"

"What about Mike Linfield?" Forest asked.

"Get rid of disloyalty in the ranks," Paul said. "And stall plans along the coastline."

"The dike delay." No wonder Ali hadn't been able to find any reason for the postponement. And Uncle Milton knew about this stuff?

"Edward referred to a plan that would solve all their financial woes. A takeover. A coup." James shrugged. "Big talker. Hot air. Sounded like foolishness."

"Edward saw us in the next booth." Paul adjusted his black-rimmed glasses.

"He paid me a visit." James patted his chest. "Him and his bully."

"What bully?" Ali leaned forward.

"The blond bombshell in tight clothes."

"Mia Till?" Forest asked incredulously.

"No. The other one." Paul rocked his thumb toward town. "That gal over in lockup."

"Evie Masters?" Forest's jaw dropped.

"That's her. She threatened me with a police stick. Knocked stuff off the shelves. Swore and yelled threats." James gulped. "Edward stood there watching and laughing."

"Same thing at my place. Only Edward and I have a past. He said he wanted payback for the bad blood. Said if I didn't remain quiet, he'd take revenge on Paisley." Paul's lips trembled. "So I didn't. Not to this day." He thrust his finger at Ali. "Don't you dare say one word of this in your uncle's paper. Hear me?"

"Don't worry. I won't use any of this information without your consent."

"Better not." Paul stood and paced across the room. "I'm not getting into why Edward hated me. He's powerful. Threatened my daughter. That was enough."

"Now, it's my uncle."

"I'm sorry. But he went along with Edward." Paul stopped walking and faced Forest. "After that meeting, Milton started praising Edward like he was his biggest supporter."

"I noticed that too," Ali said, disheartened about her uncle's about-face. "Where he'd criticized him before, suddenly he was condoning the mayor's actions."

"Would you testify in court about what you heard that day?" Forest stood.

"Only if it helps my girls." Paul opened the door like he was ready for this meeting to be over. "Then I might have to leave town."

"Me too," James said. "We all might have to leave Basalt Bay for good!"

Seventeen

Paige knew better than to be in the gallery by herself. Forest had warned her to make sure Sarah was with her. But since it was nearly closing time, and things had been quiet for the last hour, she let her assistant go home.

They'd heard about Paisley's pregnancy scare, and how she was staying at the project house. Maybe Sarah could be helpful with fixing dinner or running errands. She promised to text Paige as soon as she found out how Paisley was feeling.

A few last-minute chores and Paige would have the coffee prep area sanitized and ready for tomorrow's customers, anyway. Then she'd leave.

Hearing the door's jangle, shivers raced up her spine and neck. Too bad she didn't lock up early. Wiping her hands, she strode around the corner and came to an abrupt stop. The one person in Basalt Bay she didn't want to see walked toward her. "Mia."

"Hello, Paige." The shorter woman thrust her fingers through her long hair, swaying like a model on a runway.

"Can I help you?" Paige gripped her hands together. "Coffee, perhaps?" Although she'd already cleaned all the equipment for the day.

"No coffee. What I want, no, what I demand, is your cooperation!"

"Cooperation with what?" Who was Mia to demand anything of her? How dare she act like she could come into Paige's shop and command her to do something! "It's almost closing time. Why don't you come back tomorrow?" Then she'd make sure Sarah was with her.

"Here's the deal." Mia stopped a couple of feet in front of her and swayed out her hands. "Turn all this over to me, and we'll call it even."

Fury ignited in Paige's core. "In what world is that even? You should leave," she said with barely controlled civility.

"We have things to settle first." Mia pulsed her black-painted fingernail in the air. "I'm sick of the trouble you and your sister and that nosey detective have caused me."

Paige moved to her left and gripped the top railing of a chair closest to her. "What is it you want?"

"This building." Mia grinned assertively. "Edward promised it to me as a wedding gift."

"A wedding—? What are you talking about?"

"Everything of Edward's is mine now. Haven't you heard? I'm his blushing bride." She thrust out her left hand, showing off her giant diamond ring lined with a slim wedding band.

Paige's jaw dropped. "How—?"

"Takes you by surprise, doesn't it? I'm in charge of all of Edward's assets and properties." Mia flashed a calculating smile. "Granted, this building fell through the cracks. But the sooner you release the loan back to its rightful owner—me—the better it will be for you."

Paige grasped the chair tighter. Mia married Edward?

"In a matter of days, I'll own all the seaside commercial buildings in Basalt Bay. Then you'll wish you'd cooperated with me."

"Are you threatening me?"

"Take it how you like, honey." Mia looked down her nose at Paige, even though she was shorter.

"What about Evie?" Craig's mom had professed her love for Edward. "She'll be devastated to hear Edward married you, if he did."

"Believe me, he did. The spoils go to the winner." Mia swayed her bejeweled hand in front of Paige again. "I won the prize."

"Or lost," she muttered.

"As we speak, the bank is processing my complaint about the loan for your little gallery." Mia flicked a crumb off her sweater. "My husband owns stock in the local bank. They always do what he wants. This town was Edward's. Now, it's mine. We'll talk again soon." She finger waved and sashayed out the door.

Paige ran to the door and locked it. Then she tapped Forest's number on her cell phone.

"Hey, baby," he answered.

"Come to the gallery right now!"

"What's wrong?"

"Mia was here. She threatened me."

"I'm on my way. Paige?"

"Yeah?"

"Keep the phone connected until I get there."

"Okay." She was thankful for him saying he'd be right here, without any hesitation.

Surely, what Mia said was a lie. She wouldn't get the gallery. She wouldn't own all the businesses on the oceanside of Basalt Bay. What of her profession of marriage to Edward?

Were the rings on her finger as fake as her threats?

Eighteen

Paisley appreciated all the love and care her family and friends were showing her. Pampered by Judah, Bess, Aunt Callie, Kathleen, Sarah, and even Alison, who was staying here temporarily, everyone who walked through the room asked if they could get her anything or do something for her. Did she need a glass of water, juice, or decaf? Maybe another blanket?

Aunt Callie spent her time guarding the front door. "No one's getting past me!"

Paisley believed her. That's why she was able to relax and stay comfy in her blanket cocoon on the couch for the last twenty-four hours. She had plenty of time to mull over baby names and nursery colors, too.

But by the second day of bed rest, the warm fuzzies of everyone's care and concern, and even her daydreaming about motherhood and baby stuff, weren't enough to keep her content with sitting still.

She stood and shuffled to the window, gazing out over the trees and toward the whitecaps down on the bay. She missed walking at the seaside. She hadn't hiked down to the peninsula in weeks. Although Judah would tell her that wasn't a safe place to be right now, she still missed it.

She thought of some of the things they'd done together over the last couple of months as they fell deeper in love. The times they walked the beach and talked. Their dancing on the veranda. Walking into the waves during their special date. Just sitting together in the moonlight on the sand. So many good memories.

Thank You, God, for bringing us back together. For making us into a family again.

She rested her hand on her stomach and prayed for her baby, for the hope he or she would bring to her and Judah, and to their families. Then she silently spoke to him or her.

You are loved, sweet baby. I can't wait to see you. Daddy and Mama are so excited to get to hold you and love you.

"Are you okay? Should you be up?" Bess came down the stairs slowly.

"Just for a few minutes. I'm going stir crazy with all the resting." A smile spread across her mouth. "I was talking to the baby."

"Well, that is a wonderful thing to do." Bess walked straight to her and gave her a hug. "Hello, baby. Grandma Bess can't wait to hold you!"

"Thank you." Paisley loved how warm and supportive Bess was toward her. She was a wonderful mother-in-law and would make a fabulous grandmother.

"Anything I can get for you before I leave for work? Soup? Tea?"

"Tea sounds good." Sighing, Paisley shuffled back to the couch to continue her bed rest.

She should be grateful for this time to relax and put her feet up, but she was anxious. She wanted to move around. Do something with her restless energy. She'd like to get back home and start converting their guest room into a nursery. Maybe she'd paint it a blue-green. In her heart, she already thought this baby might be a boy.

A few minutes later, snuggled into her blankets and pillows again, she was ready for the cup of chamomile tea Bess offered her.

"I've been thinking about the trial," Bess said as she sat down on one of the easy chairs.

"Me too." Although, Paisley had tried to focus on positive things as the doctor told her to do. "I wonder if that's what's caused my body to try to shut down, or whatever it's doing."

"Are you worried?"

"Very."

"Care to talk about it?"

Paisley appreciated Bess's loving attitude toward her.

"Judah and I spoke with Pastor Sagle. And we've prayed about it." She ran her finger around the lip of the cup. "I'm nervous about how I'll react when I testify against Edward with him sitting right there. I hate to think of him mocking me or acting like he didn't do anything wrong."

"The way he came against you violently hurts my heart. I'm so sorry." Bess reached out and clutched Paisley's free hand. "Maybe if I had brought formal charges against him, what he did to you might not have happened. I regret not doing that."

"You couldn't have known."

"I knew he had violent tendencies. I just wanted out."

"I don't blame you."

"Thank you." Bess sighed.

They sat in companionable silence, sipping their drinks.

"Can I give you a little advice?" Bess asked quietly.

"Of course."

"When you're called to testify, don't look him in the eye. Look at Judah. Or me." Bess patted her chest, emphasizing her words. "Or at the lawyer who's questioning you. It's a way to stop Edward from having even the tiniest amount of control over you. I have some experience with that."

Paisley met her mother-in-law's gaze. "I'm sorry for what you went through with him, too."

"Thank you. I'm glad I escaped his abuse. Now, you're the one who matters. Your safety. And the baby's. Your health is important to all of us. I'm praying for you daily. Hourly."

"That's so sweet of you. Thank you."

After Bess left for work, Paisley spent some time talking to God and turning over her worries to Him. Questions still rambled through her mind. But as each one did, she prayed about it. What would testifying in Edward's trial be like? She asked God for His strength. What if Edward mocked her or berated her? She thought of how Jesus was mocked and berated. He would help her get through the days ahead, even if they were turbulent days.

She stroked her fingers down her flat belly, trying to imagine her tiny baby. *We're going to get through this. You, me, and Daddy. We're going to be okay. We already can't wait to meet you. Stay safe. And Mommy will try to do the same thing.*

Nineteen

Craig wore a button-up shirt and tie, hoping to make a good impression when he dropped by C-MER to see C.L. on his own. Forest hadn't approved this visit. If he knew about it, he'd probably tell Craig to stay away from his old job site. Not to make waves. Hopefully, there wouldn't be any repercussions, like his having to do even more community service hours. He needed some questions answered. Going to the source himself seemed like the best way to get those answers.

He felt such an urge to do his part in getting Edward locked away, and to make sure Al, Paisley, Paige, and Piper remained safe. He'd like to get leniency for his mom too. But based on what Al told him about Forest's and her conversation with Paul and James, and the way Evie had threatened those men, her release seemed unlikely.

"How can I help you?" The new receptionist, Betsy, intercepted him near the door. "Do you have an appointment?"

"I'm Craig Masters. I'm here to see C.L." Tempted to lie, truthfulness prevailed. "He isn't expecting me. However, I'd like to talk with him. It's important."

"Aren't you the brave one? Wait here. I'll see if he's available." She strode to the receptionist's desk and picked up the phone.

Being at his old workplace felt odd, but it was doubly weird without Mia here. Was the rumor he heard at Bert's this morning about her marrying Edward true? How could it be? She was a massive flirt. But tied to an old geezer like him for life? Why would she enlist for that kind of misery?

How would his mom take the news? Heartbroken. Depressed. Screaming denials, no doubt.

Betsy clomped back toward him. "You may see him now. Don't try anything funny. Security is on its way."

"Thanks, I guess." He marched across the room to the manager's open office door. What did he have, two minutes?

C.L. stood behind his desk, scowling. "Masters, what's this about?"

"Why haven't you fixed the dike yet?" Craig jumped right into his first question, not silencing his accusatory tone. "Who's behind that oversight?"

"I don't know what you're implying."

"I think you do."

"I've heard you called my superiors." C.L.'s eyelids lowered to small slits.

"No law against that."

"Your digging will only hurt others."

"Others, like whom?" Craig tugged at his tie that felt restrictive. "If you're covering up for Edward, you might as well stop. He's not as powerful as he's led you to believe. I learned that the hard way."

C.L. snorted but didn't comment.

"Mike Linfield got ousted," Craig continued quickly, since his time was almost up. "So did I. So did Judah Grant, twice. Someone is moving players around in this company like pawns. I'd like to find out who that person is and why they're doing it."

And what else they were still planning.

His face darkening, C.L. jabbed his finger toward the door. "If you're finished, you should go. Jeff is ready to escort you to your car. Don't come back to this building again."

"Who ordered the delay on the dike?" Craig asked determinedly. "Whose purpose does it serve? Why not do what's right for the community? For the safety of the public?"

"Why? Are you gunning for my job? Are you next in line in your daddy's queue?"

"Daddy's?" Craig scoffed. "Edward is my biological father, but he's done nothing for me."

"Didn't he keep you out of jail?" C.L. peered at him with a dark, piercing gaze.

"No. That was Detective Harper."

"When you were younger, I mean. I've been aware of Edward's and your connections ever since I arrived."

"What?" Craig staggered backward. How could C.L. know anything personal about him? Hadn't Edward promised to keep that information private as long as Craig did what he demanded? Oh, right. He had gone against him in rescuing Paisley.

"I could bring charges against you myself."

"What are you talking about?" Craig growled out.

"Doctored documents. Changes to schematics that brought the coastline's safety into question. Months of studies and reports wasted. Money sucked out of the project." C.L. verbally pounded out his list of offenses. "I could lay all of that at your feet."

"No, you couldn't. That wasn't me!" Tension throbbed through Craig's temples. "You've got the wrong scapegoat."

"Have I? See yourself out. And don't come back."

Craig heard a sound outside the door. Jeff must be here.

"Do you deny following Edward's orders to keep your job?" Craig said forcefully despite the man's threats.

"Do you?"

"I lost my job! So did my brother."

"Get to the bottom of that, then." C.L. thudded his fist against the desk surface. "And leave me alone."

"How can I get to the bottom of anything when no one will answer my questions?"

"I dare you to ask your new mommy." C.L. sneered.

Craig gulped. He meant Mia.

Jeff strode into the office and grabbed him by the arm. "Let's go, Masters."

Maybe he made a mistake in coming here. But there was something suspicious about C.L. Something deceptive.

"You did what?" Forest demanded as soon as Craig told him where he'd gone.

"I talked to C.L." Craig glanced at Al sorting through some papers at her desk. "What's wrong with that?"

"Didn't I tell you to get back to your community service detail?"

"Yes, you did." Craig debated whether he should say anything else. "C.L. avoided my questions. He said I should ask Mia for the answers."

"Right. The most evasive person I've ever had the displeasure of searching for?"

"You're not giving up, are you?"

"No." Forest took a long breath. "But Mia and Edward threw a wrench into my investigation by getting married."

"You think they really went through with that?"

"By what she told Paige, yes."

Craig groaned.

"Now she doesn't have to testify against her husband." Al tossed a newspaper onto a stack.

"I suspect it's a last-ditch effort to hide their criminal acts." Forest raked his fingers through his hair in obvious frustration. "He gets a young flirty wife. What does she get?"

"His money and property," Craig answered.

"Prestige," Al said.

"We need to find Milton." Forest nodded toward Al. "Send him a needy, coded email, will you? 'I'm in trouble. Need you. Call me.' That sort of thing."

"Lie to him?"

"Not a lie. We need answers. You might still be in trouble. Requiring his assistance."

"Okay. I'll try it." Al hustled over to her computer.

"What about me?" Craig regretted his failed attempts to help with the case so far. Was there anything else he could do?

"Get back to your community service. And stay away from the jail!" Forest lifted his finger. "Except for one last visit."

"Why is that?"

"You should be the one to tell Evie the bad news."

Ugh. "Tell her Edward married Mia? It'll kill her."

"Maybe." Forest's arms sagged at his side. "Or she'll be mad enough to tell you where we can find the vixen who stole Edward from her."

"All right. But I hate doing this to her."

"Edward did it." Forest shook his head. "Not you."

"Yeah, but I'm the one who has to tell her."

Twenty

With his thoughts on the upcoming trial, Judah was on his way to the cottage to pick up some dressier apparel for him and Paisley that he'd forgotten to pick up yesterday. How was Paisley going to react in court if Edward behaved rudely toward her? What if he acted proud of what he did? How would Judah feel about that? Could he sit through the proceedings without intervening? Without begging the judge to let him testify instead of Paisley? Not that the judge would agree. Paisley was the key witness. Still, Judah hated thinking about what his wife might still have to go through, especially in her condition.

After parking his pickup in the driveway next to the cottage, he walked down to the seashore. He needed a few minutes alone to get some of the frustration and worries out of his system before he gathered their clothes and headed back to the project house.

Swinging his arms, he strode farther south, stepping around large chunks of basalt, his shoes squishing into the muddy parts of the shore. The cold breeze coming off the ocean hit him square in the face, causing his eyes to tear up. Or maybe that was simply due to his inner turmoil.

Forest had called last night and shared what Mia told Paige about marrying Edward. What, like they were in love now? Unbelievable. Had she taken a marital vow as a precaution for herself, so she didn't have to testify? Or was it part of some bigger scheme to have control over Edward's assets?

The whole thing made Judah angry. And that fury on top of all the other annoyances he had toward his father boiled in him now. He picked up a handful of small stones and hurled them one by one into the waves.

He'd worried about Mia being too flirtatious with his father before. Then Edward referred to her as a sweet-tart to Judah. Was their marriage even real? How could it be when Edward was going to spend a substantial portion of his time in prison?

Unless he had plans to get out. That better not be the case!

Mia marrying Edward must mean the two of them were concocting more trouble. But what? What if something evil were to befall Paisley, or Paige and Piper, before the trial?

As if Mia had stepped from his thoughts, she strode down the beach toward him. "Hey, Judah."

Just great. He gritted his teeth. What was this about? Did she follow him out to this isolated location?

He was tempted to run back to the house and lock the door. She wouldn't be able to catch up with him in her high heels. How had she made it down the beach in them this far?

"I guess you've heard." A flirty grin spread across her mouth. "Can't blame a girl for wanting a Grant man. You were taken. I grabbed second best."

"Stop with the nonsense." He held out his palms. He didn't want her coming any closer to him.

"What do you think of me being your stepmom?"

"Don't even say that. Why did you marry him?"

"Edward is such a—"

"Cad? Control freak? Ancient?"

"I did what I had to do." She crossed her arms. "Now, you need to do what you have to do."

Tension tightened the nerves in his neck and shoulders. Was she here to order him around? To give him another message from Edward?

"Here's a message you can take back to your bridegroom. Leave me alone. Leave my family alone!" If Edward and Mia had a plan to hurt his family—

"Judah, you are too cute. I am your family now." She touched his coat sleeve. He jerked back. "You used to be a nicer man."

"Maybe that was before I learned about you and my father."

Her tinkly laugh grated on him like fingernails against a chalkboard.

"Can't get the picture of me and him being romantic out of your thoughts, hmm?"

"Is that all you followed me to say? If so, goodbye. Have a nice life as Mrs. Grant."

He walked away from her, but she dogged him, remaining a few steps behind him.

"We share the same last name now. I get to share your father's belongings. His wealth."

"You're welcome to it!" He pivoted back to her. "Right alongside being a prisoner's wife. The ex-mayor's temporary fascination." The words came out quickly, and he didn't have time to douse his resentment. "Someone who's fallen into Edward Grant's trap of manipulation and servitude, right where he wants you."

"Servitude?" She held up her hand and his gaze fell on her glaringly large ring. "Was all that grace and love stuff you used to talk about just an act?"

Pain shot through his spirit. "No, it's not an act." He took a shaky breath and gazed toward the sky. *Lord, help me.* "Grace is of immense value to me. Redemption in Christ is something you still need, Mia. I don't mean to be unkind, but why did you marry a man old enough to be your father? Just to have control of his property?"

"I have my reasons for being Mrs. Edward Grant."

Was she referring to the dollars in Edward's bank account?

"Lighten up, Judah." She tugged on his sleeve. "I left a note for you in your box at the house."

"What are you talking about? You broke into my house?"

"It was unlocked. I'm your stepmom. I can go into your house, silly."

He opened his mouth to argue.

"Besides, I was putting something back."

"You were the one who took what Edward left for me?" How dare she presume—

"For leverage. But since we're family now, I changed my mind. I have your best interests at heart, *Son*."

"I said don't—" Groaning, he sprinted back to the cottage, keeping well ahead of Mia's ability to catch up to him. He wanted nothing to do with her.

Stepmom, indeed!

Twenty-one

Craig waited in the interrogation room at the jail, itching to leave, and hating every second he was in this building. But since it might be the last time he saw his mom for a while, he stayed. He dreaded telling her about Edward and Mia. How could she not feel betrayed? All these years she thought they were going to get married, and Edward did this to her? What a scum!

He deserved the worst fate. Craig clenched his fists tightly. He'd gladly mete out the worst fate to his biological father, except he didn't want to end up in the same place as Edward. Didn't want to be like him, even in his temper.

Focus on a happier time. Isn't that what the counselor said? He pictured running on the beach when he was a kid, chasing a seagull, or finding a sand dollar without any chips in it. Slowly, he released his clenched hands, relaxing one finger at a time. He took a deep breath.

The door opened, and Deputy Brian escorted Evie into the tiny space. It had been only two days since he saw her, but she looked thinner, her face gaunt. Her hair was shriveled against her scalp.

He swallowed hard, concern and compassion rushing through him. If only there was something he could do to help her.

"Craigie! It's good to see you, my boy."

"Hey, Mom."

Evie dropped into her chair, and the deputy secured her handcuffs to the table. He nodded at Craig once, then left the room.

"I'm glad you stopped by again. This place is awful. Can you bust me out of here?"

"Sorry. I can't." He clenched his jaw to stop himself from saying he wished she hadn't done the things she did that landed her here.

"What about the detective? Tell him I was just doing my job."

"Your job?" He leaned forward, squinting at her. Is that all she thought she'd done? Her job?

"Doing what Eddie told me to do." She stuck out her lower lip. "I haven't heard from him in a month. Mia hasn't been by to see me, either. Have you heard anything?"

"Uh, well, sort of. I'm sorry, but I have some news for you."

"Bad news? Oh, no." Her mouth dropped open in a wailing pose. "Did Eddie get hurt?"

"No. But, um, things have changed."

"Changed how? What have they done to him? Did he go to court early? Is he in the hospital?" She was getting more agitated, her hands clawing at each other, tugging against the chains. "What's wrong with my Eddie?"

"Look, this isn't easy for me to say to you."

"Oh, no. Oh, no," she whimpered.

"Edward—" Feeling the tightness in his throat, he tugged on his neckline. "Edward and Mia got married."

"What?" Evie screeched. "Don't you dare lie to me, Craig Masters!"

"I'm not lying. It's the truth, even though I can't believe it myself."

"Edward and Mia got hitched? No way! Is this a scheme you and the detective concocted to get me to crack?" Her voice ricocheted off the walls. "Deputy! Deputy!"

Deputy Brian opened the door. "What's going on in here?"

As if he didn't know. Wasn't he listening in through a speaker?

"Get me out of here!" Evie yanked on her chains, jerking them back and forth. "He's tricking me. Lying to me. He's a wolf in sheep's clothing!"

"No, I'm not. She's upset about what I told her about Edward and Mia." Craig clutched his hands over the table. "Please, stay here for a few more minutes so we can talk."

"Why? Are you going to feed me more lies? I always could tell when you were lying! That's what you're doing now."

"Sadly, I'm telling you the truth."

"Evie," the deputy said, "what do you want to do? Stay or go back to your cell?"

Tears running down her cheeks, she sniffled. "I'll stay. But be ready to protect me if I need it."

Deputy Brian shot Craig a look of exasperation before exiting the room.

"People thought Mia was missing. Then she showed up,

saying she married Edward." Craig softened his voice. "I didn't want you to hear about this from anyone but me."

"This can't be happening." Evie lifted tear-filled eyes toward the ceiling. "After all the time I've waited for him? He loves me!"

"I doubt Edward loves anyone but himself."

"Don't say that about your father! I won't let you be disrespectful to him. He wasn't there while you were growing up because of his ex and her brat child." She sniffed noisily like she needed a tissue. "He wanted to be with us."

Craig suppressed a groan that nearly roared out of him.

"We could have been happy, the three of us," she said in a woebegone voice. "Now everything is lost. How could Mia do this to me?"

"Would you be willing to testify against him now? Against her?"

"No!" Evie pulled her shoulders in tightly up to her ears. "I'm no snitch!"

"Even if you know things that would keep Edward locked up for a long time?"

"Why would I want to hurt him? I love him!" She shrieked out a hair-raising sound. "How that tramp convinced Eddie to marry her is beyond me. But he and I will be together one day." Suddenly, she grinned. "I've waited this long. A little while longer won't hurt."

"Ten or fifteen years might hurt a lot."

"Why do you even care?"

"I care about you, Mom." He wanted to clasp her hand, but if he did, Deputy Brian would charge in here again. "You matter to me."

"Aww, Craigie."

Forest had told him to appeal to her motherhood to get answers. But Craig didn't want to toy with her emotions. She was already fighting her own demons.

"Edward promised he'd fix everything. I trusted him. We had plans."

Plans? A surge of adrenaline coursed through him. "What does Edward have planned for the Cedars girls? For the town?"

Evie stilled, her eyes looking downward.

"Considering what Mia did to you by marrying your future husband"—he tried to say this kindly—"and what Edward did to you by going along with the scheme, don't you owe it to yourself to tell me or the detective what you know?"

"I'm no tattletale!" She glared at him then. "You're the one who saved your backside at my expense!"

A sword pierced his heart. She was right. But she was guilty of crimes worthy of prison. She would have to serve time for colluding with Edward.

What if she confessed? Would the courts go any lighter on her?

"If you cooperate, it's possible things will go easier for you when you face the judge."

She slouched in her chair. "What do I even have to live for if Edward is lost to me?"

"Me." Craig's voice cracked, sounding pre-teen. "Maybe your future grandkids."

"Are you dating someone?"

"I care for someone."

"Oh, Craigie." Her chains rattled as she attempted to reach her fingers out to him. "Who is she?"

"I'll tell you another time." He needed their conversation to stay on track. "If we get married and have kids, wouldn't you want to be there for them? Being a grandma?"

"Of course." She sighed. "Mia and Edward really got hitched?"

"Yes, they did."

"Okay." She sat up straighter. "Get me the detective!"

"You'll talk to him? Confess?"

"I'll talk to anyone other than you. There are things a mom doesn't want her son knowing about her. I'll do whatever it takes to see my grandbabies." Her eyes filled with tears. "Thank you, Craigie. I didn't think you still loved me."

"Mom. I want you to get the help you need. To be stronger in here." He patted his chest but thought of her mental health too. "Are you taking your diabetes medication every day?"

"That annoying deputy makes me."

"Good for him." Craig glanced toward the window and nodded at Deputy Brian. "So, you'll talk to Detective Harper and tell him the truth?"

"If I must." Her shoulders sagged. "Can I go back to my room now?"

"Sure, Mom." Craig stood. What could he say with these last moments they had together? "I wish you well. I love you."

"Love you too, Craigie."

Even though Evie agreed to talk with Forest, Craig left the jail with a heavy heart. What hope was there for her when she'd done so many things wrong in her efforts to please one lousy man?

Twenty-two

Barely hearing the rumble of the waves barreling up the shore, Judah sat on the lounge chair on the veranda, turning the unopened metal box in his hands. Why did Mia sneak into the crawl space and steal whatever was in the box, then come to the cottage and return it? For manipulation? Just to be annoying? How could he trust that whatever was in the box now wasn't a trick of hers? Or Edward's?

Slowly, he opened the metal lid. He peered into the box like a snake might be in it ready to lunge at his hand. One crumpled folded sheet of paper rested on the bottom. Exhaling, he unfolded the paper.

"'My darling Edward ...'"

Wait. Who wrote this? He skimmed to the bottom of the letter. It was signed "Sue Anne." That name sounded familiar.

"'I'm so sorry for what I did without telling you.'"

What was this about? Why did Edward want Judah to see a letter written to him?

"'At the time, I loved you in the way I understood love. You and Paul both captured my heart.'"

Him and Paul Cedars? Oh, right. Callie had told Paisley something about Edward and Paul going after the same woman when they were young.

Judah reread the section he skipped.

"'She's beautiful. But my parents forced me to give her up. She looked like both of us.'"

Was Sue Anne saying she and Edward had a child she was forced to give up? As in Judah might have another sibling? An older sister? He groaned. Being the cad he was, how many kids had Edward sired without owning up to them?

"'I've searched and searched for her over the years.'"

Maybe this letter wasn't as old as he first thought.

"'I hope you and Paul didn't hate each other all these years,'" Judah continued reading. "'I shouldn't have let you steal me away from him. I cared for you both, but you were more persuasive.'"

Poor woman. Poor Paul.

Judah felt uncomfortable reading about his father's love affair with a woman Paisley's dad had loved first. Did Paul know of the child? Is that what drove the stake of hatred and bitterness against Edward into his heart?

"'I discovered the adoptive family has connections to Basalt Bay, so I won't mention their last name. They called her Sarah.'"

"Sarah?" Judah swallowed hard. As in the Sarah who was staying at the project house? How unlikely was that? He took a couple of deep breaths, trying to clear away his confusion. What if it were true? Sarah might be his half-sister.

What emotional or psychological control was Edward trying to pull by showing Judah this letter before the trial? Was it even authentic? Or another ploy of Mia's to cause trouble?

Twenty-three

"What can you tell me about Mia's involvement with Edward?" Forest sat in the interrogation room across from Evie. She was acting sullen and pouty, not giving him the information he hoped to hear based on Craig's claim that she was ready to confess.

"I don't want to talk about her. Other than to say she's a dirty man-stealer!" Evie bunched up her lips and stared at the wall.

"You don't feel any loyalty toward her, since she went behind your back and married Edward, right?" Forest was prodding her emotionally, but he had to say something to get her to talk.

"The way she pawed at Eddie, Craigie, or whoever, drove me nuts." Her face crumpled into a silent wail. "I don't know how she could stab me in the back like this!"

"So their wedding took you by surprise?"

She bared her teeth like a rabid dog. "Of course, it did, you toad face!"

Even though her wrists were cuffed to the table, Forest scooted back in his chair.

"I came here today because your son said you wanted to speak with me. Was he lying?"

"My son doesn't tell falsehoods like others in this town do." She glared toward the window.

"Who lied to you?"

"Eddie. Mia. That deputy!"

"What did the deputy lie about?"

"He said I couldn't receive messages from Edward," she said in a forced whisper. "That wasn't true. He's the reason Eddie took up with Mia again!"

"Again?"

"I stole him back from her when I came to town." Evie made a sucking sound against her teeth. "I did everything Mia told me to do because I thought her instructions came from Eddie."

"You don't think the messages were from him?"

"Don't you smell her perfume? It's stinking up the whole town!" She cast furtive glances between Forest and the window where Deputy Brian was watching them. "If I talk, she'll find out. She'll take revenge on me. So we're done here." She pressed her lips together so tightly the rosy flesh disappeared. "If you catch her, toss her in the slammer, will you? Then Eddie will want me again."

How insecure she must be to settle for someone like Edward. As unfathomable as it was for Forest to imagine, maybe she truly loved the guy.

"What if Mia goes after Craig?" He tried a different angle.

"She'd better not! I don't want a minx like her getting her nails into my son."

"Did you ever tell Edward of your concerns?"

"Sure. He just laughed. I told him her plans about capturing Paisley were—" She swallowed a loud gulp as if she realized she'd said too much.

"Are you saying Mia came up with the plan to kidnap Paisley?" Forest's shoulders tightened, his detective instincts on high alert.

"Don't tell!" she said in a frantic tone. "Or what she still plans to do will fall on my head."

"You're obviously afraid." He felt sorry for her, but he had to pursue answers. "What else does Mia have planned?"

"Where she's concerned, I fear for my life!" She nodded toward the door and whispered, "Her and that deputy laugh it up. Planning on how to do me in, too, no doubt."

"Mia was here with the deputy recently?" Forest lowered his voice. "Can you hear what they talk about?"

"Nope. Just laughter. Like they're pulling the wool over everyone's eyes."

Forest's heart pounded a riotous beat. Was the deputy involved with Mia's and Edward's schemes?

Suddenly, Evie laughed loudly, her face tipped toward the ceiling, her mouth open wide as if she were pulling one over on him right now.

Had she just duped him again?

Twenty-four

After Judah and Paisley discussed the letter from the box, and even though he questioned the note's authenticity, they agreed he should talk with Sarah about it. She had a right to know about the possibility of her being Edward's daughter. Judah suggested that Kathleen join them for Sarah's moral support.

He didn't want Paisley to undergo any more stress, but he wanted her in on this conversation too. Tomorrow would be her regular doctor's appointment, then they'd have a better idea of her current condition. Until then, he wanted her to remain as stress-free and relaxed as possible.

Sarah and Kathleen walked down the stairway side by side and then settled into two easy chairs.

"Thanks for meeting with us." Judah squeezed Paisley's hand. She answered back with a slight squeeze.

"How are you this morning, dear?" Kathleen asked.

"Good. Tired of resting!" Paisley chuckled.

"I bet." Kathleen smiled warmly.

"But I sure am thankful to be carrying this little one."

"I'm glad about that too." Kathleen's eyes filled with moisture, showing her compassionate nature.

"Why did you want to talk with me?" Sarah looked pale and nervous. "Have I done something wrong at the gallery?"

"Nothing like that," Paisley said. "Judah heard some news he wants to talk to you about. That's all."

"Okay." She crossed her arms over her ribs, her gaze darting between Judah and Paisley.

Kathleen linked her hand into the crook of her elbow. "I'm sure it will be fine. Whatever Judah wants to say must be important." She nodded trustingly at him.

"I think it is. Although someone I mistrust gave me a letter, so I don't know how reliable it is." He lifted the folded note in his hand. "Supposedly, it was written to my father."

"How does this letter involve me?"

"Someone named Sarah with connections to Basalt Bay might be my sister. Half-sister."

Sarah's jaw dropped. "You think that's me? I had a mom and dad."

Maybe he shouldn't have mentioned this until he talked it over with Forest, and he had a chance to investigate. But wasn't it better for them to find out the truth together? Hadn't there been enough secrets in their family? Then again, what if Mia was toying with them? Making this all up?

"I'm sorry to cause any alarm. But are you certain about your parents?" Judah asked.

"Yes. I mean, my brother and I look different. He and my parents had light hair and fair skin." She gazed up at the ceiling as if thinking hard. "My mom said I took after a distant relative with dark hair like mine. But as far as I know, I wasn't adopted."

They all sat quietly. Judah wanted to give Sarah a few minutes to process this news.

"You're not suggesting it was Bess, are you?" Sarah blinked slowly.

"No." Judah took a steeling breath before continuing. "My father and a woman named Sue Anne *may* have had a daughter after high school."

"My parents wouldn't have lied to me for all those years. They weren't the kind of people to keep secrets, either." Sarah made an anguished-sounding moan. "Unless I didn't know them at all."

"There, there." Kathleen patted her arm. "It'll be okay. We'll figure this out." She cast a concerned gaze in Judah's direction.

"I'm sorry. This must be a shock. We can have a DNA test done in case this is a fabricated story. I admit it may be a fake letter. If it is, I'll strongly regret mentioning this today. But if it isn't—" Judah shared a sad smile with Paisley, the one person in the room who understood his conflicting feelings with Edward. "I was uncertain whether I should tell you or hold off until Forest investigates the matter further."

"My mother said she hated this place. Would never step foot in Basalt Bay again. If your letter is true, perhaps she feared I might discover the truth here." Sarah covered her face with her hands. Then lowered them slowly. "My parents hiding this kind of secret from me seems impossible. And horrible. Not that your being my brother would be horrible. But Edward—?"

"I understand. Believe me."

"Are you okay?" Paisley asked softly. "It's a lot to take in."

"Yeah, it is." Sarah drew in an unsteady breath. "But I've been through worse."

Kathleen rubbed her shoulder. "We're here for you, sweetie. We care for you so much. It'll be all right."

"Thanks." Sarah met Judah's gaze. "If this is true, then Craig would be my brother too, wouldn't he?"

"Yes. He and I only recently found out we were related."

"There did seem to be a mystery surrounding Granny's place." Sarah gazed around the room. "I have good memories from here, though. If an adoption took place, my parents and grandmother kept it private. I never suspected a thing."

"If you are related to Judah, you'll be an auntie to our little one." Paisley smoothed her hand lovingly over her stomach.

"That would be the best part." A faint smile crossed Sarah's lips. "May I read the letter?"

"Oh, sure." Judah passed the crumpled note to her.

She gazed at the paper for a couple of minutes. "Was my whole life based on a lie?"

"I don't know. I'm sorry to put you this." Judah sighed. "Edward as a father figure is a poor example of parenthood. I'm sure you got the better deal in the father you had growing up. I don't know anything about Sue Anne, other than it sounds like she was forced to give you up, if this is real."

Sarah handed the letter back to him. "Could I get a copy of this?"

"Absolutely."

"I'm open to doing a DNA test." She closed her eyes for a moment. "Just when things were getting on stable footing, this is a whammy to my heart. But thank you for telling me. For being honest. I wouldn't want there to be any more secrets."

"That's how I felt too." Judah tapped the edge of the letter against his open palm, contemplating what to do next.

Hopefully, he hadn't caused Sarah undue distress.

Twenty-five

Forest leaped out of his car and ran into the *Gazette* office with more energy than he felt in a week. Even though he'd rather pursue Milton on his own, he knew Alison wanted to be a part of finding her uncle. "I have a lead! Grab your coat and come on."

"What is it?" Alison jumped up from her chair at the desk and threw on a sweater.

"Milton just made a purchase on his credit card."

"Really? This is the break we've been waiting for!"

"Exactly."

Alison locked the door on their way out. Then they both ran for Forest's car.

"Where are we going?"

"To the Beachside Inn."

"Why would Uncle Milton be so close, again, without telling me?" she asked in an exasperated tone.

"I don't know."

Minutes later they entered the Beachside Inn's office.

"What are you two doing here?" Maggie glowered at them from behind the counter.

"Task Force business." Forest extended his badge toward her. Fortunately, he was still on the timeclock. "Milton Hedge is here, isn't he? You processed his credit card minutes ago." He slid his badge back into his coat pocket.

"Don't you need a warrant or something?" Maggie twisted a watch back and forth over her wrist in a nervous gesture.

"Isn't it time you told us what's going on?"

"Where is my uncle? Tell me now!"

"Alison—"

"Don't barge in here and make demands of me." Maggie stomped her foot. "I'm a law-abiding citizen!"

"If so, why don't you prove it by cooperating with my investigation? Which room is Milton in?"

"I can't give out private information about my guests." The innkeeper tucked her arms tightly across her ribs. "There's no law against me renting a room to someone, no matter who he is!"

"No. But I told you to inform me if he showed up again. He's a person of interest in Edward's case."

"Sorry. I can't help you." She lifted her chin.

"I'll knock on every door in the place, then." Alison strode back to the door.

"Don't you dare bother my guests like that!"

"If I do, I'll find my uncle here, won't I? Because you're hiding him! When you knew we were searching for him!"

Maggie made a choking sound like her tongue got stuck in her throat. "I won't admit to any such thing. You two barged in here—"

"Why don't you do what's right by Callie's family?" Maybe if Forest appealed to her softer side, Maggie might be more cooperative. "She's your friend. Her niece must testify before her assailant in court. Why not make this easier on her? Tell us where Milton is so we can get to the bottom of the conspiracy."

"Conspiracy?" Maggie patted her palm over her breast-bone.

"Maybe she's hiding my uncle because she's a part of the cover-up, too." Alison pointed at her.

"I wouldn't have anything to do with Edward Grant if my last breath depended on it! That baboon is an embarrass-ment to our town. If only Milton—" Maggie clamped her lips shut.

"What about Milton?" Forest asked. "Did he tell you to be quiet about him? Why would you listen to anything he told you to do?" She obviously had a mind of her own.

"He said if he's found out, we'll all be in danger." Her timid-sounding voice revealed her present state of mind was one of fear.

"Why 'all?'"

"How would I know? Edward hoodwinked everyone else, not me! I never fell for his smooth-talking lies." She sniffed a couple of times. "Never voted for him either."

"But you know something, don't you?" Forest clasped his hands loosely on the counter, forcing a relaxed stance he didn't feel.

"I can't talk about it. Please, leave my premises before I have to call the deputy!" She picked up the receiver and held it out like she was going to make the call.

"You can't stop me from finding my uncle." Alison yanked open the door.

"All we need to do is talk to Milton." Forest smoothed his hands over the edge of the counter. "You would be doing a service to the town, and to Callie's family, if you told us his room number. That way we wouldn't have to bother anyone else."

"My inn is a safe harbor for the weary." Maggie set the phone back down.

"Of course, it is. You want to do right by Milton. An old friend?"

"Don't try to wheedle your way into my good graces." Maggie huffed. "That boat sailed a long time ago."

"What'll it be? Tell us where he is, or I'll go searching room by room. I don't mind bothering your customers." Alison took a step through the doorway.

"Wait. I knew you'd come," Maggie said so quietly Forest almost didn't catch it. "But you shouldn't have brought her." She lifted her chin toward Alison.

"When you ran the credit card, you mean?"

"I sent a message without actually telling you anything."

"I see. How about if you give me the last three room numbers you rented out?" Forest glanced back at Alison, hoping for her cooperation. "We'll welcome each of the guests to Basalt Bay. It won't be like you gave out specific information about anyone."

Maggie gnawed on her lip. "Perhaps offer them a complimentary breakfast at Bert's?"

"You've got it."

She wrote down three numbers and slid the paper across the surface of the counter toward Forest. "You'll be polite?"

"On my best behavior."

With Maggie's permission to knock on some doors, it felt like they were finally getting somewhere.

Twenty-six

"So, it's fine for me to resume normal activities?" Paisley asked Doctor Isabel. If so, this was an amazing answer to her prayers of the last few days. She was willing to be on bed rest for longer if that's what was best for the baby. Its health and well-being was the most important thing to her. But she longed to be able to walk and do normal things. Even to be able to go back to work would be a blessing.

"Everything appears to be fine." The doctor smiled widely. "Listen to your body. If you're tired, rest. Take a midday nap. If you want to walk, do that. Just take it easy for the next couple of weeks, okay?"

"Hard to do when I'm on my feet with shift work." She met Judah's gaze. "But I'll do my best."

"Any chance of reducing your hours?" the doctor asked.

"I can't really—"

"Sweetheart, we'll make it work." Judah clasped her hand. "If you need more rest, that's what you should do. God is our provider. I'm sure there's work for me around the corner."

She loved gazing into her husband's eyes and feeling assured of his love. He was right. They were in this together. She didn't have to carry the weight of their household needs alone. Through every aspect of marriage and parenting, they would face it together. Trusting in the Lord together, too.

"Doctor Isabel, I want to ask you about the trial." Judah's voice deepened. "What do you think about Paisley being in such a tense situation? Is it harmful to her or the baby?"

The doctor turned a kind gaze on Paisley. "How do you feel about that?"

"I was tempted to ask for a medical excuse to get out of it." She grinned sheepishly. "But it seems like the chicken's way out."

Doctor Isabel chuckled. "Understandable."

"I just want the whole thing to be over and behind me." She linked her fingers with Judah's. "Then we can get on with our life together. What Edward did to me has been hanging over our heads long enough."

"Are you seeing a counselor?"

"Sort of. We meant to go back. I was on bed rest, so we put it off."

"I recommend that you talk things over with a pastor or a counselor. Not just once. Keep a line of communication going so you aren't carrying so much stress in your system." The doctor patted her knee. "I'll see you in two weeks, okay? Just as a precaution. I don't anticipate any problems, but we'll keep an eye on things."

"Thank you, Doctor." Judah stood and shook her hand.

"Thank you," Paisley added.

"Of course. Keep breathing calmly through the days ahead. You have a lot of good things to look forward to. Stay positive." Doctor Isabel nodded once and left the room.

Paisley stood and adjusted her clothes. The baby was okay. Their lives could get back to normal. A tender feeling of thankfulness filled her. *Thank You for protecting my baby.*

"She's right," Judah said.

"About breathing?"

"About us having good things to look forward to."

"I know." She leaned up and kissed his cheek. "Thank you."

"For what?" He smoothed his hands around her, holding her loosely.

"Being here. Loving me and our baby."

"It's my honor and privilege to be here." He touched his lips to hers in the gentlest of caresses. "Loving you and our baby? Always and forever!"

Twenty-seven

Since Teal's call was the second one in less than twenty-four hours, Forest accepted the call despite the tension racing through his veins. "Hey, Teal." He stopped at the corner of the motel building, peering around the edge.

Alison bumped into him. "Sorry."

"You sound busy," Teal said. "Or stressed. Bad timing?"

"I can't talk. Things are happening—"

"I get it. Your job is important."

"No, it's not that." No time to explain. "Are you in danger? Any trouble?"

"No."

"Then I'll call you back." He ended the call, hating to be abrupt.

At the second motel door he knocked on, no one answered but he heard a rustling sound inside. Every instinct within him said someone was watching him through the peephole. He nodded at Alison and stepped back, giving her their prearranged signal.

"Uncle Milton? I need to speak with you. Please, open the door."

Nothing.

"I'll get Deputy Brian over here to break down the door. Maggie will charge us triple the cost of repairs." She met Forest's gaze with a grim look. "Listen, Uncle Milton, there are things I must speak with you about. You're afraid. I'm worried too. Let's talk."

The door cracked open an inch, the chain still attached to the doorframe. "Alison, who's that with you?"

"It's Detective Harper. Open up." Forest rammed his shoe against the door, stopping it from closing.

"Leave me alone!" Milton said in a raspy voice.

"Uncle Milton, can I come in?"

"Just you?" He sounded more like a scared boy than a man.

Forest shook his head at her.

"Sorry. The detective must accompany me inside."

The door pressed hard against Forest's shoe.

"Can we talk?" Alison asked wooingly. "Let's get out in the open whatever it is that's keeping you from speaking the truth."

"They're watching you right now."

Forest swung around, peering toward the building behind him, then toward the beach. He didn't see anything unusual.

"Who's watching us?" Alison asked.

"Look at the room across from me."

Forest and Alison both swiveled back.

"I don't see anything." She leaned toward Forest. "Do you?"

"No." He stared hard at the window, the peephole, the bottom of the door.

"I beg of you. Leave me alone," Milton said.

"If you're worried about someone overhearing our conversation, let us in." Alison rested her hand near the edge of the door. "Or else I'll have to bang on your door and shout what I have to say. That'll get everyone's attention."

The chain lock released. The pressure on Forest's shoe eased.

Alison pushed into the darkened motel room and hugged Milton.

Forest followed her inside the room, closed the door, and searched for a light switch. A quick survey of the room revealed piles of clothes, blankets heaped into a mound on the bed, and newspapers scattered across the orange '70s carpet. The open bathroom door exposed toiletries and towels spread haphazardly across the counter and floor. The TV hummed, although too low for Milton to have been listening to it.

"I'm Detective Harper with the Coastal Task Force." He pulled out his badge.

"I've heard of you." The unkempt man glanced at it as if he didn't care. "Am I under arrest?" By the looks of Milton's shaggy whiskers, he hadn't shaved in a week. His stringy, gray and black hair looked in need of a trim. He shoved his dark glasses up his nose like they didn't fit him anymore.

"Is there a reason you should be under arrest?" Forest peered around the room again, making sure no one else was there. "Hiding out in a motel room is hardly grounds for arrest."

Milton dropped onto the edge of the bed, clutching his stomach.

"Are you all right, Uncle?" Alison sat down next to him and put her arm over his shoulders. "Are you sick?"

"Sick at heart. Embarrassed. I'm sorry I left you to deal with everything involving the paper. I'm humiliated and angry. That's why I came back." He spoke methodically. "I'm being threatened. Stalked. But I don't want harm to come to you because of my poor choices."

"Can you tell me about these threats?" Forest asked.

Milton crossed over to the window and peered stealthily through the side of the curtain. "You shouldn't have come here. You've made things worse for my niece. I was told you—"

"Forest isn't the person your informant accused him of being," Alison said. "He's helping me. He found a place for me to stay. Made sure someone was with me at the *Gazette*."

"I appreciate his diligence with those things."

"What were you going to say about me?"

"That you were in league with Edward." Milton said Edward's name in a subdued tone. "That you were going to assist him in getting out of jail. Getting him out of his sentencing!"

"That's not happening!" Forest said. "I'm not involved in any of Edward's plots to absolve himself of his crimes!"

"Not yet, perhaps. They'll do anything to get you to change your mind and support their cause." Milton gazed out the window near the edge of the curtain again, his shoulders stooped, his limbs shaking.

Forest caught Alison's gaze and nodded toward her uncle. If they were going to get any information from him, they had to calm him down.

"Uncle Milton, come away from the window." Alison went to him and tugged on his arm. "Come over here, okay?"

She led him to the bed, and they sat down.

Milton's gaze roamed the space nervously. What was he looking for?

"What kind of threat did you receive?" Forest asked.

"They're listening to us." Milton peered wide-eyed at the wallpaper.

"Why do you think that?" Was he being paranoid? Had his hiding and thinking someone was watching him caused delusions and this fearful behavior? He didn't act in the right frame of mind to even be a witness.

"The calls. The texts. They keep finding me. Telling me what I'm doing." Milton stared at an aged picture of the ocean on the wall. "But I can't locate the listening device or camera."

He was searching for surveillance equipment?

Forest crossed the room and ran his fingers over the edge of the picture. He did the same thing to the mirror, then checked the router and Milton's laptop without finding a bug.

He squatted down in front of Milton. "What did these people want you to do? Did they tell you not to testify against Edward?"

Milton clenched his lips together and stared at the rug.

"Uncle Milton, who confronted you about not testifying? We must get to the bottom of this."

"They'll come after you too. I don't want you reaping the ramifications of my involvement." Milton clasped both of

Alison's hands and gazed at her with a desperate look. "You are the last of my family. I must protect you."

"Thank you for that. But what have they threatened to do?"

Milton gnawed on his lower lip.

"Alison, wait outside, will you?" Forest nodded toward the door.

"Okay, but why?"

"Don't do it!" Milton surged upward and put himself between his niece and Forest. "He's one of them. They're waiting for you to make one false move. He's plotting to get you out there alone."

"That's not it at all!" Forest palmed the air. "I'm concerned for Alison's safety. But I need the truth. Tell me what's going on here, and she can stay."

Forest and Milton stared at each other, seemingly at an impasse.

"What about your loved ones?" Milton's lips quivered. "Your daughter? Wouldn't you do anything to protect them?"

Twenty-eight

Paige strode toward the gallery distracted by a conversation she'd had with her sister. Paisley said she wouldn't be returning to her job at the diner until after her court appearance. She and Judah made the decision after seeing her doctor, who wanted her to be able to rest when she needed to take a break. And Judah was still worried about the possibility of someone trying to stop her from testifying.

That seemed like a dangerous possibility.

Here Paige was going to work in the gallery the same as usual, although Forest told her not to be here alone. He'd even suggested she close the shop this week. But how could she shut down her business and lose all that revenue? She owed it to her consignment artists to remain open.

As a compromise, she scheduled Sarah to be with her every hour of every day throughout the week. She appreciated her coworker's willingness to assist her. With the surprising news that Sarah might be part of the Grant family, Paige loved being around her even more.

As soon as she stepped into the gallery, something seemed weird. Although it might just be her edgy feelings. The main lights were off as if no one was here, yet the sounds of the coffee machine going meant Sarah must have arrived.

"Sarah?" Paige flipped the switch, turning on the lights.

No answer. No return greeting.

Was she in the bathroom?

"Sarah?"

Instinctively, Paige backed up. Should she call Forest? Go outside and wait? Was she just being paranoid? Sarah had to be here.

Suddenly, a masked man charged at her from the coffee area. She gasped. Turned to flee. The guy grabbed her by both arms and jerked her farther into the gallery.

"Leave me alone!" Adrenaline spiked through her. She yanked hard against his hold. "What do you want? Why are you doing this? Let me go!"

"Be still."

"I won't!" She tugged even harder, twisting one way and then the other. If she got loose, she'd run for help. But where was Sarah? Had this guy captured her too?

Forcefully, the guy dressed in black clothes dragged her toward the coffee preparation area. She kicked at his legs and tried yanking her arms free of his grip. Was he planning to rob her? Hurt her?

Sarah! Her assistant sat in a chair, bound and gagged, tied to her chair, panic radiating from her eyes. What was going on here?

"Are you okay?"

"Silence!" the man shouted.

"You're going to be in a lot of trouble for doing this." Paige didn't want to antagonize him, but she had to try to stop him from tying her up too. "Are you after money? I don't keep much cash on the premises. Fifty bucks. You're welcome to it!"

"Shut up!" He pushed her onto a chair next to Sarah's.

"Sarah?"

"I'm okay," she said around the cloth keeping her mouth wedged open.

The man who'd proven he was stronger than Paige fumbled with a rope, giving her time to lunge to her feet. But he pushed her back, knocking her over. She landed hard in the chair for a second time.

Panic mingled with her primal need for survival. She needed Forest! He'd know what to do.

The masked guy bound her wrists behind her, removing her ability to reach for her phone. She grimaced at the tight, burning sensation of rough rope against her skin.

Her phone vibrated inside her coat pocket. Was Forest calling her? Too bad she couldn't answer. If she could, she'd shout, "Call 911! We've been kidnapped!" Or else, she'd silently connect the phone, leave it in her pocket, and keep it on so he'd hear what was going on. Then he'd know something was wrong!

The stranger dug his hand into her coat pocket and yanked out her phone. "It's Judah. Are you two close now?"

How did this person know her brother-in-law? He must be someone local. Why was Judah calling her?

The guy hurled the phone across the room. The device slammed against the wall, breaking into several pieces. There went her only means of communication with Forest!

"Why'd you do that?" Her words came out garbled. "You should get out of here while you can! My husband will be here any minute." It wasn't exactly so, but if Forest tried calling her and she didn't answer, he'd come looking for her.

The cad laughed. His dark eyes glistened through the ski mask holes. "We both know that isn't the truth." His voice sounded familiar. Who was he?

He shoved a cell phone in front of her face. On the screen, Forest and Alison were in a motel room together. What was her husband doing with—

Wait a second. Why did her captor have a camera on them? An older man's face came into view. Milton Hedge? Forest and Alison must be there talking to him.

Did the kidnapper have something to do with Milton being missing? Or with Edward's court case? What if he was trying to keep her from testifying like Judah thought someone might do to Paisley? A sudden realization of the awful trouble she might be in hit her.

She met Sarah's gaze. "I'm so sorry."

"Silence!"

The masked man tied her legs tightly to the chair. She winced. When he wrapped the gag around her mouth and cinched the fabric around her head, she wanted to vomit.

He held out his cell phone and snapped pictures of her and Sarah. "This will sweeten the deal."

"Who are you? What do you want?"

"Be quiet and it will go easier on you."

"I don't know anything!"

"Your husband must be stopped."

Stopped? Did this creep plan to use her for leverage to keep Forest from gathering more evidence before the trial? Because he found Milton?

The guy messed with his phone, probably sending the photos to someone. Maybe to Forest.

He squatted down in front of her. If her legs weren't tied, she'd kick him so hard he'd fall backward and conk his head. Then she'd untie Sarah and run. She should have listened to Forest about keeping the gallery closed this week. If she had, she'd be safe at home with Piper.

Piper. Her sweet girl. Was she okay? This bad guy wouldn't hurt her daughter to manipulate Forest into doing what he wanted, would he?

Lord Jesus, help us. Protect my daughter.

Paige peered around her immediate area, searching for anything to protect herself or to help her get away. She eyed the masked man. Why did he seem familiar? He was tall. Craig's build and dark eyes. But that man would never tie her up or hurt her.

"No wonder the Grant brothers are so attracted to the Cedars sisters." The guy stroked her hair.

"Get away from me!"

"Leave her alone!" Sarah shouted around her gag.

He laughed and patted their knees. "If the detective doesn't do what I say, you ladies and I are going for a nice drive. Sounds enticing, doesn't it?" He stood and strode toward the window.

Paige met Sarah's gaze again and tried conveying a reassuring message. *We'll get through this. We'll be okay. Forest will come for us!*

He would come for them, right?

Twenty-nine

Forest observed Milton pacing across the motel room, thrusting his hands over his oily hair as if pressing it down. Suddenly, he came to a stop in front of Alison.

"I never meant for you to become involved. I was against Edward's scheme from the start. Wanted no part of it!"

"What scheme is that?" Alison asked.

Based on what Forest learned from Paul and James, he figured he knew the man's answer.

"I abhorred his plan to run Basalt Bay as if he had ultimate sovereignty! I decried him in my paper every chance I got."

"What changed?"

"His supporters and minions came after me. Threatened me. And you."

Forest's phone vibrated in his jacket pocket. In most interviews, he would have turned off outside communication. For some reason, he didn't this time. "Sorry."

He yanked his cell out of his pocket. "Unknown" displayed on the screen, followed by, "Look at this or you'll regret it!"

He swiped his finger across the screen. A photo of Paige gagged and bound in the gallery café appeared. "What? How did—" The abject fear in his wife's expression sucker punched him. *God, protect her. Save her.*

"What is it?" Alison stood.

Hot anger pounding through him, he thrust the phone toward her.

"Oh, Forest, I'm so sorry."

Milton glanced at the screen. "It's started. There's nothing you can do except follow whatever instructions they give you."

"Why would someone capture my wife?" Forest demanded, his voice shaking.

Milton clamped his teeth onto his lower lip and shook his head.

Forest peered at the screen again. *Paige, I'm so sorry.* Another photo blipped into view, this time of Paige and Sarah, both gagged. "I can't believe this is happening." He should have been there with his wife, protecting her. Then it hit him. Milton said, "It's started." He must know something about this abduction.

"What does this mean, Milton?" he demanded and texted at the same time.

Who is this? What do you want?

"What does it mean, Uncle?"

"It's about Edward's leverage over us. Over the town." Milton peered around the room. "They know you're here. Watching us. Listening."

Forest's phone vibrated again.

Leave town for good and I'll let the ladies go unharmed.

Quickly, Forest opened another text field and tapped a message to Deputy Brian. If anyone was surveilling this room, he didn't want to say anything aloud.

Hostage situation at the gallery. Suspect has Paige and Sarah tied up.

He forwarded the pictures to the deputy.

On it. Deputy Brian's answer came back swiftly.

Get backup. Contact the sheriff.

Roger that.

Forest returned to the text with the kidnapper. Nothing else came through.

"I must go!" He didn't know what he would be facing at the gallery. He'd call Craig en route. Maybe Judah. "They have my wife and her assistant. What are they after?"

"Your wife's silence." Milton's face looked pale, almost green. "Your efforts to find dirt on Edward and Mia stopped. Not to mention the gallery is in the center of the new Basalt Bay."

"New Basalt Bay?" Alison asked.

"Grant Bay."

"What?" Forest groaned.

"Don't leave her here. It isn't safe." Milton took Alison by the hand and led her to the door. "They'll be here any second. Go!"

"Because you told me this?"

"Yes." Milton's chin wobbled. "A group of staunch supporters has dedicated themselves to assisting in Edward's diabolical plan to restructure the town, even with him in prison. All he needed was one equally greedy person to sign legal documentation for him in his absence."

"A wife."

"Correct."

Forest's phone pinged.

Milton is a liar. He's as deep in this as anyone. Want to see your cutie-pie again? Get out of there now! Come alone. No tricks.

How did the kidnapper know what Milton told him? Milton must have been right about someone surveilling this motel room. Was the person watching them now?

Thirty

Forest clutched the steering wheel in a death grip, a breath caught in his throat. The three-minute drive from the Beachside Inn to Bert's felt like half an hour. How was he going to rescue Paige and Sarah? What should he do first?

"Do you have Judah's number?"

"Paisley's," Alison answered.

"Send a text. I need Judah at the gallery now!" He glanced at the frazzled-looking woman tapping her screen. "Say it's an emergency."

"Okay. She's asking what kind of emergency."

"Tell her briefly."

"Judah's on his way."

"Good. Text Craig." Forest pulled to a fast stop in Bert's parking lot. Deputy Brian's rig was already there. "Stay put!"

"But—"

"Lock the door. Stay in the car!"

Forest grabbed his handgun out of the glove box, jumped out, tucked the gun into the back of his waistband, and took off running. Deputy Brian, dressed in a protective vest and holding his gun at the ready, crouched at the corner of the hardware store where a Closed sign was hanging in the window.

"Have you seen anything?" Forest leaned into the alcove and peered toward the gallery entrance.

"A second masked suspect went inside."

"Male?" His throat hiccupped.

"Affirmative."

So, it wasn't Mia.

With two men inside, Forest and Deputy Brian outside, and Judah on his way, possibly Craig, those were good odds. Except for the two hostages. A hostage situation changed everything. Forest had to compartmentalize his fears for Paige and focus on how to best execute a negotiation.

"Did you call for backup?"

"On the way," the deputy answered.

"I'm going to walk in and talk with them." Forest took a step.

Brian grabbed his arm. "Negative."

"She's my wife. They're waiting for me."

"We're going to wait for backup per Sheriff Morris's orders," Brian said in a gritty tone.

"I need to go in there." Forest jerked away from him. "I must protect her!"

"Uh, Forest?"

Hearing Alison's voice, he whirled around. "I told you—"

"Sorry. It's Judah." She held out her phone to him. "There's been a development."

Forest grabbed the phone. "Yeah?"

"I've been detained." Judah sounded out of breath. "There's a roadblock. A masked figure is blocking me from getting to town. What's going on? Why are these guys wearing ski masks?"

"Don't get out of the vehicle."

"Paisley's back at the house with Kathleen and Callie. I'm worried about her."

"Turn around and drive slowly." Forest heard a sound over the phone like a car door opening. "I said stay in the car!"

The call ended abruptly.

"No!" Every fiber of his being on high alert, Forest wanted to run into the gallery, confront the kidnappers, and save his wife and Sarah. Then he'd find out what just went down with Judah. If the masked men set up a roadblock where he was, had they done the same thing to stop the other police from coming into town?

"We might be on our own," he told the deputy. "We have to get inside the gallery."

"I said—"

"Masked men have detained Judah. Maybe that's what's happening to the backup you're waiting for."

"I'm in charge!" Deputy Brian gave him a menacing look.

"Of course, you are. But this situation is a ticking time bomb." Forest pointed toward Alison. "For your own safety, get back in my car!"

"Okay." Nodding, she backed up.

Forest's phone buzzed. "Unknown" displayed on the screen again. "Yeah?"

"I told you to come alone."

"I'm here. Outside. Shall I come in?"

"Too late. You failed. This is our last communication."

Click.

Forest growled out a deep-throated moan and charged toward the gallery. Before he reached the building, Deputy Brian locked his arms around his chest, holding on with surprising strength.

"Let go!"

"What did the caller say?" the deputy asked through gritted teeth.

"That it's too late." Forest jerked against his belt-like grip. "Let me go to her!"

"Look!" Brian dragged him back around the corner of the hardware store.

Two masked figures exited the gallery, using the women as human shields.

Outrage cut a swath of warrior-like fury through Forest. When Paige met his gaze with terror in hers, a surge of adrenaline hit him. He yanked forcefully against the deputy's hold, freeing himself, and ripping his jacket in the process. He lunged into the street. But it felt like he was in one of those horrible slow-motion dreams where he couldn't reach someone in time.

"Paige!"

The guys dressed in black fatigues shoved the women into the car. Then dove into the vehicle themselves. The getaway car released a blast of black smoke and roared down the road.

"Nooooo!"

Thirty-one

"Get out of the truck!" A muscular, darkly dressed guy yanked on the truck door and dragged Judah out.

"What's going on?" Now Judah wished he'd kept the door shut and turned around as Forest told him to do. "Why have you stopped me like this?" Although nervous about the situation, he attempted to make his voice sound tough. He squinted at the military-type guy. "Why are you guys wearing masks?"

"Get down on the ground!"

"Why? What's happened?" His heart pounded as he checked to his left and right. He knew the beach like he knew his own backyard. He knew where he could run down to the dunes and hide. But what if these thugs or hoodlums back-tracked and reached Paisley before he did?

"Sit down!" The guy who was about Judah's height pulled a gun out of his pocket.

"Hey, now. No need for violence!" His option of running away just got more precarious.

"Sit down!" the guy yelled.

"Okay. I will." Judah squatted. "What's this about? Who are you?" He was tempted to grab the guy's mask and rip it off. Too bad he had a gun.

"Doesn't matter who I am. You had your chance to have an influence on this town and you blew it."

"What are you talking about?"

"You could have overseen our new government. You refused." The figure came closer, pulsing the gun toward him. "Bet you're sorry now. Sit on the ground as I said!"

Judah dropped on his backside next to the front tire. A new government? What kind of weird takeover was this?

Lord, be with Paisley, was the last thing he thought before a putrid-smelling cloth was slapped across his mouth. He fought against it until he couldn't.

* * * *

Paisley came out of the first-floor bathroom—the lights had gone off while she was in there—and heard shouting.

"Get out of my house!" Aunt Callie sounded enraged.

What was happening?

"Where is she?" A male voice yelled.

She? Paisley backed up toward the stairway. She'd gotten a text from Alison about Paige being in trouble, and Judah went to help. What if someone was here to kidnap her as Edward did before? Wasn't that what Judah had feared might happen? The air felt like it left her lungs suddenly. Should she go upstairs and hide in the attic? She crept up the stairs.

"Leave us alone!" Aunt Callie shouted again. "You're trespassing. I'm calling the police!"

The male cackled. "He's a little preoccupied. And the phones are dead."

They were? Before Paisley reached the top stair, a figure dressed in black charged into the living room with Aunt Callie hitting him with a kitchen towel. The masked guy shoved her aunt, nearly knocking her to the floor. He stared up at Paisley, an eerie gleam in his eyes.

It was too late for her to run and hide. Leaving Aunt Callie alone to defend herself was unthinkable. Where was Kathleen? Music came from the closed planning-room door. She must be doing artwork in there. Probably didn't hear the commotion.

The guy stomped up the stairs. "You're coming with me."

"No, I'm not!" The fear Paisley experienced when Edward kidnapped her rushed through her now. This guy wasn't as tall as Edward, but he was bigger and stronger than her. Considering his size, fighting him seemed foolish. But she wouldn't go with him complacently, either.

When he grabbed her arm, she jerked away from him. "Leave me alone!" She trudged down to the first floor on her own, her heart racing, her gaze meeting Aunt Callie's. What were they going to do?

Aunt Callie stomped toward the guy, hitting him with the towel again. If only she'd grabbed a rolling pin instead of a dish towel.

The assailant shoved Aunt Callie. She stumbled backward, barely catching her balance.

"Aunt Callie!"

The guy wrestled Paisley's arms behind her back and tied her wrists together, despite her tugging against him.

With the scent of fear in the air and adrenaline shooting sparks up and down her middle, she got lightheaded. Dizzy. Woozily, she swayed. Then she was falling. Everything went black.

As if in a distant fog, she heard women's voices.

"Oh, my dear. Please, wake up," Kathleen said mournfully. "Callie, she still isn't awake yet."

"This one either."

A palm slapping gently at her face made her grimace. She moaned.

"Paisley? Oh, good. She's waking up!"

"About time," Aunt Callie said.

Peeling her eyelids apart, Paisley tried to see what was happening. Kathleen peered over her, staring into one eye, then the other.

"Oh, my dear, you're awake. Thank goodness! Are you okay? Need anything? Water?"

Her head hurt. She stared up at the ceiling. Why was she lying on the floor? "What happened?"

"You fainted. There's been an—" Kathleen's voice trailed away.

"How is she?" Aunt Callie asked.

"Appears to be okay. What should we do?"

"I'm not leaving my post."

Kathleen leaned over Paisley again, patting her arm. "I'm going to get you a glass of water. Stay right here."

She fainted? Was the baby okay? Fragments of memory came back to her. She was trying to get away from someone. Who?

She leaned up on her elbow. The room swirled in a foggy haze. She peered intensely at the woman standing by the couch with a cast iron pan in her hands. "Auntie? What's going on?"

"Stay put until you're better."

Her vision cleared enough to see a man dressed in black and wearing a ski mask crumpled in a heap, passed out cold on the floor next to the coffee table. Had Aunt Callie hit him with the pan?

"How did you—"

"This twerp isn't doing us any harm." Aunt Callie grimaced. "I was worried about you, Paisley Rose. Good thing Kathleen came downstairs when she did."

"Is he—"

"Still breathing."

The guy moaned.

Paisley pushed herself to a sitting position.

Kathleen handed her a glass of water. "Drink slowly, dear."

"Thank you." She felt parched but took small sips. "Where's Judah?"

"Remember, he left to help Forest?" Kathleen asked, not filling in any details.

Paisley tried to recall what happened before the intruder entered the house. Judah had left to do something. "What was wrong with Forest?"

A look passed between Kathleen and Aunt Callie. Were they being evasive to protect her?

"You can tell me. I need to know what's going on!"

"There's been some trouble at the gallery." Kathleen took the glass and set it on the coffee table. "Are you ready to stand up? Maybe come over to the couch and rest?"

"Okay."

"If you want to stay here, that's fine." Kathleen glanced at the man on the floor. "He'll wake up soon. We've tied his hands and legs with sheet strips. But they won't hold if he jerks hard against them."

"Who is he?"

"We don't know yet," Kathleen said.

Paisley pushed herself onto her knees. Kathleen slid under her arm and assisted her in standing. Even though the older woman was small-framed, she was stronger than she appeared.

A wave of lightheadedness hit Paisley again and she swayed.

"Hold on tight." Kathleen led her to the couch.

Toppling onto the cushions, she moaned. "I must have hit my head on the fall."

Please, keep the baby safe.

Kathleen ran her fingers over her scalp. "I don't feel a lump."

"That's a relief. Now, what's the emergency at the gallery?"

"We're worried about your sister and Sarah," Aunt Callie said. "We haven't heard from them."

"I texted Judah about your condition, but the text didn't go through. Something appears to be wrong with our cell phones. Landline too. And the electricity is off. Good thing we still have city water." Kathleen snuggled a throw blanket around Paisley's shoulders. "Don't worry, dear. He's probably involved in whatever is happening at the gallery."

Paisley dug in her pocket for her cell phone, then tapped a quick text to Judah. It didn't go through, either.

The guy's legs twitched.

"Maybe we should take off his mask before he wakes up," Paisley said. "Find out who he is."

"I don't want to touch him." Aunt Callie puckered her lips.

"Something's going on at the gallery, an invader breaks in here, and the phones and the electricity are out? That can't be a coincidence." Paisley took a calming breath. "What was he after? Or who?"

"You, I'm afraid," Aunt Callie said solemnly. "But that will happen over my dead body."

"I heard the ruckus, crept down the stairs with one of my mosaics, and hit him over the head! I've never done anything like that before." Chuckling, Kathleen draped her arm over Paisley's shoulder. "Callie got her pan. End of story. You're safe now. No one is taking you from us!"

"Thank you. Both of you."

The guy's eyes opened to thin slits. He met Paisley's gaze and muttered something. He jerked against the sheet strips binding his limbs.

With each movement, she tensed up a little more.

Aunt Callie lifted the frying pan into position like a baseball bat.

Kathleen grabbed the mosaic picture. "I did it once. I'll do it again!"

These two women appeared ready to do combat to protect her. Paisley felt loved and cared for by both.

"You should have come with me." The man squinted at her. "Then it would go easier on the others."

What others? Were Paige and Sarah in more danger because this man couldn't fulfill whatever plan he intended against her?

Thirty-two

Kidnapping at gallery. Come quick!

Craig read the brief text he'd missed earlier, disbelief flashing through his brain. If Al was in danger, he had to go to her!

Be there in five, he tapped, but the text didn't work. Lousy phone.

He took off running, leaving his wide broom on the cement parking lot of Lewis's grocery. Mid-stride, the truth hit him. Al said the gallery. Was Paige in trouble?

God, save her. Craig thought the words without pausing to analyze why they came to him.

He ran in long strides. Charging into the gallery filled with art and the scent of gourmet coffee, he came to a stop as Al dove into his arms and hugged him tightly.

"What's ... going ... on?" he asked between taking deep breaths.

"Paige and Sarah were taken by two assailants."

"Taken?"

His gaze skimmed the semi-dark room. Deputy Brian shook his phone like he was angry with the device. Forest paced agitatedly—he must feel horrible. Thoughts of Paisley's kidnapping and how dreadful she looked when Craig rescued her raced through his mind. Was that what was happening to Paige? Was Edward behind her abduction too?

Craig strode over to the other two men, Al trailing him. "Why aren't you going after them?"

Forest glared at the deputy. "Yeah, Deputy, why aren't you doing something to rescue my wife?"

Deputy Brian stuffed his phone into his jacket pocket. "I was told to wait for backup and not give chase. I'm following orders. Ever heard of the chain of command?"

Forest crossed his arms over his head and let out a frustrated-sounding growl.

"What's taking so long?" Craig demanded.

"There's a roadblock. A skirmish. Cell phones appear to be off-grid."

Forest stepped in front of the deputy, almost nose to nose. "Why did you stop me from following Paige and Sarah?"

"I stopped you from getting yourself killed!" Deputy Brian jabbed his finger at Forest's chest. "The town is under siege! Before the phone stopped working, I was getting reports. Judah's pickup was seen abandoned at the roadblock. Hostiles have taken over City Hall, including capturing Bess Grant."

"Whoa. Are you serious? This is bigger than I imagined." Forest paced for a short distance then returned. "We must do something! We're wasting time here."

"Yeah, that's right." Craig rocked his thumb toward the door. "Let's go!"

"A roadblock has been set up at the South exit to Highway 101," Deputy Brian said. "Another one on the north side."

"Did Milton have anything to do with this?" Al asked, her expression forlorn. "He knew about some stuff. But criminal endangerment of residents? I seriously doubt that."

"Still judge me as the bad guy?" Forest asked her, a wild look in his eyes.

"No! Didn't you hear me tell my uncle the truth about you?"

"Besides, this isn't the time." Craig held out his palms toward Forest.

"No, it isn't. Sorry." He turned abruptly toward Deputy Brian. "I'm going after my wife. I don't care who's barricading the road. That you detained me from following her is highly suspect."

"I knew nothing about these altercations," Deputy Brian said in a weak tone. "I didn't want the hostages getting injured."

"We lost their trail because of you!" With Forest's flinty gaze and clenched fists, he looked mad enough to take a swing at the seemingly inept lawman.

"If you made it as far as the roadblock, you would have been stopped anyway." Deputy Brian's nostrils flared, and his hand pulsed over his holstered gun.

"How do you know that?" Craig rolled up his sleeves.

"Yeah, how do you know?" Al asked.

Without answering, the deputy shoved the door closed and locked it. Crossing his arms, he stood stiffly in front of the exit. "No one's going anywhere until I get an official word from the sheriff."

"With the phones not working? Think again." Craig moved forward at the same time Forest did. The two of them could take on Brian Corbin!

The deputy pulled out his gun.

Well, until he did that. Craig and Forest took a couple of steps back.

"This is how it's going to play out," Deputy Brian said in a deep tone of voice. "Grab a chair and sit your backsides down."

"You've got to be kidding me," Craig muttered.

"This is insane!" Forest shouted. "Why are you doing this?"

The deputy frisked him and grabbed his gun from his waistband.

"Are you in on this takeover? What do you get out of it?" Forest's tone got louder with each question. "A higher position in the police force? A hefty raise? Edward's undying gratitude?"

"I'm following orders. Now, sit down!" Deputy Brian rocked his gun toward a table with chairs surrounding it.

"Not until you tell me what's going on." Forest pointed at the door. "Otherwise, nothing is stopping me from rescuing my wife."

"Want to bet? What about your daughter?"

"What about her?" Forest growled.

Craig gulped. Had something happened to Piper?

"I didn't want to tell you this." The deputy gnawed on his lower lip. "Before I lost internet connection, someone reported seeing suspicious-looking men dressed in black outside Paul Cedars's house."

"What? That's not possible!" Forest pressed his fists against his forehead. "Why are they doing this? Why go after a kid?"

"I'm so sorry," Al patted his arm. "This must be the plan my uncle mentioned. It shows to what lengths those men will go for the control they seek."

"Now, sit down! Or do I have to use force?" Deputy Brian yelled.

Craig met Forest's gaze. If Forest charged the deputy and somehow made it past him without getting shot, Craig would follow and sneak beyond whatever obstacles existed to rescue Paige and Piper. They were part of his family too. So was Paisley.

Where had Paige and Sarah been taken? One probable place came to mind.

"I have an idea." Trying to appear compliant with the deputy's demands, Craig dropped onto a chair at the circular table closest to the door.

"What is it?" Forest sat down on the edge of his seat, eyeing the deputy.

Al sank into the third chair.

Since they weren't far from Deputy Brian, Craig muffled his voice. "If it's a takeover of Basalt Bay to get Edward free, they'd want to take Paige as leverage. Paisley, too. Maybe even Piper."

"Silence!" the deputy barked. "No plotting!"

"You'll have to gag us to keep us quiet."

"Craig!" Al warned.

"While he's busy tying us up, we'll grab his gun and run for it."

"That'll buy us some time," Forest said in a subdued voice.

"I think they'd take her to the Grant estate." Craig met Forest's gaze. "Like Edward did with Paisley."

"Makes sense."

"Would they take all the Grants/Cedars there?" Al asked.

"Possibly. We need a distraction. Something epic." Craig lifted his chin toward Al. "You can do this."

"Why me? Because I'm a woman? I never thought of you as a male chauvinist."

"Just do it, will you?"

"Fine. Oh, Deputy? I have to use the bathroom. Women's problems." Al squinted at Craig as if sending him a warning not to smirk.

"Stay put," the deputy said. "I know you three are scheming."

"Let me use the bathroom, okay? I'm having a problem." She stood and tugged her coat down, shuffling her feet back and forth. "I can't wait!"

The deputy strode over to her. "No funny business! I mean it."

Al met Craig's gaze, one eyebrow quirked. He shrugged. They were playing this by ear. But they needed the deputy to stay away from the door for a minute. Al put her hand to her forehead and swayed like a woman in an old Victorian flick who was about to faint.

If the situation weren't so dire, Craig would mock her terrible rendition of being weak. Instead, he pushed away from the table and said, "Al! Are you okay?"

"Sit down!" the deputy shouted.

Craig did as he was instructed but remained ready to spring for the door.

Deputy Brian put his arm around Al and assisted her to the bathroom.

Al met Craig's gaze. Then she went limp against the deputy in a fainting collapse.

Craig and Forest charged for the door. Craig hated leaving Al behind, yet he was confident she could fend for herself.

"Stop! Get back here!" Deputy Brian shouted.

But they were already through the door barreling toward Forest's car.

Thirty-three

"I wish my phone was working." Paisley sat on the bottom step of the stairway leading to the second floor. Her texts weren't going through to Judah, but she kept trying. Where was he? Why hadn't he come back here? "I'm worried about Judah."

"I'm sorry, dear." Kathleen sat next to her, clutching her arm and supporting her back.

"I have to sit down." Glaring at the intruder on the floor, Aunt Callie dropped into the chair near the corner of the couch. "Try anything, and you'll have a mammoth-sized lump on your skull."

The guy moaned like his head already hurt.

Paisley tried texting Dad's number. Then Paige's. Neither worked.

One bad guy was here. What if more were on their way? What if the rest of her family was under attack too? She stared intensely at the guy in black clothes. Who was he? She stood, debating whether she should get closer to him. She had the baby to consider. Didn't want to take any risks. Yet they had to find out who he was and what he was after. She moved forward.

"Paisley Rose, stay back!"

Ignoring her aunt's warning, she grabbed the guy's gag, jerked it down over his chin, and tugged off the ski mask.

Mike Linfield?

"What are you doing here? Were you trying to kidnap me?" Her breathing came out raspy. "Did Edward ... send you?"

"Wouldn't you like to know?"

"Yes, I would!"

"Too bad." The man who'd ordered Judah's firings stared back at her with a belligerent expression.

"Let me take care of this." Aunt Callie stood and swung the frying pan threateningly.

"Go ahead," Mike taunted. "Someone else will be here to replace me soon." He gazed darkly at Paisley. "You need to come with us."

"No, she doesn't," Aunt Callie said.

"Not as long as we're here to protect her." Kathleen stepped beside Paisley.

"It's the only way to end this peacefully."

"What is 'this?'" Confident he was tied securely, Paisley leaned closer. "Why did you invade this home?"

He licked his dry-looking lips. "I'm under orders to take you to join the others."

So he was trying to kidnap her.

"What others?"

"The rest of your family."

"You have Paige? Judah?" Her heart rate sped up and she backed away from him until she stood next to Aunt Callie.

"Of course," Mike said cockily. "We have a plan to remove you, too."

Remove her? What did that mean?

"If you didn't notice, your plan failed," Kathleen said boldly. "Paisley isn't going anywhere with you. Callie and I have seen to that."

"You're wrong. The plan didn't fail. I might have been unsuccessful. But more are coming."

Paisley ran for the front door.

"Paisley Rose—"

"I'll be right back." She made sure the door was locked, then she hurried to the back door and did the same thing.

"That won't stop anyone from reaching you." Mike made some throat noises. "They'll be here any minute. Then wait and see what happens next!"

Thirty-four

"Feeling better?"

Since he was blindfolded, Judah couldn't see who was talking, but he recognized Mia's voice. He smelled her excessive perfume scent too. She was sitting beside him in the backseat of a car that was jostling up and down a long road. By the feel of the bumps and turns, they were heading to his father's property.

"Not really." He tried lifting his hand to press it against his aching forehead, but his wrists were bound together.

Why was he tied up in a car with Mia? He'd been on his way to help Paige at the gallery. Oh, right. He'd been stopped by militants. Forced to sit on the ground. Smelled something awful. Was Mia involved in that?

"Sorry we detained you like this." She didn't sound sorry at all.

"What do you want?"

"That's a loaded question if I ever heard one." She laughed in her high tone of voice. "If I had my choice of

Grant men, I would have picked you." Her fingers trailed over his arm.

He jerked away from her touch, although it was difficult to do in the confined space. "That sounds unfaithful for a new wife to say."

"Crushes die hard. But I have one Grant right where I want him."

Did she mean him? Or was she referring to marrying Edward in jail?

"You asked what I want. I'd like the Grant/Cedars families to leave Basalt Bay immediately." She touched his hand. He tensed. "You are no longer welcome in my town."

"Your town? Why should we leave?"

"Edward will be laid up for a few years," she said matter-of-factly. "Too bad you didn't listen to him and become the mayor yourself. Then all this unpleasantness could have been avoided."

"You mean if I did everything he said from jail?" He turned toward her even though he couldn't see her.

"Or if you did everything I said from right here." She chuckled.

"Sounds like you two deserve each other."

"I got what I wanted. The town is mine." She brushed her fingers over his shoulder, up his neck. "Just a few unessential people to get rid of."

Meaning he was one of those unessential people? And Paisley? He clenched his jaw so tight his teeth hurt. "What's the plan? Escort all eight of us out of town?"

"Nine, actually."

Was she counting Paul and Callie? Judah's father-in-law wouldn't take kindly to being escorted out of town. Neither would Callie. Heaven help the masked person who tried to manipulate her!

"What then?"

"Don't worry. Eddie and I have it all planned out," she said in a whimsical tone.

When the car came to a stop, Judah said, "Why don't you take off my blindfold? I know we're at Edward's house."

"My house, now."

He didn't say what he thought. That she was misled if she believed Edward would hand over his property, or anything else, to her. Most likely, he'd use her for whatever benefitted himself, then discard her. In that, Judah felt sorry for her.

Mia led him across the gravel parking lot. A guy, probably the driver, ripped off the cloth from around his head, scraping his face. Judah winced at the pain and the sudden brightness.

They were at Edward's just like he said. A guy with a rifle stood guard by the driveway. Was Paisley here? Was this where Paige and Sarah were being held? What of Paul and Piper?

When they reached the living room, he saw Mom sitting on the couch, blindfolded and gagged. "What's my mother doing here?"

"Don't get your underwear in a knot," Mia said playfully.

"Unbind her now!" Anger throbbed through him. How dare Mia act like this was a game without serious consequences! "She's the mayor. And my mother. You can't treat her like this."

"Sorry. But her mayoral role has been commuted to, you guessed it, me!"

Mom made muffled sounds of disagreement.

"Let her go!" Judah glared at Mia.

"You are in no position to make demands of me, Judah Grant. Unless you do something for me first." She winked and rocked her eyebrows suggestively.

"Not happening."

One of the guys dressed in black shoved him harshly into a dining-room chair and bound his ankles to the wooden legs. Sunlight came in through the large living room windows, but it looked dim in the house like the lights must be off.

"Mom, are you okay?"

"Yes," she said in a muffled voice.

"Be quiet!" Mia paced in front of him. "If you don't cooperate, I'll gag you too! Or I might do other things with your mouth to stop you from talking." She winked at him again.

He clenched his jaw.

Mom yelled what sounded like "Stay away from him!"

"Silence! Or I'll put you in the closet upstairs." Mia laughed like she found the threat hilarious.

Was she referring to the closet where Edward had held Paisley captive? How dare she mention that as if it were a joke! The inference, and seeing his mother bound, twisted fury through Judah.

He'd break free if he could. But not only were his wrists strapped together, now his legs were tied to the chair. Glancing around the room, he saw things he could throw at the fellow who appeared to be a muscle-builder type, or at Mia—he wouldn't hesitate to do what was needed to protect Mom or Paisley—if he had the chance. A solid vase and a two-foot sculpture of a dog would cause some serious damage. A letter opener was on the coffee table. But first, he had to get free of the ties.

Another idea came to mind. What if he faked an interest in Mia's plans? What if he went along with her suggestions of cooperation so she'd let down her guard? Maybe she'd get distracted, even believing he was on her side, and allow him to be untied. It might not work. But it might be worth a shot.

"Why did you bring us here, Mia?" he asked softly. "What do you plan to do with us?"

Mom's muffled sounds stilled as if she were listening.

"You need to start a new life elsewhere," Mia said. "You'll be relocated far from the Oregon Coast. Guarded. Kind of like the Witness Protection Program, you'll have to swear to silence about your life here. You won't be able to contact anyone in Basalt Bay."

How could she even imagine this would work?

"I'll miss you. But it's the way it must be." She swayed her hands toward the massive windows. "This is all mine now. A twist of fate, huh? The man who refused to be mayor sitting here with the woman who stole the mayoral position from me?" Mia dropped into a chair next to him, setting her hand on his leg. "Let's get a few things straight first."

"Okay." Judah stole a glance at Mom. She was moving her arms in small increments. Was she trying to get her wrist bindings free? *Good job, Mom!*

He turned away from her, focusing on Mia so she'd focus on him. "What do we need to talk about?" He still spoke softly, using subterfuge in hopes of disarming her.

"About you following *my* orders. Doing what *I* want." She moistened her lips.

He was tempted to tell her to remove her hand from his thigh, but the sound of a car engine turning off in the driveway reached him first.

"They're here!" Mia jumped up and nearly pranced to the door.

Who was here? Paisley? He sat up straighter.

Two darkly-dressed guys with masks dragged in two gagged women. Paige and Sarah! They weren't even fighting their captors. They walked into the room as if they'd already given up trying to break free.

If Paisley were brought in like that, he imagined her fighting and jerking against the kidnapper's hold the whole way. Judah appreciated his wife's feisty spirit. But he was glad she wasn't here right now. He prayed she was still safe at the project house.

Paige met his gaze from across the room. Her eyes widened like she was surprised to see him here.

"Welcome to my home, ladies." Mia spread her arms wide.

Mom moaned.

"Paige, are you okay?" he called.

The muscled guy smacked him on the head. Judah groaned.

"I warned you to do things my way," Mia said lightly.

"Are you all right, Sarah?"

Another wallop to the head silenced him.

"Yes," she said through her gag.

Mia pointed to two dining room chairs at the side of the couch. Roughly, the women were shoved onto the chairs and tied to them.

Their captors were certainly making an escape difficult. Still, Judah would keep looking for a way out of this. Ali had texted Paisley, requesting that he head to the gallery at Forest's insistence. Where was he? His brother-in-law wouldn't allow Paige to be kidnapped without putting up a fight. Unless he was tied up somewhere too. Or injured.

Lord, help us all.

Three militant types were in the room. Judah stared hard at the tall, thin man leaning toward Mia, talking quietly. Her eyes sparkled up at the guy flirtatiously. Marriage vows hadn't lessened her amorous flirtation with whichever man she was with.

Why did the guy look familiar? Tall. Dark eyes. Somewhat muscular. Wait. C.L.? Was the current manager of C-MER in on this hostile takeover? This scheme to remove their family? The revelation stunned him. Any chance C.L. was involved with Edward and Mia's plans all along? What a rat!

During the mayoral election, he'd convinced some of the residents to trust him. Even Judah had been impressed with his speech. It was a good thing the newcomer hadn't won. If he had, or if Mia had won the election, would this shakedown have happened sooner?

Thirty-five

From the gallery doorway, Ali watched Deputy Brian marching back and forth in front of the building. He'd told her to stay inside several times, but she wouldn't. It was dark in there, plus, he'd have to hogtie her to keep her from following him outside and discovering what was going down today.

Why were the streets deserted? How did everyone know to stay in their houses? Or to keep their businesses closed? It looked like a desolate Old West town during a duel. Something sinister had to be taking place. If the townspeople were aware of what was going on, how could any of them let this monstrous plan unfold without doing something?

Did Edward wield that much power over all of them? And if not him, then who?

Ali was going to write the exposé of all exposés about this day in Basalt Bay!

"Where are the police you said were coming? Did you know this rebellion was going down? Are you involved in it?"

The deputy stopped pacing and glowered at her. "How many times do I have to say I knew nothing about this?"

"Then why aren't you going after Paige and Sarah? They were kidnapped! Why pace in front of the gallery as if you have no authority? You're a police officer, for goodness' sake! Do something." She wanted to yank on her hair because she was so frustrated.

"I have no idea where they went."

"Try the Grant estate. That's what Craig said."

"I was told—" He groaned. "What's the use?" He paced again.

"I can't fathom an officer of the law staying put because some higher-up told him to when people in his own jurisdiction are in trouble. With the electricity off and phones down? Isn't that suspicious to you?" Her voice rose with her impassioned speech. "Looks to me like you're following the wrong instructions. And the wrong leaders! Am I ever going to lambaste you in my uncle's paper!"

"No, you are not!" Deputy Brian shoved her into the gallery. "Stay put like I told you. And be quiet. The detective and Masters escaped because of your theatrics!"

She pulsed her index finger toward him. "I'm going to tell the world how you sat on your hands doing nothing, while Detective Harper and a regular citizen stepped up to the plate to rescue the victims."

"You know nothing about it!"

"I know there was a pact made between businessmen to take over this town. Are you in their group too? Were you part of this diabolical strategy to take over Basalt Bay?"

The deputy just glowered at her.

"Maybe you were promised a cushy position if you stayed here and acted ignorant."

"Be quiet!" He yanked his cell phone out of his pocket, jabbed his fingers against the screen, then growled out, "When are the phones going to work again?"

Thirty-six

Craig sat tensely in the passenger seat as Forest drove through town at breakneck speeds, then raced the engine up the winding hill toward the Grant estate.

"Stop the car!"

Forest braked, the vehicle fishtailing on the gravel road. "Why?"

"We must go on foot from here. Drive around the corner, and they'll see you."

"If they're here." Forest glared at him. "You'd better not be in on this!"

"Of course, I'm not in on it!" Craig was offended by his suggestion. "I have no idea what's going on. Edward brought Paisley here. It's his empire. Makes sense it would be Mia's domain." He thrust his hand toward the hillside that was blocking them from seeing the Grant's luxury home. "This and the money are probably the reasons she married him." Craig shoved open the door. "Come on. We don't have much time."

Forest clutched his arm. "If you're in on this, tell me now."

"I'm not." Craig shoved his hand away. "I get it. I was a rat in the past. No more. I care about Paige and Paisley. I want them both to be safe. Piper too."

"Wait." Forest backed up the car into a pullout. "Best approach?"

Craig pointed toward a cluster of bushes. "Squat and stay low."

They both exited the vehicle, staying close to the ground. Crawling all the way up to the Grant house would be cumbersome, but Craig would do whatever was necessary to rescue his family.

* * * *

Forest and Craig stayed on their haunches in the tall grasses, peering through the long blades at the guards in front of the house. When one of the thugs turned away to speak to someone or to peer down the driveway, Forest motioned for Craig to move closer to the building. The going was snail slow as they crawled and crept through the grass and over rough terrain.

There must be a back entrance. Was that guarded too?

Suddenly, the guy in front of the house charged toward them, rifle raised as if he heard a sound.

Forest dropped on all fours. Craig stilled beside him. Neither breathed a breath aloud.

After a couple of minutes, the thug returned to looking out over the driveway again.

Forest blew out a slow breath.

Craig made hand signals to go farther back through the brush. "Back door," he mouthed.

Forest nodded. His heart pounding in his ears, he let Craig lead the way as they half crawled, half squat-walked through the bushes outlining the landscaped yard. Paige and Sarah must be here by now. Was anyone else held captive inside?

Finally, they reached the back of the house. A guard stood at the door, gun in hand, just like Forest thought might happen.

Craig, sitting on his haunches, nodded toward the second floor.

Forest glanced up. A balcony! It wasn't located directly above the back door. But how could they get up there undetected? They'd have to wait for the guard to move or get distracted. If they managed to climb up, was the door locked? If Mia had been staying here since her marriage to Edward, she might have left the door unlocked.

"Follow me," Craig said.

Forest gripped his arm. "Don't try anything."

"I'm going to save Paige. Aren't you here to do that too?"

"Yes. Just don't be a stupid hero."

Craig jerked his chin toward a small building at the rear of the house. "There's a ladder. Let's use it to climb up."

A cha-chunk sound like that of a bullet dropping into a chamber made them both drop to the ground again. A sharp piece of wood dug into Forest's knee. He stifled a groan.

How were they going to get to the ladder and carry it to the balcony without being spotted?

Thirty-seven

A strong knocking at the door sent cold chills skittering up Paisley's spine. Who might be here to try and take her now?

"Don't answer it!" Aunt Callie ordered. "Probably one of this dimwit's cronies."

"What if someone has come to help us?" What if it was Judah?

"Do I look like I need help?" Aunt Callie shook the cast iron pan at Mike and gritted her teeth. She certainly looked formidable.

Paisley ran for the window by the front door to look.

"Paisley Rose!"

Outside, three men stood clustered together on the porch, hats on, shoulders bent. Oh, one held a child. Piper!

"It's Dad and James!" Paisley unbolted the door.

"We came as quickly as possible." Dad hugged her as he strode into the house.

Piper lunged into her arms. "Hey, Piper." She hugged the girl to her chest.

James stepped behind the door and peered out the window. "Coast is still clear."

The third man shut and locked the door. His hat was pulled down low enough to nearly cover his eyes. Who was he?

"Come see who we've got, Pauly!" Aunt Callie chortled from the living room.

"What's going on here?" Dad asked.

Paisley followed him and glanced back at the guy she didn't recognize. "It's Mike Linfield. Judah's old boss." She settled Piper on her hip. "Kathleen whopped him on the head with one of her mosaic pictures."

"Takes art appreciation to a whole new level, doesn't it?" Dad chuckled.

"I'll say." Kathleen smiled.

"You should have seen the two at your dad's place," James called from his guard position near the door. "The three of us took them on and left them tied to the porch railing."

"Why were they there?" Paisley glanced at Dad.

"Trying to take Piper. They weren't getting her, I can guarantee that!"

"No, sir." She bounced her niece gently. "Grandpa and James were watching out for you."

The third guy faced her then. Milton Hedge? Now, that was someone she hadn't expected to show up at the project house. Not with Dad and James, either. Since when were they buddies?

"Heard anything from Alison?"

"No. Other than her text saying an emergency had happened at the gallery." Paisley smoothed her hand over

Piper's back. "Judah went to help. I haven't heard from him since then."

"He was probably taken." Milton shuffled toward Mike.

"Taken?" Paisley followed him. "Taken where?" Her shoulder muscles tightened. Her heart pounded in her ears.

"I don't know for certain."

Was he telling her the truth? Or did he know more than he was letting on? She forced herself to breathe normally and silently prayed for Judah and Paige. Sarah too.

"Are you okay?" Dad asked her.

"Yeah. I fainted and I'm tired. But I'm thankful Kathleen and Aunt Callie didn't let someone steal me away from here."

"I'm thankful for that too." He rested his hand on her back as if supporting her. "We stayed off the main road. Took some backroads James and I know about to get here. But I was determined to check on you."

"Thanks, Dad."

Milton stood over Mike, scowling down at him. "What's next? Who else is coming?"

"What's this about?" Callie demanded.

"He knows." Milton pulsed his finger toward the man on the floor. "What's going to happen next?"

"You mean he was right? There are more intruders on their way?" Paisley felt a surge of panic.

"Two tried to subdue us and pull Piper from my arms," Dad said. "Would have too, if James and Milton hadn't intervened."

"Tied them up with every piece of rope in the house." James chuckled from the doorway.

"Get back to your post!" Milton ordered.

James whirled around but paused before leaving the room. "You okay, Cal?"

"Better now that this fiend is under my shoe."

"That's the spirit!" Grinning, James marched back to the front door.

A rosy hue crossed Aunt Callie's cheeks. Even in this tense situation, her caring attitude toward James, and his toward her, was obvious.

"There's another wave coming." Milton squinted down at Mike. "When should we expect more trouble?"

Paisley leaned against Dad. Having him here, and having more people in the house, made her feel safer. But what kind of wave was Milton talking about? How did he know this stuff?

"Speak up!" Aunt Callie shook her pan at Mike. "Have you organized some other vile scheme against us?"

"It's her we want." Mike nodded toward Paisley. "Give her up and it will go easier on the rest of you."

Everyone's gaze flicked toward her. She held Piper even closer.

"You leave my daughter and granddaughter alone!" Dad stepped forward and shook his fist at the bound man.

Milton held out his palms toward Dad. "He'll get what's coming to him. First, we need information. Not more violence."

"I'll give him what he deserves!"

"So?" Milton squatted down beside the prisoner. "Your men took some captives. Failed at capturing others. If they want the rest, they'll be here soon, huh?"

"You'd know that better than anyone," Mike said.

Was he saying Milton was in on this? If so, could they even trust him? Maybe they should tie him up alongside Mike Linfield!

"What does he mean?" Dad moved to stand protectively beside Paisley, who was swaying with Piper. The girl had fallen asleep on her shoulder.

"I confess I was aware of certain things that might happen today." Milton stood slowly. "I doggedly trailed Edward's group. But I'm not one of them. My niece is in danger now, too!"

"Right." Mike scoffed. "You wanted the property or funding you were promised. You craved power and prestige like the rest of us!"

"That true?" Dad demanded. "Are you a part of this takeover?"

"Of course, he is! Edward swore I'd get my job back. What did he say you'd get, Milton?"

Milton's face hued red. "What matters is how to protect the innocent. Paisley and the girl are their controlling cards. We must keep them hidden. Keep them safe."

"Like you care," Mike said scornfully.

Milton kicked him in the knees. Mike groaned.

"Where are Paige and Sarah?" Paisley demanded.

"Captured, no doubt."

Captured.

"But their coup didn't go as planned." Milton glanced around the room. "They didn't envision senior citizens standing up for their fellow residents."

"You thought we were weak?" Aunt Callie's face contorted. "Thought you could bust into our houses and take what you want? Is that why they sent only you after Paisley? If anyone else comes here, they're in for a treat too."

"That's right." Kathleen lifted her mosaic piece.

Only then did Paisley notice the ocean scenery made of cut glass that had become Kathleen's weapon. It was much like the beautiful nautical mosaic she'd given Paisley and Judah as a vow renewal gift.

"You might as well tell us who's coming." Milton nudged Mike's black shoe. "You aren't getting out of this unscathed."

"Five old fogies can't stop a tidal wave," Mike said mockingly.

"Let's show him what we're made of!" Dad rubbed his hands together. "Whoever's on their way expects easy pickings? They have another thing coming."

The talk of more men coming to try to capture her caused more panic to race through Paisley. But instead of giving in to it, she turned to prayer. *Please, God, protect my family. Be with all of us.*

Thirty-eight

The ties around Paige's wrists hurt and the cloth rubbing the side of her lips chafed. Worried sick about Piper, she felt her stomach lurch. Was her daughter safe with Dad? If these insurgents had the gall to abduct her, Sarah, Judah, and Bess, what else might they be willing to do? Would they kidnap Piper, given the chance? What would Dad do if they attempted something so despicable?

Dear God, please watch over Piper. Help my father to keep her safe.

"Judah, are you hungry? Want a snack?" Mia grinned at him like she meant something other than food.

"No, thanks."

Mia's ongoing flirtations with Judah grated on Paige's nerves. Wasn't she married to Edward now? Why was she acting like a single woman who was a wanton flirt? And why wasn't Judah objecting to it?

He turned his face away from Mia, but she kept smiling flirtatiously at him and walking her fingers up his arm like she had a right to do such things.

"Stop!" he said finally.

Mia whispered something in his ear and giggled. How dare she flirt with him like this! How dare she act like she was the victor in a game. While Mia held them captive, Paige considered her the worst of enemies. She deserved to be locked up for years, right alongside Edward and Evie.

Somewhere out there, Forest was trying to rescue her. Paige knew that like she knew her next breath. This situation might look disparaging, and yes, she was fearful for her daughter, but it wasn't hopeless. They were not sitting here without anyone on their side. God was watching over them! And maybe Forest was somewhere close.

She glanced over at Bess whose eyes and mouth remained covered. Why didn't Mia let her see into the room? Did the troublemaker feel guilty having Bess tied up in her previous home? Maybe Mia didn't want to look the current mayor in the eye. That made Paige want Bess's eyes uncovered even more.

Bess's arms moved jerkily behind her, then stilled. She made the sneaky movements again. Paige observed her actions, then periods of stillness. Was she trying to free herself? Paige glanced at Judah a couple of times, hoping to catch his eye when Mia wasn't looking. Could he see what his mom was doing?

Trying to break free sounded like a smart idea. Paige would try to undo her bindings too, but she'd reefed on them without any luck when the guy tossed her into the backseat of the car.

How were they going to get out of this mess?

Lord, You see what Mia and these guys are doing. Don't let them get away with such cruel behavior. Keep my family safe. Tell Forest where we are. Help us. Please—

A silent sob erupted from within her. She wasn't normally a crier, but her daughter might be in trouble. Paisley might be in trouble too. She was the witness with the most influence in Edward's trial. Was she the one these people wanted to do away with like Edward had tried to do away with her before?

Perched on the edge of his chair, Mia nearly sat on Judah's lap. Paisley would be enraged if she saw Mia's cat-like movements as she petted his arm and leaned close to his ear, whispering. Then grinning at him possessively. Or was it obsessively?

Why didn't Judah yell at her to get away from him? Was he trying to distract her so Bess could break free? Mia pointed toward the big windows as if showing him the view. He acted interested, but then he met Paige's gaze and nodded slightly at her. Was he telling her not to worry? That his tolerance of Mia's behavior was a ruse?

She hoped that was the case. She trusted her brother-in-law. But if she had to endure watching Mia fawn over him for another minute, she might be sick.

Thirty-nine

Paisley sat on the stairs in the shadows, rocking Piper as she slept. The rest of the group, other than James who still stood by the front door, were discussing options for staying here and protecting themselves, or else leaving together. They spoke of roadblocks. Hiking down the beach. Possibly borrowing someone's boat.

"Paisley Rose should go up to the attic with Piper." Aunt Callie pointed toward the ceiling. "Two of us can guard the second floor. No one's getting past me!"

"Might work." Dad stroked his chin. His agreeing to anything Aunt Callie said was like a miracle.

"If they breach through those of us on this floor"—she shook her pan as if to show that wouldn't happen easily—"those on the next floor can fend them off." Aunt Callie nodded toward Paisley and Piper. "We must protect those two. Paige and Judah are counting on us."

Paisley thought of the baby in her womb. She must do everything in her power to keep him safe, too.

"Someone's coming!" James hollered.

Paisley tensed, ready to flee up the stairs.

Dad picked up a sculpture off the bookcase. Milton grabbed a vase. Kathleen lifted her mosaic again. Aunt Callie stood like a warrior, her legs braced, her cast iron pan clutched in her hands.

If anyone came through the door, he'd have to overcome James, who carried a thick stick he retrieved from outside, then prevail against the others to get to her. They were a small group, but she was proud of them for being willing to fight for her and Piper.

"False alarm!" James called in a relieved tone. "It's just that reporter."

"My niece?" Milton set down the vase and marched toward the door.

"What if they've put her up to this?" Aunt Callie asked in a huffy tone. "She might be leading a whole slew of bullies right to our house."

"She'd never do that!" Milton said over his shoulder.

"I wouldn't put it past her," Aunt Callie muttered.

Milton opened the front door. "Alison! I'm so glad to see you're all right."

"Uncle Milton, what are you doing here?"

He embraced her as she walked through the doorway. "I came with Paul and James."

"When the deputy let me go, I had no idea I'd find you here." She spoke quickly. "There's a roadblock, so I ditched my car and hiked the rest of the way on the beach."

They strode into the living room with their arms linked.

"Did you see Judah?" Paisley asked.

"No. He never showed up at the gallery. Do you think—"

"Yes." She bit back the urge to sob. "I think they must have him."

Alison clutched Milton's arm. "You knew this was going to happen, didn't you?"

He mumbled something to her that Paisley didn't understand.

Ever since Milton arrived with Dad and James, the group had trusted him. But what if he'd participated in the awful things being done today as Mike alluded to? What if he was the one who was leading others here?

"Milton, please tell us what you know," Paisley urged him.

"Keep your trap shut," Mike said gruffly.

"So what if I lose the paper? The plan failed! These women's safety comes first!"

"It didn't fail." Mike squinted at Milton. "Is Judah here? Craig? Neither are present to rescue her this time."

Paisley gulped.

"So this is Mike Linfield?" Alison asked. "What's he doing here?"

"Good question!" Aunt Callie said.

"Let me go free, and I'll bring her to the others." Mike's voice rose dramatically. "We'll get what we've been promised. We'll be set for life. Nothing will stand in our way!"

"It's over!" Milton said. "The plan failed!"

"You're wrong. Others will be here any second."

"What's he talking about? Why does he keep saying that?" Aunt Callie asked.

"Callie." Dad scowled at her. "If you listened more and talked less, you'd learn something."

"Don't you tell me anything!"

Paisley groaned. This wasn't the time for one of their squabbles! Who were the others Mike spoke of? Where did they plan to bring her?

"Edward's been preparing this for years, right down to the software hacking of the substation phone grid and the electricity being down for repairs today. Believe me, when I say someone is coming to get you, it'll happen." Mike stared intensely at Paisley. "If I take you to headquarters now, there will be less of a struggle. Less collateral damage."

"You're not taking her anywhere!" Aunt Callie yelled.

"Edward didn't plan for every contingency. He didn't expect the detective to be digging up the past." Milton glanced at Alison with a glimmer in his eyes. "Nor for my niece to be mining through my newspapers to discover the truth."

"How did you know about that?" Alison asked.

"You never gave up, even when I told you to. I'm proud as can be of you."

A soft smile crossed her mouth.

"Stop with the emotional rubbish. Do what you are supposed to be doing!" Mike's wide eyes reamed Milton with accusation. "Unless you're a turncoat?"

"I'm doing what I should have done all along—standing up to you bullies!" Milton jabbed his finger at Mike. "You and Edward are the schoolyard tyrants, only grown up and just as mean! I won't bow and scrape to your demands any longer."

"You can't stop now! You're in too deep."

"Watch me." Milton's eyes looked clearer as he gazed at each of the room's occupants. "Come into the kitchen. Let's make plans without him hearing us!" He marched out of the living room, and Alison followed him.

"I'll stay here and watch this one." Aunt Callie shook her pan at Mike.

Paisley carried Piper down the stairs and hurried after the others moving into the kitchen. The six of them circled the butcher-block island. Kathleen set a battery-operated lantern on the center of the island and turned it on.

"We need to leave quickly and hike down the beach," Milton said in a hushed tone. "He's right about more men coming. They know Paisley and the girl are here."

Why was all this happening? Just so Edward could get away with the charges against him? So he could be mayor again like he told Judah? If Paisley were captured and sent away like Edward tried to do with her before, did he imagine Judah would forget about her and go along with his grand scheme? That would never happen!

Still, her heart beat fast at the thought of men dressed in black clothes and masks coming after her. But she didn't want to give in to panic. She had to keep her head. Do her best to keep herself and Piper safe.

Breathing slowly, she pictured the ocean waves, the sea-foam bursting over the rocks. She thought of her spot on the peninsula where the water poured over her like a cool shower.

The Lord is my strength and my shield; my heart trusts in him, and he helps me. Reciting the Psalm comforted her.

"I'll stay here with the prisoner," Dad volunteered. "I'm not afraid to face Edward's minions. I want my girls to be safe."

When his gaze met Paisley's, she smiled at him, appreciating Dad standing up to protect Piper and her. He'd come a long way from the weak man she thought him to be four months ago when she first returned to Basalt Bay.

"Is hiking on the beach our best option?" Alison asked with doubt evident in her tone. "The terrain is difficult."

"That would be hard for Callie," Kathleen said softly. "I'll stay with her. Paul, you should go with Paisley and Piper."

"You're probably right."

"With the roadblocks in place, driving out by car is impossible. Leaving on the beach is our only option," Milton said quietly. "We'll have to secure Mike with more than sheets. Left to his own devices, he'll be out of the fabric binding and following us too quickly."

"Whatever we do, let's do it and stop talking about doing it!" James said with urgency. "It's time for action!"

Paisley agreed. It was time to do something.

Forty

Foremost in Forest's mind was rescuing his wife, then ensuring Piper's safety. He and Craig reached the shed on their knees, crawling through brush and over rocks and sticks. Fortunately, the ground was dry. But their pants were torn and bloody at the knees. Every few seconds they froze and waited, listening, steeling themselves. How much longer until they were discovered?

Craig met Forest's gaze with a questioning look. Forest nodded, his emotions caught in his throat.

How could this standoff end well? The guards carried guns. Forest didn't, thanks to Deputy Brian taking his handgun. If the armed men saw Forest and Craig hauling the ladder to the balcony, what would they do other than shoot them on the spot?

Lord, help me rescue my wife. My daughter too.

The guard at the back door pressed his fingers against his ear like he was listening to a device. Receiving instructions, perhaps. Suddenly, he jogged around the corner out of sight.

This was their chance!

Taking a deep breath, Forest picked up one end of the ladder at the same time Craig grabbed the other end. Expecting the guard to come back at any second, they rushed across the open space.

Somehow, maybe God placed a supernatural curtain around them, they reached the house without being detected. They butted the ladder against the outer wall between two bushes so it wouldn't be seen by casual observance.

Forest pointed at himself. He wanted to go up first. His body tight against the perpendicular ladder, he crept up. The toe of his shoe skimmed the metal, making a soft clink. He forced his movements and breathing to remain silent.

More creeping. Almost there. At the balcony ledge, he crawled across the wooden railing like a snake slithering over it. He hunkered down. Was the door locked? All their efforts would be for nothing if he couldn't get the door open. Otherwise, he'd have to break the glass, which would bring the guards down on them.

Craig slid over the railing and landed on the balcony with a soft thud. He crouched beside Forest. Had anyone heard them?

Standing slowly, Forest pressed himself against the glass door and peered inside. No one was in the room. He gripped the handle and pulled. It didn't give. He reefed harder. A soft click. A grinding sound followed like the hinges hadn't been used in ages, but the door gave way.

Incrementally, he tugged the glass door open enough for him to slip inside. He crawled into the large bedroom with Craig a couple of feet behind him. He saw the open closet door. Was that where Edward imprisoned Paisley? He swallowed hard. Where was Paige being held now?

He squatted next to the bedroom doorway and made hand signals to Craig. *I'll go first. Wait here.*

Craig shook his head. He made signals. *Wait. I know the way. I'm tougher than you.*

Forest gritted his teeth. Paige was *his* wife. He'd reach her first.

Craig held up his hand in a shushing gesture. They both stilled.

Voices came from below.

"Let them go." Judah's voice. So he was here.

A snarky female laugh came next.

"Mia," Craig mouthed.

"You sure are cute," she said. "But under no circumstances would I let any of these women go."

Questions pulsed through Forest's mind. Was Judah trying to coax Mia into letting the women go? How many were captured? Anyone besides Paige and Sarah? Was Paisley here?

Craig pointed toward the stairway, making it obvious he wanted to go first.

Forest shook his head. Taking the lead, he crawled forward. The floor squeaked beneath him. Teeth clenched, he stopped, hoping no one downstairs had heard that. If they did, this rescue mission was a bust.

Craig tapped his shoulder. Forest glanced back and saw a gritty determination in his expression. Craig's rescue of Paisley, and his entrapping Evie, both revealed his bravery—and his reckless nature. Forest didn't want him charging into a volatile situation and losing the upper hand they had now.

Upper hand? At least, no one had spotted them yet.

Forest palmed his chest. He'd go first. He had surveillance experience. He knew how to wait for the perfect moment to attack.

This time Craig didn't balk.

Taking a deep breath, Forest crept a few more feet.

"Sit still!" Mia shouted.

He dropped to the floor. Who was she yelling at?

"I see what you're doing!"

He tensed. Did she mean him?

Muffled voices rose in a concert of barely discernible commands—"Leave her alone!" "Stop that!" "Let us go!"

"All of you, be quiet!" Mia yelled, sounding like a five-year-old kid demanding her way.

At least she hadn't seen him. Taking advantage of the noise and the upheaval, Forest and Craig advanced to the top of the stairs, then remained flat on their bellies, peering over the edge. Without lights on, the shadows along the stairway might keep them hidden.

A man dressed in a black hoodie and ski mask trudged past the bottom stair, a gun in his hands.

Unable to view the whole living room from this angle, Forest couldn't see how many guards were present. It looked like he'd have a clear shot to the kitchen. If he sneaked into the living room and untied Judah, assuming he was bound, that would make three of them against the rest.

"What are you planning to do with us?" Judah asked.

If Forest could communicate with his brother-in-law, he'd tell him to keep asking questions. Keep Mia talking. A diversion might give Forest and Craig a chance to sneak downstairs without being seen. A loud noise or distraction would buy them a few seconds to clobber the first guard.

Mia answered Judah in subdued tones that were difficult for Forest to decipher.

Craig made small jerky hand signals. He wanted to go downstairs first. He'd take the risk. Forest grabbed his wrist. No. This was his family. Craig eyed him savagely. It was his family too.

Fine. They were in this together. Still, for their attack to be successful, they needed a momentary lapse in the guard's attention.

"Tell us what you're after, then this tomfoolery can be done with," Judah said.

"Tomfoolery?" Mia laughed. "Is that what you think this is? You had your chance. This all could have been avoided if you would have taken over the mayorship instead of her!"

Did she mean Bess?

If Judah, Paige, Sarah, and Bess were here, that meant four captives. Forest counted at least six captors, including the four outside, and Mia. Although there might be more. Still unable to see into the living room, he guessed he and Craig would be facing an uphill battle. Was Judah still tied up? Had he been able to work his ties loose at all? They could use his brute force if a fistfight followed.

A rifle fired outside!

Forest froze. Whose shot was that?

Multiple shots resounded!

"Now!" Craig growled.

It was time for them to make their move.

Forty-one

"Who fired those rounds?" Mia screeched.

At the report of gunshots, every muscle in Judah's body tightened. He jerked hard against the ropes binding his wrists together and the ones tying his legs to the chair. If he had any chance of getting free, this was it. He'd take it!

The two guards and Mia dove forward, crouching near the window ledge and peering out.

"Looks like the deputy," one of the criminals said. "What's he doing here?"

"I thought you took care of him!" another guy said accusingly.

"He was told—"

"Shut up." Mia grabbed binoculars and peered out the window. "That's him, all right. Well, well. I didn't think Brian had it in him."

Yanking against the ropes at his wrists, Judah heard a creak, an off sound among the other noises in the room. He glanced toward the stairway. Forest and Craig glided down the steps on their backsides, crouching low. Forest shook his head at him.

Judah glanced away so as not to bring attention to the two men, but his heart pounded. He had to be ready for anything. He'd do what he could to keep Mia preoccupied so she didn't notice the rescue team. If Forest and Craig's plan failed, what then?

Had Mom gotten her ties loose yet?

"Now what?" one of the guards asked.

"We wait for the others just like we planned. Nothing's changed!" Mia growled out. "Get back to your places! Move, you fools!"

The masked guards scrambled to do her bidding.

In a different scenario, Judah would have found humor in the ex-receptionist taking command like this. Not today.

"What others?" Judah asked her. "What's going on out there?"

"Something interesting." Mia stood and dusted off her hands.

Forest and Craig were out of sight. Hiding in the kitchen, most likely.

"Too bad you aren't one of us." Mia strode back to Judah. She smoothed her palm over his shoulder, making his skin crawl. "Things could have been different. You and I could be running the town together, following Edward's blueprint."

Judah forced himself not to shudder. To speak softly. "That would have been something."

Paige and Mom groaned.

"I wouldn't have minded sharing the spotlight with a handsome man like you." Mia danced her fingers down his shirt's button line. "Too bad you chose your wife's family instead of your own."

"What do you mean? You have my mother tied up! And my sister-in-law."

"Not to mention your half-sister. Don't forget about her."

"I didn't. What about my wife? Where is she?" Judah kept his voice quiet so Mia would stay close to him, her back facing the kitchen.

"If you want to be with her, it'll have to be far away from here." She caressed his arm like she was petting a dog. "In a matter of minutes, Deputy Brian and his little posse will be hemmed in on all sides." She laughed as if she had everything plotted to the last detail.

If that were so, where was Paisley? Where was Piper? Did other guards have them isolated somewhere? Were they okay? Judah ground his teeth together, wanting to demand information from Mia. But he had to appear passive. Keep her distracted, talking to him.

"Mia," he said softly. "I want to ask you something."

"What is it?" she asked breathily.

"Why did you marry my dad?" It was the only question that came to mind.

"Jealous?"

"No, but I'm concerned about you. I care for you as a … friend."

"More than friends, Judah." She leaned her cheek against his. "We could have been way more than friends."

Ugh. Why weren't Forest and Craig jumping out and grabbing her?

Come on, Forest!

Forty-two

Crouching behind the massive kitchen island, Craig made succinct hand movements to Forest. He pointed at himself then at the masked guard by the stairs. He'd take that guy. Why did Forest shake his head?

The detective held up his palm. Wait? No. They'd waited long enough. If they missed their window—

Mia's voice hit him with acidic familiarity.

"Oh, Judah. This is the way it should have been all along. You and me. Us leading Grant Bay. Judah and Mia sound sweet together, don't they?"

Was Mia cuddling with Judah? Why would his brother allow her to go on romantically like that? Paisley would—

Oh. Judah was going along with Mia's delusional attempts to seduce him to give Craig and Forest time to get the upper hand, right? Craig nudged Forest's shoulder and jabbed his finger toward Judah in quick stabs at the air.

It was time. Do or die.

Forest nodded.

Craig gulped. *Help us.* A silent desperate prayer.

Taking a breath, muscles taut, fists clenched, ready to pummel the guard with the gun by the stairs, yet hoping to take him down unawares, he rushed around the island.

Everything in the room imploded at once. In high-speed velocity, or slow-motion clarity, he saw snippets of action. Mia lunged away from Judah. Another woman—Bess?—charged forward blindfolded, ramming against Mia, knocking her to the floor. Mia screamed. Forest let out a bellowing howl and barreled toward the other guy holding a gun.

Craig's fist rammed his guy's jaw powerfully. Not fast enough. The gun in his hand discharged an ear-ringing rapport. A firebrand of burning pain seared through Craig's chest. Stunned, falling, crying out in a silent wail of agony, he toppled over.

He hit the floor, a fog engulfing him. The noise faded into oblivion.

Forty-three

Forest heard his voice yelling out a guttural war cry. He had two goals. Subdue the thug. Rescue Paige. He barreled into the guy before the guard pulled the trigger. Hit him hard in the face. Rammed his gut.

A shot cracked in the room! Not his guy's weapon. Craig?

Desperate to subdue the guard he was fighting, and check on Craig, Forest punched the masked man's face again and again. The thug stumbled backward, his weapon crashing to the floor. He toppled over into a heap.

Forest huffed out a hoarse breath.

In the next second, the guy Craig had been fighting hit Forest solidly in the gut, his eye, his gut again. The room turned fuzzy, a haze filling his brain. He was still standing on his feet, but his torso reeled back and forth, nearly careening to the floor. He couldn't take much more of this beating. A far-off voice in his mind chanted, "Fight. Rescue. Fight. Rescue."

He heard Paige's muffled voice calling, "Foorreeest!"

He inhaled a painful breath. The guy belted him—one, two, three. Forest reciprocated. Things crashed to the floor as they wrestled and punched each other. He'd never struggled against anyone so desperately and forcefully before. It felt like a fight for his life. For his wife's life. For Craig's life.

He heard another scuffle going on across the room. Judah? He didn't have time to evaluate. More crashing. More falling and hitting the other guy.

"Call 911!" someone shouted.

When the guy he fought lay crumpled on the floor, Forest drew in great gulps of ragged air. Hands on his knees, he would surely vomit. He peered at Craig on the floor. Someone was bending over him, helping him. Sarah? The man lay still on the wooden floor with blood pooling around his chest. This looked serious. How did Sarah get free?

Only then did Forest view the room in its entirety. Hands clutching his ribs, Judah bent down, gulping air like he might pass out. He'd obviously been involved in the other fight. On the floor a third guy was lying face up, unconscious.

Bess sat on top of Mia who was kicking, screaming, and calling her crude names. Paige—*Paige was safe!*—was tying up Mia's legs with the ties she must have had on her limbs.

Judah shouted into his phone in phrases—"Send an ambulance! Or helicopter! Get through the barricade. A man needs medical assistance, now!"

Thank God the phone was working!

Paige met Forest's gaze and her face creased into a sob.

Oh, baby. Breathing raggedly, he stumbled over to her and dropped onto the floor. She curled up in his lap, crying against him. Then she hugged him, kissing his cheek, his mouth. He saw blood on her clothes. Oh. His blood. Not hers.

"Thank God you're okay," he said.

"You, too. I'm so glad to see you." She sobbed into his shoulder. "Poor Craig."

"Judah, help me!" Sarah cried out. "He's slipping away."

Judah stumbled across the room, an anguished look on his face.

Forest heard him counting out numbers as he performed CPR and Sarah administered puffs of breath in between. Brother and sister, most likely, trying to save their brother.

God, help him. Save Craig.

Mia wrestled against her ties, yelling, "You're all going to be sorry! Let me go! You can't tie me up like this! I'm the mayor! I'm in charge here!"

"You're in charge of nothing," Bess shouted back at her. "I need some help!"

Paige crawled over to her. Forest followed on his knees. Grabbing the ties the others had dropped, he secured Mia's legs and wrists tightly. In the process, one of her high heels clipped his nose. He sucked in his breath and yanked on her ties again.

"You can't do this. I must meet the others. I'm their leader!" Mia turned her head and shouted to her fallen guards. "You're all useless! Pathetic. You call yourself patriots? Get up now. Be ready for the next phase of our fight!"

"Next phase? Where are the others?" Forest demanded, barely recognizing his ragged voice. "What else do you have planned for Basalt Bay? Tell me. What else is about to happen?"

He met Paige's fearful gaze, their thoughts probably coinciding. Did this have anything to do with Piper?

"You think you're so smart," Mia yelled. "But you don't know the great ideas Edward and I have planned for our city!"

"Your city?" Bess made a scoffing sound. "If you're the one who masterminded this hostile takeover, the kidnapping of citizens of Basalt Bay, you're going to prison!"

"That's right," Forest added. "You should stop mouthing off and start trying to make a deal." He held a cloth above Mia's mouth threateningly. "Who are you supposed to meet up with?"

Squinting at him, she showed her teeth in a grimace. "I'm not talking to you, Detective!"

"Fine. Mia Grant, I arrest you for the kidnapping of Paige Harper, Bess Grant, Sarah Blackstone, and Judah Grant." He finished reciting her Miranda rights.

"You can't do that to me!" Mia screamed. "Deputy Brian will let me go! Judah, help me!"

"By the authority given to me by the Coastal Task Force, I just did. And no, he won't let you go! No one's going to help you." He made sure the ties were secured around her legs and arms. While he was tempted to cover her mouth so he didn't have to listen to her, he didn't. That would be a cruel punishment.

Clasping Paige's hand, Forest drew her away from Mia and over to where Judah and Sarah were laboring over Craig's still body. They both prayed quietly and waited.

"A pulse!" Judah shouted.

Sarah laughed and cried at the same time.

The whirring of helicopter blades sounded above them. More shots were fired.

"See!" Mia said in a confident tone. "My people will fight for me!"

Her people?

Groaning, Forest dropped onto the floor, holding Paige's hand. Judah had his palm on Craig's shoulder, praying for him. Craig's chest rose and fell in slight movements.

"How can we get him out to the chopper?" Judah asked. "I'm guessing there's more rebellion going on outside."

"Forest?" Paige shot worried glances toward Craig. "What are we going to do? He needs help!"

"Come on," he said to Judah. "Let's do this!"

As Forest stood, his legs wobbled and nearly buckled under him, but he forced himself to jog up the stairs. Judah's uneven footsteps pounded the treads behind him. Once they reached the door to the balcony, he lunged over the side of the railing and crept down the ladder. Without discussion, Judah followed.

They had a common purpose—get Craig to that helicopter! Then they'd get the women off this mountain.

Forty-four

Leaving Aunt Callie behind was one of the hardest things Paisley ever had to do. But one look at her aunt's determined grimace and the heavy pan in her hands, and she knew someone would think twice about barging into the project house when Callie Cedars was on duty.

"Go! Find shelter and safety for you and our treasure." Aunt Callie stroked Piper's hair lovingly. "Keep her close to you, Paisley Rose."

"I will. I promise I won't let her go." She tugged Piper's sleeping form closer to herself. She thrust one arm around her aunt's body. "I love you, Auntie. Stay safe."

"Love you too, precious girl."

"We have to go!" Alison said. "Come on, Paisley."

Glancing between Aunt Callie holding the pan and Mike, still tied up on the floor, Paisley prayed for a safe resolution to the turmoil they'd experienced today. She prayed for Piper's safety and her own child's, too. For peace for them all.

James clasped Aunt Callie's hand and whispered near her ear. Aunt Callie nodded. The two of them looked sweetly at each other.

"Paisley!" Alison said gruffly.

"Coming." Paisley followed her out the door, along with James who locked and closed it firmly behind him.

"Stay close together," he said.

James and Dad took the lead as their group traipsed in a huddled formation down the trail toward the ocean. Paisley held Piper. Alison and Milton brought up the rear.

Paisley felt safe, sandwiched between the four. But what might they face up ahead along the southern shores of Basalt Bay? How long could they fend off an attack, if one came?

Thoughts of her previous abduction flashed through her mind. She hated the thought of experiencing any of it again, even mentally or emotionally. She didn't want Piper or Paige to endure anything like she'd gone through, either.

Where was Judah? By now he should have returned to the project house. Nothing would have stopped him from reaching her and protecting her from Edward and Mia's plot. Unless he couldn't get back to her. She pictured him tied up. Or worse, wounded.

Trying to not panic, she focused on walking down the sandy trail. She needed to do everything in her power to protect Piper and herself. To that end, she prayed with every step.

"You okay, Paisley?" Dad asked over his shoulder.

"I'm okay." She was tired and worried. She wasn't used to packing a child like this, but fortunately, Piper was light. She wouldn't hand off her charge to anyone else. Not when a creep might be lurking behind one of the bushes or a boulder. And she wasn't going to complain. Not when these four were risking their lives to protect her. So were Aunt Callie and Kathleen back at the project house.

When their group reached the beach, Paisley sighed, thankful for a full view of the shoreline. If anyone came toward them, they'd have the advantage of some warning. And this ... the ocean waves churning up the seashore ... was a natural calm for her. She took a couple of deep breaths and let them out slowly.

"Now where?" Alison asked.

"Head south," Dad said between hoarse breaths.

"Are you okay, Dad?"

"Been better. We'll get through this, Paisley-Bug."

She smiled slightly at the endearment.

"Walk faster," Alison said in a brusque tone. "We must keep moving."

Paisley gazed at the waves rolling up the beach and continued at the same pace. Alison was the one in the best shape in their group. The three men were in their sixties, some of them not in the greatest physical condition. Paisley had been on bed rest for a couple of days, and now carried Piper. There would be no fast walking, despite the newspaper reporter's orders.

"Want me to take a turn holding her?" Alison asked.

"No thanks." Paisley still hoped to carry Piper the whole way herself.

They crossed the mudflats without conversing. The air around them felt thick with potential danger. Were they walking into a trap?

Whoever was involved in trying to control Basalt must have another plan in mind as Mike said. Would they wait until after dark to try capturing her? He'd mentioned someone hacking the phones. Was that why her texts to Judah and the others hadn't gone through?

With two days until the trial, was this attack about stopping her from testifying? What did Edward hold over so many people's heads to get them to do his bidding when he was such a scoundrel—and in jail?

"I wonder what happened to Craig and Forest." Alison broke the silence.

"Maybe they're still trying to rescue Paige and Sarah," Paisley said around her fatigued breathing. "They won't stop until they succeed. Judah too."

"Unless something's happened to all of them."

She had to mention that.

James stopped suddenly, and Paisley almost ran into him.

"I saw a figure up ahead. At least, I thought I did." He put his hand over his forehead as a sun shield. "Up by the tree line."

Paisley repositioned Piper on her shoulder. The girl was still asleep. "Should we turn back?" She glanced at Milton, then beyond him to the seashore they'd already crossed.

"We have to keep going," he said.

"Maybe we should have stayed with Cal," James said.

"We agreed." Dad eyed him. "I don't see anyone. Maybe it was your imagination."

"Maybe. Looked like someone to me." James huffed out a breath.

Tensely, they continued. Their previous walking had spread them apart. Now they clustered together again with Paisley and Piper in the middle. The others took backward glances, tight scowls on their faces, their shoulders stiff. They all looked as fatigued as she felt.

Finally, they took a break and guzzled from shared water bottles. Piper awoke and stared at Paisley as if she didn't know who she was. She wailed loudly. "Mommy! Mommy!"

"Shhh. Shhh." Paisley jostled her.

Dad clasped Piper's hand and said, "Hey, little girl. You're okay. Grampa is right here."

Piper lunged toward him, and Paisley let her go into his arms. They needed her to stop crying. Otherwise, her noise might give away their location.

Fortunately, she settled down and took a drink of water. By the look of exhaustion on Dad's features, he wouldn't be able to carry the two-year-old for long.

"I see it!" James said, pointing ahead.

The camp shack Paisley hadn't been to in years came into view. It looked broken down. One corner of the gaping shelter rested on the sand while the other corners were supported by damaged cinder blocks. The whole thing seemed about to topple over with a wind gust.

"That's where we're going to stay?" Alison asked incredulously.

"Just long enough to get our bearings," Dad answered.

Paisley held her hands out to Piper. The girl stared at her like she was going to cry again.

"Are you okay with carrying her?"

"For now," Dad answered.

Piper wrapped her arms around his neck even tighter.

They continued walking, their pace slower than before.

"Why don't we break into one of the summer homes?" Alison asked. "I doubt anyone would care. It would be better than stepping foot in a shack that looks as dilapidated as that."

"There's an unwritten code here about not breaking into the summer houses. But I'd go along with your idea for our safety." Paisley glanced at Dad. "What do you think?"

"Let's rest. Catch our breath. Then decide."

They approached the shelter that had obviously received severe beatings by Hurricanes Addy and Blaine. At least it was semi-dry. Paisley needed to rest. The others did too.

A few minutes' delay wouldn't hurt, would it?

Forty-five

At the front of the house, Judah punched a masked guard then shoved him, his energy dwindling. He barely caught his breath before the next guy charged at him. The assailant struck him in the head with his gun. Judah toppled to the ground, crawling backward, the world spinning. Any second the gun report would sound, and he'd be dead or seriously wounded.

Acid filled his throat. His vision blurred. He imagined Paisley, her hand reaching out to him, calling his name.

Judah.

Paisley, my love. I'm so sorry I didn't see this coming.

Despite his pain, if he had breath in him, he'd keep fighting to save Craig. And to reach his wife. He forced himself to stand, his hands on his bent knees. He might be sick. Man, his head hurt. Still, he clenched his fists.

"Hands up!"

He did what the guy said.

"This is bigger than you, Grant! You've lost." The gravelly male voice sounded familiar. "You should have done what

Edward and Mia tried to get you to do before. You only have yourself to blame."

Why was that? He tried focusing. Where had he heard this guy's voice before? Why was he even fighting when he believed in mercy and grace?

Craig. He had to get his brother to the helicopter. Then find Paisley.

The guy dressed in black fatigues touched the back of his hand to his nose where Judah's fist must have connected. "All you have to do is agree to leave with the others, and this will be over."

That voice. Jeff's from C-MER? He peered at the masked man. C.L. and Jeff were both involved in this bizarre takeover?

"Jeff?"

The guy chortled.

Scuffling and grunting sounds were going on behind them. Forest must still be fighting.

"We need to get Craig to the helicopter," Judah yelled over the noise of the whirling machine below. "He's hurt."

"Masters?"

"One of your comrades shot him."

"No kidding?" For a second, the guy almost sounded like he had a heart. Then he shouted, "Get down on the ground with your hands behind your head."

"Help us get Craig to the chopper first."

"No can do."

"We have to try to save him." Judah clutched Jeff's arm. "Please. He used to be your friend. He needs medical attention!"

"No!" Jeff jerked away from Judah's grip.

Gulping down the bitter taste in his throat, Judah did what he had to do. He rammed his fist into his previous coworker's gut. Jeff retaliated by chopping the side of his hand against Judah's neck and shoulder. With each hit, he moaned.

Gunshots rang in the air.

Judah ducked behind a vehicle. As did Jeff.

The gunfire resounded again, this time from guards emerging from the bushes.

A group of townspeople with Deputy Brian leading the charge marched farther up the driveway.

"Stand down!" Deputy Brian shouted. "This is over."

"Mia was right," Forest muttered from where he lay on the ground, wiping blood from his face. "Our deputy has arrived!"

"Craig Masters is in need of immediate medical care!" Judah shouted to both groups. "Let us carry him to the helicopter. Please!"

"I told you no about that!" Jeff said through gritted teeth.

"Where's your sense of compassion?" Judah breathed hoarsely. "Haven't you done enough harm here?"

"Not nearly enough. I'm waiting for orders."

"From whom?"

Jeff jabbed his finger toward Edward's house.

"Mia? She's been arrested. She's going to prison right alongside her new husband."

"Then C.L. is calling the shots."

"C.L.? You've got to be kidding me." Judah sucked in a breath. "Please, Jeff, let me get Craig to the chopper. Save his life."

"No!"

"I thought you were an honest person."

Jeff barked out a laugh. "Shows how dumb you are. Mia was right. She bragged she could get you and your father to do anything she wanted. Believe anything she said."

"She was wrong about that, too."

"We'll see. This isn't over."

Was he challenging Judah?

Focus. Help Craig. Find Paisley.

A line of six black-dressed guys guarded the road, guns facing Deputy Brian and the dozen people from town, all residents Judah recognized. He hated the thought of anyone else getting hurt.

The helicopter blades still whirred. No doubt the pilot wouldn't wait long since this looked like a war zone.

Craig desperately needed medical attention.

"Sorry, Jeff." Using his remaining strength, Judah rammed his shoulder into the man's chest as hard as he could, knocking him to the ground. Then he ran for the helicopter, his hands flailing to get the pilot's attention. "Don't leave! A wounded man is inside. Needs help."

The chopper pilot gave him a thumbs up. Then two fingers. Two minutes? Not much time.

With his hands raised, Judah backed up. "Listen, all of you! I'm going to help Craig into the helicopter. Tell your men to stand down. Do this one humanitarian thing. Don't shoot. I beg of you."

He took a couple more steps. No one fired at him. But Jeff followed him every step of the way, his gun barrel aimed at Judah's chest.

Forty-six

The rough, uneven floorboards of the one-room cabin weren't comfortable, but Paisley appreciated the chance to sit down and rest. Alison sat on one side of her, Milton on the other. Dad and James knelt on the floor, peering out the glassless windows, mumbling quietly. Making plans, no doubt.

Piper sat still in Paisley's arms as if she sensed something was wrong. Quietly, Paisley sang nursery rhymes to her, trying to distract her and keep her calm.

"We should push on." Dad sounded extremely tired.

"At least this place is sort of dry." Paisley smoothed her palm over Piper's thin blond hair. "Aren't we too visible out on the beach?"

"Not really." James shook his head. "The shore is more protective than this."

"How so?"

"Out there we can hide behind boulders or driftwood. Even the monolith might be a defense for us."

"That's right," Dad agreed. "James and I know the best places to hide."

"But with Piper? We must keep her safety a priority."

"And yours," Dad said. "She's doing okay, isn't she?"

"I think so." Paisley hugged her. Thankfully, Piper was more relaxed around her now.

"Are we rested enough to push on?" Milton sounded like he was saying they'd better be ready to move on.

Everyone shrugged or nodded.

"We'll stick to our plan. Stay on shore. Get as far as we can." Gripping the window frame for balance, Dad stood. "Hopefully, Judah and Forest will find us before night-fall."

Paisley silently agreed.

"It's foolhardy to assume anyone's coming for us." Milton clucked his tongue against his teeth. "Wouldn't they be here by now if they were physically able to? Getting to the next town is our best bet."

"Or finding an empty house?" Paisley asked, reminding them of Alison's previous suggestion. "I'm not going to make it twenty miles."

"The terrain is difficult," James said. "And the tide is coming in."

"Then why not stay here?" She cast a pleading glance toward Dad.

"Whoever is taking over the town means business." He lifted one shoulder. "We can't stay in one place. Moving is essential to our safety. To your safety."

"Okay." She sighed.

As they left the beach shack, Dad stayed by her side, even putting his arm around her back. She appreciated his comfort and concern, especially when he was tired too.

Piper moved restlessly in her arms. *"Pway?"* She pointed at the sand.

"Not today, sweetie. We're going for a nice walk."

"No. *Pway.*"

"Sorry, kiddo," Dad said.

Paisley pointed at the water, then at a bird, trying to get the girl's attention off playing in the sand.

James led their motley crew along the rocky beach where they'd soon have only a narrow opening between the seawater and the large rocks bordering the trees up ahead. He increased their walking pace. If they didn't hurry, the tide would get too far up the shore, and they'd miss their window.

Piper felt heavier in Paisley's arms now. But everyone else must be as tired and worried as she was.

"How about if I carry her?" Alison held her arms out toward Piper.

Paisley stopped walking. "Piper, do you want to go to Alison?"

"No." She buried her face in Paisley's neck.

"Thanks anyway. She's shy around strangers."

"Come on," James said gruffly. "The tide won't wait for us."

"Hold your horses," Dad called, breathing noisily. "We're all beat."

"If we don't get through that space right away, we'll be forced to walk in the dense forest," Milton huffed out. "Or wade through seawater."

"Okay, okay," Dad grumbled.

With exhaustion on their faces, and tension swirling around them like foul air, the group trudged onward. Yet with their slower strides, how were they going to make it through the gap in time?

Suddenly, shouts rang out from down the beach behind them.

"They've spotted us!" Milton said.

"Come on." James waved them forward in agitated movements. "Hurry. Hurry."

"We won't make it to the cutoff in time. Let's fight them off here." Dad braced his legs and raised the stick he was carrying, but his arms shook.

"Maybe I can go back and talk with them," Alison said. "Why don't I try appealing to their sense of decency?"

"No!" Milton said. "You're staying with us. Only by remaining together do we stand a chance of holding our ground. First, we need a hiding place for Paisley and the child." He gazed toward the ocean as if seeking a solution.

"Besides, do those men look like they'd stop for a chat about decency?" James asked.

Paisley glanced over her shoulder. Five guys dressed in black clothes were running through the sand straight toward them. Toward her, probably. They looked muscular. Some held guns. All wore masks.

They had someone with them too. Kathleen? Oh, no! She appeared to be wrestling against their hold. Slowing them down, perhaps.

Maybe they could make it to the cutoff if they tried.

Paisley walked faster with Piper squirming in her arms. If those men had Kathleen, what had happened to Aunt Callie?

"This way!" Milton waved his arms toward the sea.

"What? No!" She couldn't carry Piper into the waves. Besides, did she trust Milton? What if he was leading her into a trap?

"Milton's right." James stomped through water up to his knees. He wobbled in the pounding waves and nearly fell over. "Come this way!" He pointed at an outcropping of basalt rocks that looked like a small island with seawater surging around it.

Paisley remembered something from years back when she and Judah explored those same rocks at low tide. Hadn't they found a hideaway nestled among them? Maybe she could make it out that far with Piper. But the water was rushing in hard, and it would be so cold.

Dear God, please protect Piper and my baby. Keep us warm enough.

Grabbing her by the elbows, Dad and Milton propelled her forward, carrying her and Piper out into the churning sea. The waves rolling up her legs nearly took her breath away. Normally she wouldn't mind the chilly waters. This time, carrying a fussy two-year-old and knowing she needed her own body temperature to stay normal for her baby's sake, she prayed she could find stable footing on the ocean floor.

Once they reached the far side of the rock pile, Paisley passed a whimpering Piper to Dad. Then she climbed up on the wet rocks. Water poured off her jeans. Her feet slipped on the basalt. Her teeth chattered with each splash of the waves hitting the boulders.

James scrambled ahead of her, surprising her with his agility, and thrust out his hand. Gripping his wrist, she pulled upward and then lowered herself into the hiding place among the rocks. Dad handed Piper to Alison, but Piper let out a scream and reached back for him. Alison quickly passed her to Paisley.

With white foam and sea spray shooting into the air, she hunkered down, clinging to her niece, whispering, "It'll be okay. It'll be okay." Thankfully, the cave-like boulders surrounding them seemed to emanate some warmth.

She prayed again for protection and that Judah would reach them.

How would the three older men withstand the five who were coming after them? Could their little group hold off the men who seemed determined to capture her?

"Love you." Dad reached down and clutched her hand. He patted Piper's back as if he were telling her goodbye.

"Love you too," Paisley said.

Dad shimmied around the basalt formation like he was going to make his last stand.

Please, God, help us.

James crouched in front of her, a thick stick in his hands, a grimace lining his face as if he'd fight off the very powers of darkness to protect her. She appreciated Dad's friend at this moment more than she ever had. If Aunt Callie could see him now, she'd be so proud of him.

"You're surrounded!" a familiar male voice yelled. "Return to shore."

Mike Linfield? What had he done with Aunt Callie?

"Come down from those rocks!" another man said. "Or else we'll come out there and drag all of you back here."

"We only want Paisley and the child," Mike said.

She bit back a sob. *I will not fear. I will not—*

"Basalt Bay is under Martial Law," Mike said firmly. "Do as we say! Return to shore now."

Piper made fussing sounds. Paisley pulled her snugly against her chest, smoothing her hand down her back. "We're going to be okay." She shivered and tasted salt on her lips. "We're going to be okay."

James peered over the rocks. "I see Kathleen. The guy we tied up is here. Poor Cal. This isn't good at all."

Had Mike hurt Aunt Callie? She wouldn't have let Kathleen go without a fight.

What could their motley group do against such strong men? Paisley didn't want her dad or James to get hurt. But she didn't want her and Piper getting captured, either.

"What's this about, gentlemen?" Alison called out in a diplomatic-sounding voice. "Can't we discuss this like mature adults? What good are one woman and a child to your cause?"

"Return to shore!" Mike shouted. "Or else we're coming out there. We will get what we want!"

"That wouldn't be wise. Surely, you want a peaceful settlement?" Alison's voice rose above the sound of the waves beating the rocks. "Isn't there room for negotiation?"

"We're taking Paisley and the girl!" another male voice said. "Either come back to the beach on your own, or we're coming out to get you. You have five minutes!"

Five minutes? Paisley's stomach clenched.

"Who is your supervisor?" Alison yelled. "Who's in charge of today's unrest? May I speak to him?"

A few of the men chortled.

"We're not here to talk, lady!"

"Stay back!" Alison shouted as if the men had advanced.

"Stand your ground!" Dad commanded.

"I'm not moving." James bared his teeth, his hands gripping the stick.

Paisley didn't want anyone getting hurt on her account. She should shout for them to stop. She moved to do so, but James clamped his hand over her mouth. Shaking his head, he pointed at Piper, silently reminding her the child was worth this standoff. That she was worth whatever it took for them to delay longer.

But would a delay make any difference? What if it was already too late?

Forty-seven

Moments after Judah returned to the house, Forest joined him, his face bloodied and bruised. Somehow, he'd broken free from his captor.

Then, with armed militants and the deputy's posse observing, Judah and Forest carried Craig outside on a make-shift stretcher made from a throw blanket. As they approached the chopper, they exchanged furtive eye signals despite Jeff traipsing alongside them.

Judah glanced toward the helicopter, the house, the helicopter. Did Forest understand what he was trying to communicate? That he was going to hitch a ride, if possible? Forest glanced at the house, downward, at the house again. Judah interpreted that as him saying he'd stay here.

The escape Judah hoped for would have to happen fast and right under Jeff's vigilant watch. He'd have one chance to make his move.

As they approached the helicopter, he made sure he was on the side of the faux stretcher closest to the door. One mistake and he'd lose his chance to find Paisley. Or risk Forest getting shot. Before he reached the whirling beast, he fake stumbled, barely catching hold of the edge of the blanket. Acting fatigued, he backed into the doorway and collapsed onto the helicopter floor, dragging Craig along with him.

"Go, go!" he shouted at the driver.

The whirring grew loud and intense as they lifted off the ground.

"Grant!" Jeff bellowed. "Get out of there! I trusted you. Get down here now!"

The medic closed the door, then turned his attention to Craig.

Judah exhaled a long breath.

Shots rang out. But none of the bullets hit the helicopter. Did Forest get injured?

Judah ran his hands over his bruised and swollen face. "On your way to the hospital, drop me off on the beach on the south side of town, will you?"

The pilot nodded.

Judah peered out the window. Down below, Forest fought with Jeff and another masked guy. He prayed for his brother-in-law. For Craig. For all of them.

After a short time, the driver shouted, "Nowhere to land! Tide is coming in. Strong winds."

"Can you get low enough for me to jump out?"

"One pass."

"Okay. I'm ready." He set his hand on Craig's shoulder, praying for him again. Then he crouched next to the door. The helicopter swayed with the powerful gusts coming off the ocean. The medic released the door, opening it enough for Judah to slide through.

"Stay low," he shouted.

"Will do. Thanks."

Taking note of his intended landing spot in the narrow strip of sand below, he tucked and lunged out of the vibrating machine. He dropped six feet, then hit the ground rolling. Umph. Ugh. Groaning at the impact and the sharp pain in his ribs and shoulders, he hunkered low and waited for the helicopter to lift and veer away.

As soon as it did, he ran for the bushes that weren't far from the project house. Was Paisley still there? Who else might be guarding her and the others?

On the trail leading up to the house, he saw footprints where hiking boots had tromped through the wet dirt. The tracks went in both directions. Had Paisley already been moved? If so, where?

Cautiously, he approached the house. Dirt clods on the porch revealed more hiking boot prints. Several sets by the looks of them.

Tensely, he peered into the windows. No movement. He nudged the doorknob. It gave easily. Not a good sign. The women would have locked this door to protect themselves.

Despite his fatigue, he clenched his fists, prepared to fight again if necessary. He tiptoed a few feet across the dining room, then stopped and listened.

A murmur. A moan.

Who was that?

He lunged into the living room. "Callie?" His wife's aunt was on her side on the floor, gagged and bound, her eyes squinting up at him.

"Judah—" She spoke around the cloth. "They're going after Paisley!"

Swallowing back a groan, he dropped to his knees and worked to untie her gag. "Are you okay? Where'd they take her? How was she?"

"Thank God you came!" she said as soon as her mouth was free. "She was okay. She and Piper left with Pauly, James, Milton, and Alison. But those bad men went after them!"

"Where?" At least Paisley wasn't by herself. He tried releasing the ties binding Callie's wrists, but his fingers fumbled with the knots.

"They fled down the beach, south."

"How many guys went after them? Did you recognize any of them?"

"Five." She rubbed her wrists and whimpered. "Mike Linfield included."

"Mike?"

"He's the one who came here to get Paisley."

"What?" Jeff, C.L., *and* Mike were involved in this? He could hardly believe it.

"Kathleen conked him on the head." Callie pointed at a frying pan on the floor. "I kept him subdued with that until the others showed up. Then I was outnumbered." Wincing, she touched the back of her head, and her fingers came away with blood on them.

"That must hurt. Let me help you to the couch." It took all he had in him, but he helped her get on her knees, then moved her to the couch. She climbed onto the cushions, moaning.

Too much time was passing, but he had to help his wife's aunt before he searched for Paisley and Piper. He ran to the kitchen, grabbed ice cubes out of the freezer, and dropped them into a towel. On his way back to Callie, he tied a knot with the cloth. "Here." He handed her the pseudo ice bag.

"Are you okay?" He gazed into her eyes, checking for dilation.

"I'll be all right. I'm furious they got the jump on me. They took Kathleen hostage, too. Something about using her as leverage against Paisley."

"That's terrible. This whole thing is unbelievable. You say they're heading down the beach?"

"That's right. A motley crew if there ever was one. Three old men ready to do battle against gangsters?" She winced like the ice hurt her head. "How do you think that's going to turn out?"

"Better than with my wife being alone. God is with her," he declared. "With all of them."

"I would have gone too, but I stayed here guarding Mike. A lot of good that did."

"You did your best." Judah checked her rapidly beating pulse. "I'll get you a glass of water. Then I must go." He hurried into the kitchen again, grabbed a glass and filled it, then rushed back. "Here." He handed it to her. "Sit up and don't fall asleep, hear me?"

"Yeah, yeah."

"Stay safe." He ran out the door, locked it, then dashed for the trail. If he paused to think about the pain in his body, he wouldn't be able to keep going. But the adrenaline pumping through him and his desperate need to find his wife would help strengthen him.

Prayer, too. God was with him. God was with Paisley and their child. He'd see them through this.

With a prayer in his heart, he raced across the sand, staying between the tree line and the waves rolling up the shore. He didn't see anyone along the beach up ahead. Whatever shoe tracks may have been here before were washed away by the seawater.

Every few minutes he stopped and leaned over, clutching his ribs and breathing hard. Everything seemed to hurt. Despite his agony, he wouldn't give up. He had to find Paisley.

God, please, help me.

He took off running again. Rounding a patch of deciduous trees, he spotted a cluster of men in dark clothes up ahead. A woman sat on the sand. Kathleen?

He ducked behind a tall boulder. Peering over it, he saw three men and a woman out on a grouping of large, piled-up basalt rocks that rose out of the water like a miniature island. Must be Paul, James, Milton, and Alison. Where were Paisley and Piper?

Were they hidden among the rocks? How could he get out there without being seen by the men on the beach? How much longer would those guys wait before wading out to the boulders and fighting for what they wanted?

If he swam out to the rocks, he might draw gunfire from Mia's insurgents. That would make it even more dangerous for his family on the pile of boulders. Maybe he could talk some sense into the men on the shore. How had Mike Linfield gotten caught up in this bizarre overthrow? Could Judah sway him to let Paisley go?

Making a quick decision, he strode out from behind the boulder, hands raised. Even holding his hands up like that hurt.

"Hey!" "Who's that?" "Someone's coming!" "Grab him!" "It's Judah Grant!" Shouts rang out.

He walked faster toward them.

"Hold up, Judah!" Mike's voice.

"What's going on here?" Judah glanced toward the rock pile. Paul, Milton, and Alison appeared bedraggled and exhausted, the same as he felt.

Two insurgents grabbed his arms, nearly dragging him to his old boss. He winced at the pain shooting up his ribcage.

"Can we talk? The takeover at the Grant residence failed! It's over. Let these people go."

"Not what I heard!" Mike said. "You aren't calling the shots. Mia is."

"I was there. She's been arrested."

"I doubt that!"

"It's true." Judah met Kathleen's weary gaze. "Are you okay?"

"Yes. But I've been in nicer company."

"Enough prattle." One of the guys yanked on his arm.

He muffled a groan. "What's the plan? What can we agree to do that will stop you from trying to take any more hostages?"

"Your arrival is perfect timing," Mike kicked the toe of his boot into the sand. "Head out there and convince your wife to come back to shore. Bring the kid too."

Tension spiked through Judah. "Why do you need Paisley? Now that your plan has been foiled, there's no need to go through with whatever action you planned. Flee while you have a chance. Better yet, avoid more jail time by turning yourselves in."

Mike laughed raucously. "If Mia is gone, her second will take over."

"C.L.? He's probably been arrested by now too."

Mike jerked like he was surprised Judah knew about C.L.

"Just coax your wife and her senior citizen pals to wade back here," Mike growled. "A swim won't stop my men. But it will go easier on the others if they come back on their own. Any resistance and we'll do what's necessary to apprehend them. Anything."

One of the guards patted his weapon as if making a point.

"Craig's been seriously injured. This nonsense must stop!"

"It isn't nonsense." Mike spit on the sand. "Casualties were expected."

His cold response stung.

"This is my family we're talking about. I want them to be safe."

"Tough. Now, do what I said!"

"Have you heard from Craig?" Alison yelled from the rocks. She obviously hadn't heard his comment.

"Don't answer that." Mike jabbed Judah's chest with his gloved finger. "Doesn't matter who got injured or what you say happened on the hill. What matters is what goes down right here." He pulsed his finger toward the rocks. "Talk to your wife, or else wait here while my men walk out and get her. If she goes underwater, too bad. Serves her right for what they did to me!" He touched his head and flinched.

Judah forced himself not to defend Paisley verbally or to fight with his old boss. "Why are you doing this? I thought you were smarter than to get caught up in Edward's stuff."

The guard next to him rammed his elbow into Judah's gut. Groaning, he buckled over, the pain in his ribs almost unbearable.

"Now, call the lady and tell her to come with us, nice and easy."

"I can't do that."

The guy rammed him again.

Bending over, gasping in ragged breaths, his vision blurred. His thoughts became hazier than before. He shook his head.

"Judah!" Paisley's voice reached him.

"Paisley!" Mike barked. "Come to shore! Or else, we'll beat up your husband until he can't stand up. Then we're coming after you."

"Stay there!" Judah yelled hoarsely. "If they thought this was an easy task, they would have done it already."

Mike slugged him. Judah toppled over into a heap on the sand. They left him there as if he wasn't a threat anymore.

"Judah!" Paisley screamed.

He took a few shallow breaths. He was still alive. Still had some fight left in him.

"It will go easier on her if we don't have to make her swim through the seawater," Mike said, lacking a caring tone. "Easier on the kid not to get dunked, either."

Judah tried standing but couldn't get off his knees. "Have some compassion, will you? My wife is pregnant. Let her go. I'll come with you."

"How can I trust anything you say?"

Judah tightened his chest, trying to catch his breath. "I'll go with you and talk to whoever's in charge. Do whatever you need me to do. Just let my wife and niece go."

Mike and one of the guards dragged him to his feet.

"As in you'll govern the town according to our rules? The way our group wants things done?"

For his wife and niece's safety, he had to appear compliant. "Let them go. And we'll talk."

"We're not here to talk." Mike nodded toward the guards.

Four masked men sloshed into the waves.

"No!" Judah cried out.

Shouting erupted from the trees! The rumble of voices and the sounds of sticks and metal being beaten together sounded like a lot of people were approaching.

Staggering, Judah gazed back to where the noise came from. A group of about fifty people charged toward them from the direction of town and from the trees, waving sticks and gardening implements. Callie was right in the center of the mob!

"What's this?" Mike swore.

"What now, Captain?" one of the guards standing in thigh-high water shouted.

"Over here!" Alison waved her hands toward the towns-people. "Help us! Hurry!"

More shouts followed. Another group of thirty or so people emerged from the woods and south beach. No one came barehanded either. The crowd marched straight for Mike and his cohorts with scowls and grimaces lining their faces.

Judah threw his coat on the sand and staggered into the water. One of the guards came at him, but a yell from the beach stopped him.

"Swim for the boat while you can, men!"

The guards plunged through the water, churning their arms through the waves like they were in a race.

Judah waded toward the rocks, trying to keep his footing as the waves hit him, but he was so tired. His tender ribs were killing him. But he was determined to reach Paisley or pass out trying.

Clutching a boulder, he heaved himself upward but only made it halfway onto the rock. Paul and Alison grabbed his elbows and helped him get up onto the mound of wet basalt. He still didn't see his wife or Piper. From his prone position, he inhaled and exhaled shallow breaths.

Out in the cove, the assailants swam hard, making their escape. Mike glanced back over his shoulder, scowling at Judah as if sending him a warning.

Judah clutched the next rock and pulled himself up. Paul helped him stand to his feet.

Then Paisley was beside him smoothing her hands over his wet face, kissing him. "Oh, Judah, my love! I'm so glad to see you. You came for me. I knew you would. Are you okay?"

He hugged her to him, even though he was soaking wet and in wretched pain. Piper was safe in Paul's arms now. They were all safe.

The townspeople gathered on the shoreline cheered, thrusting their fists, rakes, shovels, and sticks into the air.

"That'll teach you to mess with us!" Callie shook her cast iron pan at the men who had escaped into the water.

"Look!" Alison pointed out toward the middle of the cove.

Their attackers were crawling into a waiting skiff.

Judah watched them with his arms around Paisley, both shivering and wet. He didn't tell her how badly his ribs or shoulders hurt. He just held her to himself and thanked God for His mercy and help.

Then he called out, "Someone, call 911. Tell them what's happened and to contact C-MER! They'll know what to do to stop that boat!"

"I was so scared," Paisley said against his neck. Her warm breath on his skin tingled. "Thank you for coming for me. For saving us."

He pointed toward the group. "They did it. They rescued us. But, of course, I had to find you." He smoothed his hands over her damp back. "I'll always find you, sweetheart." He kissed her softly.

"Judah, what you said about Craig?" Alison asked. "Is it true?"

"Yeah. He's hurt badly. Shot." He pictured the way his brother looked in the helicopter, unconscious and bloody. "I'm sorry, but I don't know if he made it."

"What?" Alison gasped, her eyes filling with unshed tears.

"I'm praying he did. It was bad. He lost a lot of blood."

Her lips trembling, she nodded.

Some of the townspeople waded into the rolling waves, forming a human chain. The tallest ones stood in the deepest water with waves rolling up to their chests.

One by one, the six adults, with Paul holding Piper, were guided back through the surf by helping hands. Drenched, tired, and shivering cold, they were met by people hugging them and cheering them on.

"We're proud of you."

"You stayed strong."

"We're getting through this together."

"Our town is stronger than those guys thought!"

Fatigued and hurting with every breath, with every step, Judah kept his arm around Paisley's shoulder to try to keep her warm as he led her back along the seashore. He heard a speed boat out in the bay. Must be the C-MER crew. Someone with a megaphone called out orders he didn't understand. He imagined they were telling the escapees to stand down and lower their weapons. How humiliated Mike must be to have his old crew arresting him.

The journey back toward the project house was exhausting. Many of the townspeople accompanied them as if guarding them the whole way.

Even though Judah was weary, and his adrenaline had tanked, he paused on the beach in front of the trail and addressed the group. "I want to thank all of you for what you did today." He couldn't speak loudly or with much effort. "Coming to our rescue like you did changed the outcome of what those men planned to do. Edward and Mia Grant"—he cringed at saying "Mia" and "Grant" together—"were the masterminds behind this takeover attempt. I'm sorry for the harm they did."

A few people grumbled or made derogatory comments.

Paisley smoothed her palm along Judah's arm, giving him encouragement through her touch.

"Another standoff took place at Edward's house," Judah continued. "My mother, our current mayor, was held captive. As were others in my family. I pray it ended peacefully."

"Me too." Callie harrumphed.

"I have no idea how all of you knew to come and—"

"It was Callie!" Maggie Thomas called out.

Callie palmed the air like she didn't want the attention.

"She sent an emergency text that we sent to others," Maggie said with a proud tone. "We came right out here!"

"Thank you, Callie. Thank you all for rescuing us!" Judah inhaled a raspy breath. "You saved us from more harm. We shall always be grateful for that."

"Yes, we will." Paisley tugged on his arm. "We should get you to the ER."

"And you need to rest."

"What now?" Maggie questioned.

"We're a resilient bunch!" James said from where he stood next to Callie. "We're going to keep Basalt Bay the way we want. Not how Edward and Mia tried to twist it into being."

"That's right!"

"It's our town!"

"No one is taking Basalt Bay from us!"

"Judah, we should go," Paisley said quietly. "Let all these people get back to their homes so they can get warm and dry."

"You're right." He waved at the group. "Thank you!"

He clasped Paisley's hand and trudged up the trail, so thankful to be with his wife and family, knowing they were safe. Hopefully, they'd hear good news about Craig soon.

Forty-eight

Despite the aching in his head and upper torso, Forest helped Paige out of their car. Together, they hurried toward the front door of the project house with Sarah following close behind them.

Paul opened the door and Piper lunged for Paige from her grandpa's arms. Forest wrapped his arms around his family, thanking God for keeping them safe through all they experienced today.

Other arms came around them too. Paul, Callie, Kathleen, and Sarah all group hugged with them, shedding tears of thankfulness and relief.

"I'm so glad you're okay." Paul hugged Paige on their way inside the house.

"Me too." She held Piper close. "Thank you for watching over our girl."

"Of course. Paisley held her most of the time." Paul nodded toward the living room. "She carried her across the beach and then hid with her out on the rocks. We weren't letting anything bad happen to our Piper girl."

"I'm so grateful."

"Any news about Craig?" Forest asked.

"He isn't out of surgery yet," Paul said with a worried tone. "Judah's about to head to the hospital."

In the living room, Paisley was lying on the couch, her head against Judah's lap. Resting sounded good. Forest couldn't wait to relax his tired muscles. Maybe sleep for a week.

Paige leaned over her sister and kissed her forehead. "Thank you for watching my baby."

"Sure. Are you okay?" Paisley gripped her hand. "Judah told me about your being tied up and taken to Edward's. I'm so sorry that happened."

"It was scary, but I'm okay. We're all okay." Paige glanced back at Forest and their gazes met.

He loved the sweet smile she gave him. He wanted to hold onto his family and stay close together. Somehow, they had to try to put today's chaos and pain behind them. It would take time and God's peace, but they'd get there.

"Looks like you got beat up, pal." Forest almost laughed at the frown on Judah's bruised face, but his insides hurt too much. So did his swollen face.

"You and me both," Judah said around small gasps.

"You need a doctor?"

"Yeah." Judah winced. "I hoped to hear about Craig's condition before I go to the ER, but I can't wait." His hand rested on his lower chest.

"Broken ribs?"

"Maybe just bruised." Judah shook his head slightly, making it obvious he didn't want to discuss what happened during their fighting in front of Paisley.

"Need me to drive you?"

"I'm going to do that," Paul said with a tone of authority.

Judah didn't argue. "I'm giving Paisley a minute to rest. Making sure it's all over, too. Then we'll go."

"The standoff ended without more gunfire. Mia was taken into custody, shouting threats." Forest winced at the pain in his nose. "Seemed to think she'd get away with this. Queen Mia of Basalt Bay, no matter her crimes. What a pack of lies and false hope Edward evoked in her and in others who wound up as disillusioned as he is."

"It's a shame," Judah said in a ragged voice. "Can you believe C.L. was involved?"

"No. That was weird."

Paige clasped Forest's hand and tugged him toward the recliner. Sitting down slowly, he quenched a moan as pain shot through his sides. Even so, he pulled his wife and daughter down next to him and sighed.

"So, Deputy Brian came through?" Judah asked.

Forest adjusted himself so Paige's elbow wasn't digging into his ribs. "In the end, he brought the whole thing crumbling to the ground. His boldness surprised me. I had my doubts."

"You and me, both." Judah coughed and cringed.

"Are you okay?" Paisley stroked her palm down his face. "Let's get you checked out. Your face looks so sore."

"I'll be okay." He was obviously downplaying his misery, not wanting his wife to worry. "I guess your dad's going to drive us."

"That's good."

Forest closed his eyes, then caught himself falling asleep. He pried his eyelids open slightly.

"My mom texted me that she's going to be at City Hall for a few hours." Judah inched forward on the couch. "Doing a news report. Sounds like she hit the ground running."

"It's a good thing Bess subdued Mia," Forest said sluggishly. "Her quick response helped us get Craig out of there."

"I'm thankful." Judah stroked some hair back from Paisley's face. "Ready to go?"

"Yes." She stood slowly.

"Where are you going?" Callie asked as she entered the room from the bathroom. Her hair was wet like she just finished showering.

"To the hospital, Auntie. Do you want to get your head injury checked out? You had a rough day too."

"We all had a rough day. I'm fine. Now it's time for some comfort food." Callie headed toward the kitchen. "I could use a piece of chocolate cream pie."

Me too. Forest sighed.

Paisley reached out a hand to Judah. "Let me help you this time."

Paul and James hurried to the back of the couch, the two of them assisting Judah into a standing position. Paisley slipped under his arm, and they shuffled toward the door.

"I'd come with you guys," Forest said around a yawn, "but I'm going to stay put. Watch over my family."

"It's okay if you want to go," Paige said.

"I'm staying with you, baby. You and our little princess." He kissed Piper's head.

Paige pushed up from the chair and caught her breath like something was hurting. "Piper and I are going to rest on Aunt Callie's bed."

"Are you okay?" Forest stood beside her.

"Just sore from the manhandling and being tied up." She nodded toward Callie's room. "A rest sounds good, doesn't it?"

"Sure does. I'll come with you two." He wouldn't be far away from Paige and Piper for the rest of the day. Maybe not until the trial was over.

As he followed his wife into the other room, a rush of thankfulness hit him that God had helped him find Milton. That the trouble at the Grant estate didn't get any worse than it did. And that Paisley would finally get justice.

Forty-nine

Paisley sat in a chair in the hospital lobby, mulling over the events of the day, and thanking God for keeping her family together and alive. Keeping her and her baby safe too.

"You're going to be fine," she whispered to her unborn child and rested her hand on her stomach. "We both are." She was so relieved the baby's heartbeat had tested normal. She wasn't spotting anymore, either, despite her activity today.

Thank You, Lord, for being with us. For protecting our baby. For having a good plan for our lives. Thank You that Mia and Edward's destructive plans didn't succeed.

After being checked by the doctors, she and Judah were told Craig was out of surgery. The attending doctor said the bullet went through his lung, causing it to collapse and nicking a rib. There were some complications, but he was going to be okay.

Something else to thank God for.

Paisley and Judah decided to wait here for Craig to wake up. Someone from the nurse's station would let them know when he could have visitors.

Dad said he was going to take a nap in the truck. That after today's events, he needed one. A nap sounded good to Paisley, too.

Judah hobbled over to her from the beverage vending machine. He handed her a juice bottle then moaned as he sat down incrementally on the lobby chair. Apparently, he'd be moaning like this for a while. Possibly six weeks to heal, since he had two cracked ribs and others were bruised. He didn't have any wrappings around his ribs, but he was going to have to take it easy. He wouldn't be doing any strenuous activities for a while.

Even with his face battered and bruised, her husband had never looked more handsome to her than now. Earlier, when she saw him getting beat up on the beach, him crumpled on the sand, and her not knowing if he was even breathing, her heart had cried out in agony.

Then, when he waded out to the rocks despite the pain he had to be enduring to reach her, so much tenderness and warmth toward him engulfed her. How she loved and appreciated this man—her husband! She wanted to stay close to him until the end of time. Them cherishing each other, loving each other, and building a family together.

Blinking back emotional tears, she teased, "So, I get to be your nurse, huh?"

"That has possibilities." He grimaced. "If it didn't hurt so wretchedly badly, I'd like it better."

"I'll enjoy feeding you broth. Fluffing your pillow. Filling ice packs. Taking your temperature." She winked at him.

"That sounds nice." He linked their fingers together. Then sighed. "I need to tell you something about today."

"Okay." She watched as his expression turned somber. "What is it?"

"Mia flirted with me."

"What's new?"

"It was, uh, more than usual." He grimaced. "I, sort of, let her."

"What do you mean?" She let go of his hand and turned to see him better.

"Not 'let her,' exactly." Judah shook his head. "The medicine they gave me is kicking in, making my brain foggy. I pretended to be okay with her flirtation so she'd be distracted long enough for Forest and Craig to take down her guards. And her." He squinted at the ceiling. "I didn't want her touching me. I hated it, but—"

"She touched you?" All her old irritation toward Mia rushed to the surface of her emotions. That woman—

"I'm so sorry. But faking an interest I didn't feel was the only thing I could think of to distract her and appeal to her vanity. I am sorry for even the appearance of flirtation with another woman."

"That makes sense, I guess. Not that I like it." It led to the right result. Mia had been apprehended. But Paisley hated the thought of her flirting with Judah at all. And touching him? She shuddered. "Thanks for being honest with me about it. Imagining what happened bugs me. But at least we won't have to worry about her flirting with you for a long time."

"Hopefully, never." He linked their fingers together again. "I love you. You're my sweetheart. You're the only one I want to flirt with. All I want is to be with you." He sounded sleepy. "I sincerely apologize, though."

"Thank you. I happen to feel the same about you—only wanting to be with you, that is."

His honest confession, and her visualizing the tense situation he'd been in at Edward's house, made it easier to let any offense go. He played a part in Mia being arrested and in Craig getting the medical care he needed—both honorable things. She took a sip of her juice. "Have you heard anything else from your mom?"

"She's reaching out to citizens who were confused by an official-looking letter supposedly from City Hall telling them to stay indoors due to a dangerous solar eclipse."

"We never received such a letter."

"No, we did not. Others were bullied by phone calls from Edward's group claiming financial retaliation if they didn't close their businesses, stay home, etc. Some were told Martial Law was in effect." Judah moved and grimaced. "Mom's planning a town meeting to field questions and discuss what happened. Also, it was rumored the town's name was going to be changed."

"To what?"

"Grant Bay."

"Oh, brother." Paisley rolled her eyes. "Do you think we should attend the meeting?"

"Probably. But I still plan to stay clear of the city's governmental affairs."

A few minutes later, he breathed deeply like he was falling asleep. He must be exhausted.

Judah's phone buzzed and he flinched. He squinted at the screen. "C-MER headquarters? That's weird." He cleared his throat and accepted the call. "Judah here." He mumbled "Mmhmm" a few times like he was barely awake. "Sure. I'll, uh, give it some thought. I appreciate the consideration." He ended the call.

"What was that about?"

Before he could answer, a nurse strode toward them. "Craig is awake. If you want to see him, follow me."

"Okay. Thanks." Judah stuffed his phone into his jacket pocket.

Paisley sent Dad a quick text, letting him know what they were doing.

They both stood slowly.

"The call was from Adam Campbell, C-MER VP, offering me a job." Judah chuckled quietly as they walked. "Is that a strange turn of events, or what?"

"Or an answer to prayer?" She tugged him to a standstill. "A job with C-MER as what?"

"Manager. Taking over C.L.'s position."

"You're kidding! Congratulations, Judah!" She hugged him before remembering his sore ribs.

He groaned.

"Sorry."

"It's okay. I didn't accept the offer yet."

"Excuse me?" The nurse strode back to them. "Are you coming?"

"Yes. Sorry," Judah said.

Paisley clasped his hand, and they followed the nurse down the hall.

Judah might go back to work for C-MER again? What unusual timing! Or, with her being pregnant and needing more rest, it might be perfect timing. A blessing of provision. *Thank You, Lord!*

Fifty

From his hospital bed, Craig peered through barely opened eyelids as Judah and Paisley shuffled into the room. Judah's face was bluish-green. It looked like he'd been in a terrible fight.

Oh, right. They both had been.

"Taking it easy, huh?" Judah asked teasingly.

"Why not?" Craig's throat felt scratchy and dry. Every inch of his body hurt or else was numbed by painkillers. "Paisley," he said without moving his neck or torso.

"Hey, Craig."

"Where's Al?" Her face was the first one he thought of when he came to.

"She and Milton went to the newspaper office. They must get tomorrow's paper out with all the details of the failed takeover." Paisley smiled pleasantly. "She's been texting me often for updates. She'll be here as soon as she can. Sorry."

Disappointed, Craig schooled his features. No doubt, Al was writing the news articles of the century! He didn't blame her for not hanging around here waiting for him to finish sleeping.

But he had been shot. Wasn't that newsworthy? Or at least worthy of her caring?

Judah patted his arm. "Thanks, man. You did an admirable thing today when you risked your life to protect Paige and Sarah."

"Or stupidity?" His words came out thick-sounding.

"That too." Judah grimaced and tapped his own chest like it hurt.

"Looks like you took a few for the team."

"Yeah. We'll all be hobbling for a few days."

Craig chuckled and groaned. "No laughter allowed in this room."

"Thank you for helping rescue our family, again," Paisley said. "That means so much to me."

He nodded, feeling awkward about her praise.

"I got a job offer." Judah exchanged glances with Paisley.

"What's that?" Craig flinched at a pain in his chest.

"C-MER manager."

"Why would they want you back?" Craig asked mockingly. "More Grant trouble?"

"Something like that. I'd be taking C.L.'s place."

"Huh." Craig closed his eyes. Drifted off. Awoke suddenly. "Sorry. What were you saying?"

"It's okay." Judah had propped himself against the wall with Paisley under his arm as if she were holding him up.

Unexpected emotions hit Craig, nearly choking him. His brother and sister-in-law had kindly come to the hospital to see him, even when Judah wasn't feeling well himself, acting like true family members. He didn't deserve their kindness and grace. But he sure appreciated it.

"You should go home and rest. You look like trash," Craig said to lighten the mood.

"Thanks a lot." Judah pulled away from the wall. "You'll be okay?"

"I'll sleep it off." He inhaled, then gasped. "So, what do you think?"

"About—?"

"The C-MER position." Judah shuffled to the end of Craig's bed. "About us being a team again."

"Are you offering me a job?" He was so tired he could barely think straight.

"Would that be so bad?"

"Not bad. Just—"

"I haven't accepted. We still have to talk it over." Judah rested his hand on Paisley's shoulder. "You'd be the first person I'd hire if I take the position."

"Thanks, man."

"Get some rest," Judah said on his way out the door.

Craig thought of something. "Hey, Judah?"

"Yeah?" He glanced back.

"If you see Al, tell her I said hello."

"Will do. Talk to you later, bro."

Craig fell asleep. Woke up. Fell asleep. Each time, the last thought on his mind was of Al. Why wasn't she here?

Fifty-one

Forest finally had five minutes to return his sister's call and explain what had transpired since he ended their call so abruptly.

"Oh, Bub, you have been through the grinder. Is Paige all right? Are you okay?"

"We're sore and tired. But it's over. Paige must testify the day after tomorrow. Then it'll be my turn. Once that's done, we can get back to normal life."

"Can I come for a visit then?"

"Sure, anytime." He heaved a breath despite his sore ribs. At least, his weren't as bad as Judah's. However, his nose might never be the same again. "Now, what's going on with you?"

"The marriage counseling is stirring up bad vibes between Danson and me."

"Probably has to get worse before it gets better." Forest cringed at the platitude. "I don't mean to say the wrong thing. Sorry."

"That's okay. I doubt it's worth it. I mean, the emotional baggage, you know?" Teal paused. "I'm not one of those women who can let a man back into her life once he's cheated."

"I'm sorry. Whatever you decide, I'm here for you."

"Thanks. I appreciate that. I'm trying to figure out what to do next. Still living with Mom and Dad." She chuckled. "That can only go on for so long before I lose my mind."

"They're not so bad."

"I'm thankful for their generosity, but I need my own space."

"What about the boys?" Forest asked guardedly, not wanting to cause any offense.

"They're spending half the time with their dad, the other half with me and the Grands." Another sigh. "I don't like it, but it is what it is."

"Has he, um, stopped seeing the secretary?"

Silence greeted him, and he regretted asking the question. "Sorry."

"He says he's not dating her. Never was." She made a grumbling sound of frustration. "In counseling, he described her as a supportive coworker. A woman he met up with after work a couple of times. The kiss was a mistake. Blah, blah, blah. Making excuses doesn't cut it with me."

"I understand."

"We're at a standstill. I must find my own way."

"Sorry, sis." He wished things were going better for her. "I'll be praying for you and the boys." Danson too. But he figured she wouldn't appreciate him saying so right now.

"Thanks, Forest."

"I'm here for you." He took a steady breath. "If you need another place to hang out, let me know. You're always welcome here with us."

"Except for when you can't answer your phone, right?"

"Yeah, except for when I'm chasing some bad guys."

"Since you put it that way, I'll let it go." It sounded like she smiled. "Thanks for the invitation to stay with you guys. I may still look into moving to Basalt Bay."

"I'd like having you and the boys living closer to me again."

"Thanks. Love you. Talk to you later, Bub."

The call ended, and Forest spent a few minutes praying for a peaceable outcome for Teal and Danson and their twins.

Fifty-two

Barely keeping his eyes open during the community meeting, Judah wished he'd stayed at the project house. Why did he think coming to this event when he felt so lousy was a good idea? He wouldn't stay long. But he came to support Mom. However, observing her at the front of the room, dressed in a navy jacket and slacks, smiling and looking confident, he doubted she needed his moral support.

"Thank you all for coming tonight," Mom spoke into the microphone without her voice wavering, even though she must be fatigued too. "I thought it would be good for us to meet and discuss what transpired today. It will be in tomorrow's newspaper. But you can ask questions and get answers here." She smiled reassuringly at the audience.

Five hands shot up in the air.

Maggie Thomas stood. "Will businesses be reimbursed for lost revenue during today's fiasco?"

"No, I'm afraid they won't be." Mom gave her a sympathetic expression. "Many of our businesses were falsely told to remain closed. The perpetrators used the City's letterhead to make the order sound authentic." She snorted quietly. "They even used my signature to back their claims of Martial Law being in effect. On top of that, the electricity was off. As were phone services. I'm sorry all that happened. But the town treasury cannot cover revenue losses."

"Such a pity."

"Miss Patty?" Mom called on the hardware store owner.

"What's to keep other insurgents from infiltrating our town? Or to keep them from sending out false notifications again? I've heard there are residents who bowed to the ex-mayor's wishes for a decade before this went down today." Miss Patty glared around the room as if spotting a few of those she was referring to.

Was anyone here a part of Edward's group? Judah glanced around too.

"I'm glad you mentioned this." Mom swayed her hand toward Deputy Brian seated on the front row. "That's why I asked Deputy Brian to address you tonight. Deputy?"

The lawman strode to the center of the room. Was he walking taller than usual? Proud of today's actions, perhaps?

Come to think of it, Judah was proud of him too. His storming the castle, so to speak, had helped Judah and Forest get Craig to the helicopter. He deserved some honor. Standing slowly, Judah clapped for the deputy's bravery under fire. For ten seconds, he was the only one clapping. Then others joined him in applause. A few called out words of thanks.

Deputy Brian held up his hand to the group, silencing them.

Judah sank back down onto the folding chair, wincing at the pain in his ribs. He couldn't wait to get back to the project house and close his eyes for the night.

"Thank you," Deputy Brian said. "I was just doing my job. Fortunately, only one person had serious injuries. The agitators were subdued by law enforcement and members of the community without any casualties." He crossed his arms and glanced around the room. "To answer your question, there have been behind-the-scenes investigations going on into Edward Grant's affairs for some time. However, this uprising took us by surprise. I'm sorry to say I was taken aback by the strong use of force by Mia Grant's rebels."

"Even the roads being blocked and shut down? Our cell phones out of service?" Maggie said in a shaming tone. "How did that happen right under your nose?"

The deputy's face reddened. "These things are under investigation. I will be stepping down for a month during an official inquiry." He nodded toward the mayor. "That's all I have to say for now. Thank you for your time and support."

Hands shot up around the room.

The deputy walked down the aisle, his shoulders a little more stooped, and exited the building. Whatever he did or didn't do in the past, if he hadn't stepped up earlier today, Judah might not have gotten away. Mia might not have been taken into custody. Who knows what the outcome might have been for Craig?

Since Mom was doing fine, Judah decided to leave before he fell asleep en route to the project house. He was bruised and a bit broken. But thankfully, the day was ending peacefully.

Fifty-three

Ali shuffled in the uncomfortable hospital chair where she'd slept the last couple of hours. It had been a difficult decision for her to go to the newspaper office yesterday afternoon and work for eight hours straight before coming here. Then, when she finally got here, Craig kept sleeping without realizing she was in the room. Not that she faulted him for that. He needed every minute of sleep and rest he could get.

But she wanted to talk with him. To hear his voice and know for herself that he was all right.

Last night, she and Uncle Milton worked together like the team she always hoped they could be. They released today's paper filled with data and first-person accounts of the hostiles' plans for 'Grant Bay,' their unlawful takedown, and the capture of innocent residents. They even included the mayor's thoughts on what the town could expect from here on out.

Bess had called Ali and provided a quote that stated she welcomed calls from residents with questions about her leadership, even publishing her phone number! Ali was impressed with Mayor Bess's heart for service. Maybe she'd interview her for a future article.

Her thoughts skimmed over the editorial she'd included in the paper about Forest. She wrote a sincere apology for her part in previously misrepresenting the facts about him and fully endorsed him as a man of integrity in Basalt Bay. If her word was worth anything in this town, he should have folks lined up outside his house for his investigative services soon.

"Hey." The low timbre of Craig's voice washed over her.

"Hey, yourself." She sat up straighter, cringing at the kink in her neck from sleeping cockeyed in the straight-back chair. "How are you?"

Craig's face was pale with dark shadows beneath his eyes. A large bandage covered part of his chest. Various tubes with accompanying machines were hooked to him. But even with his injuries and all the medical paraphernalia, he looked wonderful to her.

"Better than yesterday," he said with a thick voice. He slowly reached his hand out to her, his fingers shaking.

"Glad to hear it." She intertwined her fingers with his. Holding his hand gave her such a feeling of peace and belonging.

"I missed you," he said softly.

"I missed you, too. I'm sorry I couldn't get here sooner. I had to write some articles. Get the paper out with Uncle Milton. However, my heart was here with you." She squeezed his hand slightly. "I got regular updates from Paisley, but I wanted to rush right over to the hospital." She shrugged. "My uncle needed me."

"Is he … is he in trouble?"

"He's under orders not to leave town, so I guess he is." She took a long breath. "He told Forest what he knew about the takeover. Hopefully, he'll get some of those community service hours the detective is so fond of—without jail time."

"Let's hope."

"I'm sorry for all you went through." She smoothed her thumb over his palm. She'd come to care so much for Craig. "I was worried about you. If I lost you—"

"Yeah, me too."

"What now?"

He pulled his hand away, his eyelids drooping. "Whenever they let me out, I'll get back to keeping the streets clean."

"The town needs you."

"No humor in here."

"It's hard not to be funny when I'm around you."

He gazed at her tenderly. "I like that about you, Al. Your way of making me laugh. Viewing life through a lighter lens."

"Who sounds like the writer now?"

"Maybe you're rubbing off on me."

"I'm serious about the town needing people like you. You did an honorable thing by standing up for your family." She felt her throat tighten. If she'd lost him, she didn't know what she would have done. "Forest told me about your heroic efforts."

"It was nothing." He closed his eyes for a moment. "After this, want to go out on a date with me?"

His off-topic comment made her smile.

"You mean somewhere other than to the newspaper office?"

"Yeah. Like out for a nice dinner and a movie."

"Sure. I've been hoping you'd ask."

"Want to marry me too?"

What?

In the next second, he was snoring!

Did he mean it when he asked her to marry him? Or was that just his medicine-induced stupor talking?

Fifty-four

The day Paisley had dreaded for three months arrived. Despite her and Judah practicing potential questions like Pastor Sagle suggested, she trembled in the witness box. She clutched her hands tightly in her lap so Edward wouldn't notice and prayed she wouldn't gag. She could claim pregnancy difficulties, maybe even get excused for a day, but the truth was her stomach roiled with nerves, not from morning sickness.

Max Fenwell, the state attorney, seemed like an honest man who was sincerely trying to search for the truth. While Edward's lawyer asked annoying, probing questions that didn't seem to have anything to do with the case or to be of a judicial nature. His inquiries had to do with Paisley's past. Her character. Her supposed gold-digging into the Grant fortune.

Did you break into Edward's office when you were in high school? Did you try to cause trouble for him even before you got together with his son? Did you pursue Judah with the purpose of having sticky fingers with Edward's wealth? Isn't it true, that even though both sets of parents were against the marriage, you demanded to go through with it?

Each time, Max stood and objected or said the lawyer was being argumentative or the question was irrelevant. But the opposing lawyer argued for his reasoning, and the objection wasn't sustained. Paisley still had to answer all the questions. However, she did so without glancing in Edward's direction even once, just like Bess counseled her to do.

Answering questions and giving her testimony in front of the lawyers, the judge, the jury, and an audience, including Edward, wasn't an easy thing for her to do. But so far, she was holding her emotions in check. She hoped to get through this as confidently as possible—without giving in to tears or having a panic attack.

Yesterday, she and Judah attended another counseling session with Pastor Sagle. They prayed together for her to have strength and wisdom in the courtroom. She journaled about her hopes and fears. She wrote down some of her longings for an outcome to this trial that would glorify God. She wanted to get through this difficult experience with a heart of faith, trusting in Jesus as her greatest strength.

She'd been told Edward had the right to face his accuser— her. But she had the right to address her kidnapper and tell him how his wrongdoings had harmed her. The emotional wounds he inflicted on her affected other people too. Judah, their future children, her father, and her sister. Even Aunt Callie.

Her aunt sat in the courtroom so red-faced Paisley wondered whether she'd be able to continue listening without saying something rude. But somehow—maybe because Dad sat on one side of her and Paige on the other—she kept her lips pressed together. Although, someone made a couple of loud moans that sounded suspiciously like Aunt Callie's.

What did the jury members think of her explanation of how Edward roughly tied her up in the gallery? How he hauled her to his house and kept her bound in his closet? Did they sympathize with her? Believe her? Her voice shook through some of her responses. During those times, she met Judah's gaze and drew inspiration from his calm, gentle expression. When she turned toward him, he always met her gaze as if he were watching her constantly.

She knew he was praying for her too. Along with Dad, Aunt Callie, Paige, Bess, Kathleen, and Sarah, who all came to support her during the trial.

Last night, Peter called from Alaska, reminding her that he and Ruby were praying for her, too. She asked him questions about the house they bought, thankful to hear of anything normal that might get her mind off the trial. It sounded like they were doing well, getting ready for one of the fishing openings they'd take part in this year.

She asked him when they'd be coming back to Basalt Bay. Peter said maybe for Christmas, which would be exciting for their whole family.

The afternoon wore on with more questions. More intimidation. More avoiding Edward's gaze. Judge Greene or members of the jury called for several breaks. During those times, Paisley wanted to rest her head on Judah's lap and take a nap. Maybe ask for an extended break. But she kept returning to the courtroom on time, fulfilling her duty, and praying she'd get through it all.

Finally, her time of testifying and being questioned by both lawyers was finished. Although she was warned she might be called back, being done, or almost done, gave her immense relief. Before she left the witness stand, the judge reminded her that if she wanted to avail herself of the opportunity, she could express herself toward Edward on another day. She was still uncertain about that.

Next, the bailiff called Paige to the witness stand. While Paisley was thankful for her sister's poise and calmness, she was nervous for her. She knew firsthand how tough it was to sit in the witness box and have everyone's gazes on her as she answered personal or pointed questions.

But Paige did fine. She never broke down. Never seemed rattled, even by Edward's lawyer's questions. Paisley was so proud of her.

The next day, none of their group attended Edward's questioning phase. Why put themselves through the misery? Paisley didn't wish to hear him possibly denying allegations or flat out lying about what happened during her kidnapping. Maybe he'd be honest. She hoped he would be. But considering everything that had transpired, she doubted it.

Others in the community would be called on to testify also, including Forest, Milton, and Deputy Brian. While she was curious about what they had to say, she and Judah were only going to attend the portions she was required to be present at.

Resting in the guest room at the project house, she and Judah spent time praying about the trial's outcome, for Edward's salvation, and about whether she should speak directly to him. Judah said it was up to her, but he encouraged her to do so because it might be a healing step for her.

"Lord, we want Your will," he prayed in a hushed tone. "We want to live in love. Paisley and I admit to having a difficult time forgiving Edward. But with Your help, we can do anything. You can do anything in our lives, and in Edward's life. Please bring healing and peace to our families."

"Amen," Paisley added. "Oh, and please bless our sweet baby. Help him to be strong and well."

Sitting close together on the guest bed, not having any tasks to attend to, it felt like a good opportunity for them to share their hopes and dreams for their future. Time to just relax and talk.

"What do you think we should name the baby?" Paisley smoothed her hand over Judah's arm.

"We'll have plenty of time over the next months to ponder that, right?"

"True. But I need a distraction today. Could we talk about it?"

"Oh, sure." He linked their fingers together and kissed her softly. "What names do you like, sweetheart?"

"I've been thinking of nautical names. Like we chose Misty Gale, what if this baby's middle name was Bay or Sea?" She gazed into his moist eyes. "What do you think?"

"Yeah. I like that."

"Really?"

"I do. Since we both love the ocean and our lives at the seaside, we could name all our kids something to do with the sea."

She sighed, thankful for him being okay with her idea. So thankful for him. For their love.

Oh, he'd said "all our kids."

"So you still want to have more children?"

"Yes," he whispered.

"Good. Me too." She rested her head lightly against his. "I love you."

"Love you too." He toyed with her hair, wrapping a strand around two of his fingers. "So, let's say a boy's name was Judah. It would be Judah Sea Grant, right?"

"Yes. I think so. Do you want him named after you?"

"Not really. Maybe we can make a list of our favorites."

"Okay. Let's make a list and pick something that sounds great with Sea or Bay."

"Sounds good."

After their baby names discussion, they spent some more time praying together about the remaining portions of the trial. Paisley was still undecided if she should speak directly to Edward the way Judge Greene said she could. For now, praying about it seemed like the best solution.

On the following afternoon, she was called back to the courtroom. Edward's lawyer had more questions for her. Then she'd be given the opportunity to address Edward if she wanted to.

As she was sworn in again, she noticed Bess, Kathleen, Aunt Callie, and Sarah were there, holding hands, praying, and showing a unified front. God bless them!

With her ordeal nearly over, after this she and Judah could go back to their own house and get on with their life, preparing for their baby. Imagining their little family, maybe with two or three kids, gave her the courage to face what was still to come.

Fifty-five

From his front-row seat in the courtroom, Edward swiveled around and stared hard at Judah in the audience section. Judah clenched his jaw, fighting the urge to scowl back at his father. This man had caused immense pain to people he loved. All for what? A quest for power? Manipulation? Greed? Unfortunately, too many in Basalt Bay had been swayed by his false promises. His corrupt misuse of the town's and C-MER's money too.

Were Mike, Jeff, C.L., and the others sitting in their jail cells bemoaning their stupidity in listening to anything Edward and Mia told them? They'd all have criminal records. And prison sentences.

What Edward did was despicable. Too bad he thought he could get away with it in Basalt Bay. As did Mia. Would their marriage even last beyond the next years in lockup, however many that might be?

Yet even with his plethora of flaws and multiple offenses, Edward was still Judah's father. Craig's father. Probably

Sarah's father, too. Somehow, they'd have to try to overcome his brand of parental lineage.

For Judah, the heritage of bad fathering, lousy leadership, and the lack of paternal love stopped here. That was a promise he'd keep for his children. He vowed to be a loving husband, a caring father, and a good human, to the best of his ability. Power and prestige would not be his goals. Grace and mercy would continue to be his mantra. Love would be at the center of their home. Hopefully, he'd have a healthier legacy to leave his kids.

Could his honest attempt at leading a kind, godly life help erase some of the vile acts his father had perpetrated in the Grant name? Could he extend that ideal to Craig and Sarah too?

Mom's hand gripped his like she understood the struggle he was going through.

His gaze locked on Edward's, Judah silently spoke to him. *You messed up as bad as any man could mess up. You failed at being a dad, a husband, a mayor, a friend, a neighbor. Yet even you can receive grace and God's love if you ask for it. I'll keep praying for you. But it will take some time before I'm ready to visit you. Before I'm ready to talk with you about forgiveness and grace again.*

Edward broke the invisible tie between them and faced the judge. Had he sensed what Judah was trying to convey?

Judah let out a long breath, his heart beating rapidly, the pain in his chest reminding him of his recent injuries.

"Do you wish to address Edward Grant?" Judge Greene asked Paisley.

Mom let go of Judah's hand and clasped her hands together, her lips moving in silent prayer.

"Yes, your honor."

"You may do so now."

Paisley stood slowly, her palms coming to rest against her stomach. By the familiar gesture, Judah knew she was thinking of their baby.

Lord, be with her. Give my wife the strength to say what she needs to say and for her heart to be healed.

He tried staying relaxed. He only wanted Paisley to experience strength and hope coming from him. *You can do this, Pais.* He met her gaze and smiled. *I love you. Say what you need to say. Then this will be over. Our future is in God's hands. Not in Edward's. Not based on fear. But built on love. On hope. On Jesus.*

"You can do this," he mouthed quietly.

Her chin rose. She nodded.

"When you're ready, you may begin," the judge prompted her.

"Thank you." Paisley clutched her hands together, turned, and gazed straight at Edward.

As far as Judah knew, this was the first time she'd looked at him during the trial.

"Edward, you are my husband's father. I should be able to say I respect you. That as a member of Judah's family, I care for you. But I ... I can't." Paisley swallowed hard. "The Bible says I should love my neighbor as myself. Where you are concerned, I struggle with that."

Aww, Pais. Judah's heart ached for her.

"When you kidnapped me, you stole something precious from me." She drew in a breath. "Trust. Belief that there's good in everyone. You harmed the part of me who used to trust more freely."

The courtroom stood silent other than her voice. Her breathing.

Lord, help her.

"I never understood why you hated me so much, even when I was a teenager. Why did you despise me?" She paused as if waiting for Edward to speak. "Old grudges toward my father? Your animosity toward people with poorer living standards? Or maybe it was because my father knew the worst about you."

Edward jerked like she hit a raw nerve.

"The loss of your first love must have eaten you up. Not knowing where she went. Did you blame my dad for that? Were you trying to make everyone else feel as badly as you did about your life?" She gulped. "Why weren't your son and your wife enough for you? Why wasn't running the town enough?"

She stared boldly at Edward. "Why did you think you had to manage my relationship with Judah? To control him like a player in your wicked scheme?" Her voice broke. "You nearly ruined everything. I took your dirty cash and fled. The worst decision of my life was listening to you!"

She pressed her lips together, whimpering. Tears flooded Judah's eyes.

"You are mean and violent. Part of me wants to hate you for what you did to me. But then you would win. Hate would win."

Judah wanted to go to her. Comfort her. But he had to let her do this. It was good for her to know she was strong enough. Expressing herself to Edward was a stepping stone in her healing. A stepping stone in their family's healing.

God, help her. Strengthen her.

"But you didn't win. You failed." Her voice turned whimsical. "God had a bigger plan than yours. What do you know? *He* is bigger than Edward Grant! *He* is bigger than your goals of ruling Basalt Bay and the people who call it home."

She leaned forward as if demanding that Edward's eyes train on hers. "You brutally hurt me." She pointed at the scar on her face. "This mark is proof of what you did to me. It will probably be here for the rest of my life. A reminder of your evil against me. Someday, I'm going to point at this mark and tell my son the truth."

Edward muttered an oath.

"Don't worry. He won't consider you a monster. He'll only hear that his grandfather is greatly flawed and in need of redemption." She drew in a long breath. "Even those who have hurt us deserve a second chance and grace. Someday, I hope I'll feel more gracious toward you. More loving. With prayer and God's love working in me, I believe that will happen. I'm not there yet."

She gazed intently at Edward as if pondering what was left to be said. "I hope this court finds you guilty and that you spend a long time in prison. I want you to have lots of time to ponder what you did until your heart changes, and you find the ability to be sorry."

Head bent down, Edward shuffled on his seat like he was uncomfortable.

The pain over his father hurting his wife hit Judah again. He clenched his fists in his lap. Mom patted his shoulder. He leaned into her slightly, sharing in their mutual grief.

"I didn't know if I could do this," Paisley continued softly. "Whether I'd be brave enough to stand here and look you in the eye. I'm glad I did. Your son and I are praying about forgiveness." She clasped her hands in a prayer pose. "We'll keep praying about it, praying for you, every day. Because forgiving you is letting the hurt go from inside me. It's helping me be free so my child can be free."

Edward's shoulders slumped.

"I wish you'd never taken it on yourself to try to destroy what Judah and I had together." She met Judah's gaze and a soft smile crossed her mouth. "Fortunately, you failed. We are more in love now than ever. Together, we are going to raise children who have grace and hope and love in their hearts.

"We are resilient. *I am resilient!*" Her gaze turned upward. "God has made me strong, despite the evil you planned for me. I will thank Him for that every day of my life."

Paisley faced Judge Greene. "Thank you for this opportunity, Your Honor."

"You're welcome." The judge wiped his knuckles beneath his nose as if getting his emotions under control. He nodded and waved for the court officer to escort Paisley from the stand.

As soon as she reached the first row of the audience, Judah leaped up and met her in the aisle, hugging her close. She clung to him, both weeping. The buzz of the courtroom went on around them. Judge Greene gave remarks Judah didn't hear.

Thank You, he silently prayed. It was finally over.

Fifty-six

A week after Craig's injury, Ali was surprised to get a text from him, asking her to meet him at the beach for lunch. Was he strong enough to hike down the trail? When she inquired, he said if he took things slowly, he'd be fine.

She donned jeans, a tan cashmere sweater, and ankle boots before heading to the driftwood log near City Beach where they met before. Sitting down, she inhaled deeply of the sea air, loving the feel of the cool wind blowing her hair back.

"Hey, beautiful." Craig's voice sounded teasing and serious at the same time.

"Hi."

She watched him shuffle through the sand, methodically moving toward her carrying two bags with "Bert's Fish Shack" and a salmon logo on them. He set those on the driftwood before sitting down slowly.

"I cheated and snagged food from the diner."

"Good. I like Bert's food."

He rested his hand on his chest. "With the decrepit way I'm walking, I must look like an old geezer."

"Can't say I ever thought of you as a geezer." She winked at him.

"No?" He grinned.

Right then, his smiling mouth looked too inviting to resist. It was great to see him outside, looking like he felt better, and grinning at her! During his hospital stay and, even before that, when they were searching for Uncle Milton, she'd kept herself from falling into his arms and kissing him. Now, smoothing her hands over the shoulders of his golden sweater, she leaned up and kissed him fully on the mouth, initiating some tender, romantic contact between them.

He chuckled between smooches. With his arms around her, he pulled her closer to him, like no post-surgery pain was stopping him from kissing her back.

"There." She settled on the driftwood again. "I got that out of the way."

He laughed and clutched his side. "Go easy on me with the laughter."

"I'll try to be good."

"Don't get me wrong. I like what you did. In fact, let's set aside this food and just spend the afternoon kissing."

"While that sounds delightful, I'm hungry for the salmon sandwich I smell." She reached for the diner bag.

"All right. Eat first. Then kiss later."

"Deal."

In a lull between eating the delicious sandwich and sweet potato fries, Ali asked, "Are you going to accept the job with Judah?"

"I guess. He and I met at Bert's to discuss it." He drew in a shallow breath and gulped like the movement hurt. "My brother is going to be my boss. The arrangement didn't work well before. Although, there were hurtful things between us, and we didn't know the truth about us being related."

"And now?" She dipped her fry in ketchup then put it in her mouth.

"He and Forest risked their lives to get me on the helicopter." He put his hand on his chest again. "I'm thankful for them doing that. I'm glad to have a family. So, sure, I'm open to working with Judah again."

"And Sarah might be your sister?"

"Yeah. We're waiting for DNA results."

They ate in silence for a few minutes, but Ali's thoughts kept replaying Craig's haphazard proposal in the hospital a week ago. Did he even recall asking her to marry him? She'd thought of little else in the interim.

"What's on your mind?" He tilted his head and stared at her. "You look so serious. Did I say something wrong?" He took a small bite of his food. Apparently, he didn't have his appetite back yet.

"No. Something you said in the hospital is stirring around in my brain."

"What did I say?" He set his sandwich on the wrapper lying on the driftwood.

Never one to hold back the truth, she said, "In your meds-induced state, you asked me a personal question." She grinned at his befuddled expression. "You don't remember, do you?"

"Personal, huh? Was it important?"

"Life-changing, if you meant it."

His lips spread in a wide smile. "Then I surely meant it."

"Craig, you asked me to marry you." The words felt like taffy in her mouth.

"I did?" His cheeks darkened.

"Yes. But in the next breath, you fell asleep." She smoothed her fingers down his jawline. "Don't look so alarmed. I won't hold you to it."

"What did you do when I asked you that?" he asked with a hint of flirtation.

"Oh, the usual. My heart pounded like crazy—until I heard you snoring."

"Sounds like the worst proposal ever."

"Pretty much." She fingered another fry. "But you were sweet about it."

Suddenly, he slid off the driftwood and landed on his knee in the sand with a soft moan.

"Craig?" She dropped the fry. "I wasn't hinting for a real proposal."

He clasped one of her hands. "Will you marry me, Al?"

"Craig—"

Was he serious this time? The gentle, wistful look on his face said he was.

"I love you." His softly spoken words sent joy and hope dancing through her heart. "I've had a lot of time in the hospital and since I've been out to think about you. About us. Even if I was in a meds-induced stupor the other time I proposed, I mean it now." Still on his knee, he asked, "What do you say? Will you go on a lifelong adventure with me?"

Her heart pounded a chaotic beat right alongside the happiness rushing through her. "I love you too, Craig. But marriage?" Staying in Basalt Bay? Being his wife?

"Al? My chest is killing me here." He grabbed his side and coughed. "Will you marry the grownup version of the boy you had a crush on in elementary school?"

More like a crush she'd had forever.

"Come on. Let me help you." She got under his arm and helped him stand.

"Does this mean you're turning me down? I realize you don't know everything about—"

"No, it's just that—" She laughed. "Yes! I will marry you. Yes, I will go on a lifelong adventure with you!" As she said the words, she knew she meant them. She wanted to be with him for the rest of her life.

"That's more like it." A wide grin crossed his lips, and he took her in his arms.

Before she let him kiss her, she said, "I love you with all my heart. Really, I do. But do we have to live in Basalt Bay?"

"You love me, Al?" He chuckled as if he hadn't heard the last part.

Then he kissed her passionately, heating her up right down to her toes.

She leaned back to look him in the eye. "Do we have to live here?"

"I'd like to work with Judah." He still held her loosely around her waist. "Would it be possible for you to stay on with your uncle for a while?"

"Meaning someday we could move to Portland?"

"I'll go wherever you go, Al. Maybe we could stay here for a year or so?"

"That sounds reasonable, especially if I wind up covering for my uncle. Maybe I'll grow to love this hamlet by the sea." She smoothed her hands over the arms of his sweater. "Do you want a quick engagement?"

"Sounds like my style."

"Mine too."

They sat down closely on the driftwood and kissed and made plans. Ali was thrilled to be in the arms of this man she'd dreamed of for so long.

They were going to get married! Craig and Ali Masters. That had a nice ring to it.

Fifty-seven

Judah sat beside the fire he built in the pit in front of his cabin. Any minute Craig and Sarah would be arriving. Paisley would join them shortly, then they'd speak to the attorney. But first, he wanted this opportunity to talk with Craig and Sarah by himself.

A car pulled into the driveway. Minutes later, Craig hobbled toward him with Sarah walking beside him, her arm clutching his.

"Hi, you guys." Judah stood and waved.

Craig chin nodded in greeting.

"Hey, Judah," Sarah said.

They all sat down, staring into the fire and the smoke rising from it.

Judah longed to open a door of healing in his family. That included talking honestly with Craig and Sarah. "Thanks for coming over."

"Sure. What's this about?" Craig made a slight groan.

"Still hurts, huh?" Judah semi-chuckled, since his ribs ached at the oddest times.

"Yeah, unfortunately."

Judah tugged the sheet of printer paper he'd copied from an email out of his jacket pocket and handed it to Sarah. "I wanted you to read this with both of us present."

"Okay." She unfolded the paper. Her eyes widened. "Ohhh. You guys really are my brothers!"

"Yep." Judah took a breath. "For better or for worse, the three of us are siblings. Different moms, but Edward is our biological father."

"Not much to celebrate about that." Craig glanced between them. "This is why you called for us to meet you?"

"Thought we should make it official."

"A gathering of Edward Grant's hapless brood?" Craig said sarcastically.

"More than that. To, uh"—Judah glanced toward the blue sky—"to make this a new beginning for the three of us as we try to forge a new family. You know, brothers and sister like we didn't get the chance to be before."

Craig tilted his head. "Still trying to fix things, brother?"

Judah silenced a laugh. Not worth the wretched ache in his ribs. "Sarah?" She met his gaze with tears in her eyes. "I'm sorry your family didn't tell you about being adopted. I don't know if it was because of Edward's demands or not, but I want to say I'm truly sorry."

"Thank you. You've both been kind to me." She sniffed. "Kinder than my real brother ever was. Oh, I didn't mean 'real' brother." She cringed.

Judah smiled. "I always wished for siblings. I was lonely growing up. Longed for brothers or sisters to run on the beach with me." He cleared his throat and a clog of emotion with it. "The three of us are family now." He eyed Craig, then Sarah. "It may take some time to work it all out, for us to feel like siblings. But with our successful Christmas Eve celebration, all that happened with the rescues, and even the trial, it's a beginning, right?"

"Could have done without some of this." Craig pointed at his injured chest.

"I hear you." Judah smiled, avoiding a laugh.

"I wish I knew about you two a long time ago." Sarah patted Craig's arm. "You could have been allies against my other brother."

"Was he mean?" Craig sounded protective like he'd speak to this other brother if Sarah wanted him to.

"Controlling. Selfish. Aloof." She stared out toward the incoming waves. "Kids running on the beach and having fun together sounds amazing. I would have liked that."

"Yeah, me too." Craig shuffled slightly. "Not on the run. Or being alone. Not celebrating birthdays and Christmases with just my mom."

"Things will be different now. You both are a true part of my family." Judah clasped his hands together, glancing back and forth between the other two. "I promise to be here for both of you. If you need anything, call me. I hope we can be friends for the rest of our lives. And when we all have our own children, they'll be cousins, running and playing together on the beach. A family bond that goes beyond the name of Edward Grant."

"Thank you, Judah," Sarah said softly. "Your family has already done so much for me. Been such a blessing in my life."

"You're my sister forever," he said with a choked-up feeling in his throat. In his heart, too.

She reached for his hand and gave it a squeeze. "You're my brother forever."

"What am I? Smashed up clam shells?" Craig said.

"You are our brother for the rest of our lives too." Judah reached out his hand.

Craig stared at him for a couple of seconds as if pondering what this handshake meant. Then grimacing, he reached out and gripped Judah's hand. "Brothers."

Sarah stood and leaned over Craig and hugged him. "Welcome to my life."

"Thanks."

Paisley walked through the sand toward them holding out Judah's phone. "It's Max."

"This is the other reason I asked you guys to meet with me." He waved for Paisley to join them. Then he clasped the phone and turned on the speaker.

"Hi, you guys," she said as she sat down beside him.

"Hey, Paisley." Sarah smiled.

Craig nodded at her.

"This is Max Fenwell, the state attorney." Judah held up the phone. "Okay, Max. Paisley and my siblings, Craig and Sarah, are on speakerphone with me."

"Hello, all. The verdict has been reached. Two, actually," the man said in a rumbly tone. "Mia's trial is still a few weeks away. I expect her outcome to be the same as Edward's. The others who were involved will have separate trials."

Sarah clasped Paisley's hand, and so did Judah.

"We're ready." Judah pressed his lips together, waiting. Even though his father deserved a long prison sentence, he dreaded hearing the final ruling.

"For kidnapping in the first degree, twenty years for Edward, with no time off for good behavior."

Judah gulped. Twenty years.

"Ten for Evie. With time reduced for her confession and cooperation with the state."

Craig pressed his palms over his eyes. Judah felt compassion for him. He was losing his mom for a decade.

"Edward yelled denials throughout the sentencing portion." Max sighed. "He assumed someone was going to rescue him. He demanded leniency considering his years of public service. He was the Basalt Bay mayor, had influence with the governor, etc."

Judah could imagine his rantings. "Thanks for letting us know, Max." He ended the call and hugged Paisley. "It's really over, sweetheart."

She cried softly against his sweatshirt. "I'm sorry it came to this. I'm sorry your dad was—"

"I know. None of it is your fault." He drew in a long breath. "He is reaping the reward of years of wrongdoing. I hope in prison he sees the error of his ways. I pray he turns to Christ."

"Me too."

They sat in silence for several minutes, giving each of them time to process, time to grieve for Edward and Evie, and the negative effects they had on each person sitting around this fire. Thankfully, their faith in God would strengthen them, heal them, and give them hope for the future.

"Thank you all for being here with us today." Paisley sat back in her chair. "I'm thankful we heard the news together."

Craig sighed. "What now?"

"I have an appointment with the regional director of C-MER tomorrow." Judah met his brother's gaze. "I plan to accept the position. I hope you will too."

"Never thought I'd work for C-MER again. Or you. But I need a job. There's the matter of my community service hours that were put on hold during this ordeal." Craig pointed toward his chest. "Otherwise, I'm ready to go back to work."

"Good. Tackling the dike delay will be my first order of business."

"It's about time someone prioritized it."

"Will Alison still work with the *Gazette*?" Paisley asked.

"We don't know what Milton's sentence will be. Al may have to run the paper for a while." A grin crossed Craig's face. "Keep this under your hat. I asked her to marry me."

"What?" Paisley said.

"Seriously?" Sarah placed her palm on his arm.

"And she actually said yes?" Judah asked teasingly.

"Yep. We're getting hitched."

"This is good news." Judah grinned and held out his hand toward Craig again. "Congratulations, bro."

Craig shook his hand quicker this time. "Thanks."

"I'll look forward to having another sister-in-law," Sarah said.

"Thank you," Craig said softly. "I think I'm going to like having a sister."

"You bet." She play punched his arm. "Until I start telling you what to do!"

Craig smirked. "Yep. That's what I missed during my childhood."

Judah clasped Paisley's hand. "Are you okay?"

"Yeah. I'm good. The trial's over. The unrest is over." She gazed around at the small group. "I can't wait to see what God is going to do in all our lives. It's like we're starting over."

"I was thinking the same thing." Judah smiled. "In spite of some of the things that brought us to this moment, it's a wonderful new beginning for our family."

Fifty-eight

One week after Edward's verdict was announced, Paige, Bess, Kathleen, Aunt Callie, and Sarah made a feast that looked big enough to be a Thanksgiving dinner. The others thought they were coming to dinner to commemorate the trial being over. And they were. But Paige had something else in mind too. She would have liked to make her announcement to Forest and her family out at the gazebo. But since this dinner was planned for today, why not spring her good news here?

She settled Piper into a high chair between her and Aunt Callie who sat at the head of the long table. Dad sat at the other end with Paisley on one side of him and James on the other. When Paige set the table for twelve, she was tempted to place James at Aunt Callie's right side. But that might have been pushing things a little. Maybe someday they'd acknowledge their romantic feelings for each other. Until then, Paige would have to wait.

"Shall we say grace?" Aunt Callie pegged Dad with a look. "Food's getting cold."

"Maybe someone else should say grace this time," Dad said with a merry expression.

It was nice to see him looking so happy. Paige prayed her news would make him even happier.

"Who's the most thankful person at the table today?" he asked.

Glances were exchanged. Paisley and Judah both raised their hands. Sarah timidly raised hers. Paige was thankful for so many things in her life, she had to raise her hand. Then she saw Craig lift his hand. A breath caught in her throat. He'd come so far in the last four months. Noticeably in his kindness and integrity, and in his willingness to risk his life for members of the Cedars and Grant families. Beside Craig, Alison leaned into his shoulder and a soft smile crossed her mouth.

Aww. Paige was glad these two were finding happiness with each other.

"Lots of thankfulness here today," Dad said.

"Amen," Bess added.

"Craig?" Dad nodded toward him. "Want to say grace for us?"

A meaningful look passed between them.

"Uh, sure. I'd be honored." Craig coughed. Then he haltingly said, "Lord, thanks for, uh, helping us through the difficulties … we've faced. I don't deserve this family's mercy and friendship. But I appreciate it. So much. Bless the food. Amen."

"Amen!" resounded around the table.

A few people wiped their fingers below their eyes or sniffled.

"Now, pass the food!" Aunt Callie ordered.

As if she'd shaken them from their contemplations, everyone passed platters and bowls of yummy-looking food in a clockwise circle. Laughter and comments ensued as plates were filled with turkey and salmon and buttered potatoes. Then the room became silent while everyone ate.

"This is great!" Judah finally said.

"Absolutely." Paisley grinned. "Since I've been pregnant, I can't get enough of eating."

Paige chuckled along with the others. While she enjoyed the meal, she felt eager to share her news. It was hard not to jump up and say what was on her mind before everyone was finished.

When their plates were empty, Sarah and Kathleen removed the dishes and silverware. While they were doing that and preparing dessert, Paige turned her back to Forest and set up a prearranged video call with Peter and Ruby on her new phone.

As soon as her brother and sister-in-law appeared on the screen, Paige stood and called out, "Could we wait a couple of minutes before we have dessert? Peter and Ruby are on the phone."

"They are?" Paisley asked.

"Yep."

"Oh, good." Kathleen rushed back to her seat.

Sarah sat down too.

Paige held out the phone to each person so they could send greetings or wave toward the screen. Peter and Ruby sat together on a loveseat and waved back or commented.

"Thanks for letting us join you guys!" Peter said. "Hello, Craig. Glad to hear you survived your ordeal."

"Thanks."

"We're so excited to get to be a part of this celebration." Ruby grinned. "See our living room!" She moved their screen around the room, showing off one of Paige's paintings on the far wall.

"Oh, nice!" Paige said.

Others oohed and aahed over the one-bedroom house they purchased in Ketchikan. "Our little bungalow," Ruby called it.

"You guys look so happy," Paisley said.

"We are." Peter kissed Ruby's cheek. "Now, tell us what this celebration is about. What's the news?"

"We're so glad you're able to be with us even from afar!" Paige laughed. "One, we're thankful that the trial is over."

"Right," Peter said. "We've been praying for all of you."

"Your sisters made it through their turns on the witness stand." Judah clutched Paisley's hand on the table. "It was tough, but I'm proud of them!"

Paisley kissed his cheek. "Thank you."

"Sarah," Ruby said. "We heard about you being Craig and Judah's sister. Welcome to the family!"

"Thank you." Sarah grinned and waved at Ruby. "I miss you guys!"

"We miss all of you too. I can't wait to come back to the project house for a visit."

"I look forward to that also," Aunt Callie said.

A few other comments were made.

Paige passed the phone to Sarah. "Can you hold this facing me for a minute?"

"Sure." Sarah aimed the phone screen toward her.

"I have an announcement to share with all of you." Paige met Forest's questioning gaze with a wide smile. She didn't get the chance to do this with him when she was expecting Piper. Since he'd missed her first reveal, she wanted this time to be special for him. "Forest, my sweet, precious husband, and my dear, supportive family, I want you all to know—I'm pregnant!" She squealed.

"What?" Forest lunged to his feet and hugged her. "Really? You're pregnant?"

"Yes! We're going to have another baby!"

He kissed her, his palms cupping her cheeks, his eyes sparkling with moisture. Then he kissed her again.

The group clapped and cheered.

From her high chair, Piper laughed and pounded her tray with her spoon. She didn't know what Paige's announcement meant, but she seemed happy about it!

Grinning, Paige gazed around the table. She met Paisley's gaze. Both nodded. Two sisters pregnant at the same time! Cousins close together in age. Paige wiped tears from her eyes. She sure was much more emotional these days.

Dad stood and tapped his knife against his water glass. "I'm proud as punch. Two more grandbabies? Who could ask for more?"

"Dad! Dad!" Peter's voice came through the phone.

"Wait, everyone! Peter wants to say something." Clasping Forest's hand, Paige sat down.

He let go of her hand and put his arm over her shoulder, tugging her close against his side. "I'm so happy. Thank you, baby."

"Me too." She kissed his cheek.

"Go ahead, Peter!" Paisley said. "You have the floor. Or the phone screen!"

"Dad asked who could ask for more." Peter chuckled throatily and wrapped his arms around Ruby. "We have an announcement also!"

"What?" Paige asked.

It seemed everyone in the room held their breaths, waiting for Peter to continue.

"Ruby and I are going to be parents too!"

Bedlam broke out as everyone clapped and cheered. Someone whistled. Paige was surprised to find Alison with her fingers in her mouth, making the shrill sound.

"Three babies?" Dad said in a shocked tone. "I am blessed beyond measure. It'll be like triplet cousins!"

"That's right." Paige laughed giddily.

Craig stood, bringing Alison to her feet beside him. "I'm new to this family. But for those of you who haven't heard yet, I asked Al to marry me. And she said yes!" Making a whooping sound, he tipped her back and kissed her thoroughly.

More clapping and congratulations ensued. Chatter broke out, everyone talking at once.

Three new Cedars/Grant/Harper babies and a wedding?

Dad was right. Who could ask for more than such an amazing blessing of family and love as this?

Epilogue

7 months later

"On the next contraction, push," Doctor Isabel said from her position near the foot of the birthing-room bed.

Paisley drew in deep breaths, preparing herself mentally and physically for the work yet to come.

"You're doing amazing!" Judah stood by her side, holding her hand or wiping her forehead with a cool cloth. "I'm proud of you, sweetheart."

"Thanks." She felt the familiar spasm building in her middle. "Here it comes."

Judah helped her get into position for pushing, her hands clutching her thighs. Finally, she was nearing the moment she'd get to see her baby, the child she'd cherished and prayed about for nine months.

After the pushing contraction ended, she sagged against the pillow. "That was a tough one."

"Good job, Pais! You're doing it!"

"Not long now," Doctor Isabel said. "This one won't take many pushes. He or she is eager to greet you."

Paisley grinned despite her fatigue. "I can't wait to meet this one either."

She and Judah had agreed to not find out the gender of the baby in advance. Either way, he or she was loved and longed for. They prayed together for their child, and for their families, every day.

Twice in the months since the trial, and since Mia was found guilty of being a co-conspirator in Paisley's kidnapping, Judah traveled to visit his father in prison. He hoped for a way to present the gospel and share grace with him. Both times he returned downhearted. But they were still praying and trusting God about forgiveness. They would continue to pray for healing and peace for their families in the days ahead, too.

Another spasm started. Paisley pushed through the contraction.

"Dark hair!" Doctor Isabel called excitedly. "Okay, Paisley, stop pushing. Just breathe. We're almost there."

Sinking against the pillow, she breathed slowly, zonked beyond belief. She'd been in labor since midnight. It was around noon now.

Judah wiped her forehead again. "You're doing great. I can't wait to hold our baby."

"Me too," she said while exhaling.

The short rest sped by. She moved into position for the next pushing contraction. Giving her all, she pushed her child out of her body and the baby slid onto the sheet.

"A boy!" Doctor Isabel announced.

"I knew it," Paisley said happily in between taking breaths.

Judah wrapped his arms around her, holding her weight as she sagged against him, kissing the side of her head, sniffling, and laughing. "It's a boy!"

"Oh, Judah. He's beautiful."

They both gazed at their son, enthralled as their baby squalled and squirmed.

"Do you want to cut the cord?" Doctor Isabel asked Judah.

"Yes." He accepted the scissors she held out to him.

He met Paisley's gaze. They'd talked about this, so she knew this was a momentous step for him. He clipped the cord between the two clamps marking the spot, then he passed the scissors back to the doctor. A wide grin crossed his mouth. "Welcome to the world, Son."

Such deep emotion welled up in Paisley's heart.

The nurse lifted the baby and settled him into her arms. Warmth against the warmth of her body. Her precious baby boy was finally here in her arms, safe and well and perfect!

"Is he okay?" she asked just in case.

"He's fine," Doctor Isabel said. "Strong heartbeat. Good coloring."

Paisley kissed his soft forehead. "Welcome to our family, Tanner Sea Grant."

"Hey, little guy." Judah sniffed, his head resting against Paisley's. "We've waited a long time to meet you." He smoothed his fingers over the baby's skin. "He was worth the wait."

"He sure was." Paisley sighed contentedly.

The nurse helped her get adjusted on the bed, then assisted with getting the baby ready to feed for the first time.

Peace and thankfulness filled her as she gazed into Judah's eyes. She was so thankful for God bringing them back together, making them into a family again, and giving them a child. "We are three now," she whispered.

"Yes, we are." He kissed her lips softly. "You've made me the happiest of men."

She chuckled. "I'm pretty happy too."

While the nurse and doctor finished their cleanup tasks and checked Paisley's and the baby's stats, Judah stayed close to Paisley.

"Want to hold him?"

"I sure do." He grinned.

She nestled Tanner in his daddy's arms. Then, grabbing her cell phone off the mobile tray, she snapped a couple of pictures of him holding the baby for the first time. She took a couple of selfies of the three of them also.

Even though she was exhausted from labor, a new strength filled her. Motherhood! The hope and thrill of parenting gave her such an urgency to tell someone their good news.

"Shall I tell them?" She held up her cell phone.

Judah, who gazed adoringly at Tanner, nodded. "Yes! Tell them our good news."

Paisley tapped the app they were using now for a family texting group.

Tanner Sea is here! Celebrate with us!

A cheer rang out from somewhere down the hospital hallway where hers and Judah's families were gathered. Paisley and Judah laughed.

Leaning toward her, he kissed her softly again, gazing into her eyes. "I love you, Pais. You are amazing. This experience of us being parents together is just so—" He swallowed hard, his eyes filling with tears. "It's wonderful. I can't wait to spend the rest of our lives together."

Deep blue sea in the morning! She loved him so much. "I love you too. I always will. Forever and ever."

And she loved their sweet, precious baby, born of their love and restoration.

Thank You, God, for all the beautiful things You've done in our lives!

Thank you for reading *Shores of Resilience*!

This book concludes the Restored series!

Author's Note:

I hope you have enjoyed this eight-part series about grace and restoration in a small town by the sea! I loved creating the town of Basalt Bay on the Oregon Coast. I had fun writing this series like a TV miniseries in that it had ongoing elements, we got to know the characters more fully with each part, and some of the books had surprise endings. I hope you enjoyed Judah and Paisley's story, along with Forest and Paige's, Peter and Ruby's, and Craig and Ali's, as they journeyed toward restoration and love.

In late 2017, following the conclusion of my first series, I felt wrung out emotionally. I didn't have the desire for writing as I did before. But by early 2018, God was filling me with inspiration for another series, and the heart for writing hit me again!

This story would be about a woman coming home to a husband she didn't know was waiting for her, a dad she'd abandoned, a town she needed to make amends with, and a life she desperately needed. Because restoration takes time, this wouldn't be a short story. It would be a tale woven with emotion, adventure, family, romance, and reconciliation. And mixed with a dash of suspense!

I published *Ocean of Regret* in December of 2018. It's been a four-and-a-half-year journey for these eight books. Thank you for joining me on this adventure into the hearts and lives of the people in Basalt Bay!

Now, for some news:

While this series has officially ended, there are a few characters in Basalt Bay who I'd like to find out more about.

Some readers have asked about Callie. Some told me she and James should have their story told.

I agreed! I set aside some time earlier this year to write the rough draft for Callie's story, and a spin-off series was born. Each book will be a standalone novel, but some of the people we've come to love in Basalt Bay will be seen as part of the background mosaic of life in the coastal town.

You can look for *Callie's Time*, Basalt Bay Women, Book 1, coming in Fall 2022! Followed by *Sarah's Design* in Spring 2023.

Blessings.

~Mary

Thank you for reading the Restored series!

If you are interested in hearing more about Mary's writing projects, sign up for her newsletter at

www.maryehanks.com

Thank you to these wonderful people!

Paula McGrew ... Thank you so much for helping me with this part of the project! You have been an amazing blessing on this journey into Basalt Bay. Thank you for your critique, suggestions, and encouragement in *Shores* and in the other books in this series. I'm so thankful for you!

Suzanne Williams ... Thank you for your cover design on this project and with the whole series. I appreciate you so much!

Mary Acuff, Kellie Griffin, Beth McDonald, Joanna Brown, and Jason Hanks ... Thank you for reading this book and this series! Your advice, suggestions, and letting me know what your reactions were while you were reading have meant so much to me. Thanks too for the cheers and encouragement along the way. God bless you!

My family—Jason, Daniel & Traci, Philip, Deborah, Shem, & Lala-girl—Love to you all!

Thank You, Jesus, for blessing me with creative ideas!

(This is a work of fiction. Any mistakes are my own. ~meh)

Books by Mary Hanks

Restored Series

Ocean of Regret, Sea of Rescue, Bay of Refuge, Tide of Resolve, Waves of Reason, Port of Return, Sound of Rejoicing, Shores of Resilience

Second Chance Series

Winter's Past, April's Storm, Summer's Dream, Autumn's Break, Season's Flame

Standalone Novel

Liv & the Preacher A Marriage of Convenience for a Good Cause Novel

www.maryehanks.com

About Mary ...

Married for 40+ years, Mary Hanks loves to read and write Christian fiction married romances. She has written thirteen books in the second-chance inspirational Christian fiction genre so far. *Liv & the Preacher* is her first standalone novel.

Thank you for reading the Restored series!

Made in United States
Orlando, FL
02 December 2022